DEATH'S REALM

TALES OF THE SUPERNATURAL

DEATH'S
REALM

TALES OF THE SUPERNATURAL

CURATED AND EDITED BY BRAM STOKER AWARD–NOMINATED
ANTHONY RIVERA AND SHARON LAWSON

GREY MATTER
PRESS

CHICAGO

DEATH'S REALM: ISBN 978-1-940658-33-9
First Grey Matter Press Trade Paperback Edition - January 2015

Anthology Copyright © 2015 Grey Matter Press
Design Copyright © 2015 Grey Matter Press
Short Stories Copyright © 2015 their individual authors
Additional copyright declarations can be found on page 301.
All rights reserved.

GREY MATTER
P R E S S

Grey Matter Press
greymatterpress.com
facebook.com/greymatterpress
twitter.com/greymatterpress

DEDICATION

This is for all of those who have left us behind,
but who have yet to step beyond the veil.
The tingle you feel on the back of your neck
is one of them reading over your shoulder.
Raise the book up a bit higher.

TABLE OF CONTENTS

ABOUT THE AUTHOR
RHOADS BRAZOS

Author Rhodes Brazos claims to lack his wife's classiness, his son's genius and his house cat's fearsome nature. His life is a simple one, Rockwellian with a touch of morbid fancy.

He is an amiable enough fellow who never quits watching and listening, always imagining what his neighbors must be thinking. This is a dangerous path for the foolhardy—Brazos chief among them—who come to believe their own guesses have truth and that passersby are living by proxy within them. The cautious should study his mistake from afar, as he courts madness.

Brazos transcribes these dreams into prose and shares them with unsuspecting readers. His work has appeared in venues that include *Apex Magazine*, *Demon Rum and Other Evil Spirits, Gaia: Shadow & Breath* and *Spark: A Creative Anthology - Volume V.*

Brazos currently lives in Colorado Springs, Colorado and has no plans to move. Although his neighbors grouse and grumble over this fact to no end.

OMNISCOPIC

RHOADS BRAZOS

"Eternity can be measured."

It was exactly the kind of thing Boas would say after a few stout drinks, of which he'd tenaciously partaken. I should know, I had been graced with the bill. It was a lost wager, the nature upon which I'd rather not elaborate.

"Infinites of scale?" I asked. "Cantor beat you to it."

"Honestly, Davis, that's so pedestrian."

We sat at an out of the way table at Schrödinger's. It was crowded that night. With finals done, the university students were seeking inebriation and like company. The pub, with its bygone *mise-en-scène* of copper and rosewood, was the favored hangout for all physics graduates. They crammed themselves elbow to elbow at the ice-top bar and drank in boisterous clusters across the floor. Gas chandeliers cast down a warm light the color of straw. Atmosphere was important here, maintained at an antique yesterday.

Boas took a long drink from a chrome flask, ellipsoidal with three finned feet—a Buzz Bomb, if I had heard his order correctly. He downed its contents with a flourish and motioned to a server. I held my tongue. Boas was likely to choose an expensive jeroboam if I protested.

"Consider this," he said, tipping his wiry frame over the table. He looked down his long beak of a nose and squinched his eyebrows down so low that I questioned whether he could even see. "Perception is immortal. As it seems to fade—"

"Death? This again?"

"There is no death. Perception seeps out of reality. This reality. This eternity."

"And is projected into another. Yes, yes. My god, Bowie, we've had this conversation so many times."

As intriguing as Boas's metaphysical jaunts could be, this particular path of inquiry had been tread into dust.

"Ah," Boas said, "and you only accept the imperial."

"Empirical. You've had far too much to drink."

"Agreed. But is evidence all that convinces you?"

"What more is there?"

"Theoretical proof."

"Theoretical," I said.

"Proof!" Boas slammed his fist to the table and grinned as he caught our neighbors' curiosity. There were mumbles about the former professor, and what he must have done to lose tenure, before the din rose once again.

I dismissed him and breathed in deeply of the pub's heady atmosphere: alcohol, tobacco, perfume, old leather. There was a pleasant thickness to it that swaddled one's senses. It anchored you, compelled you to stay.

Boas snapped his fingers, inches away from my nose. "I have something you simply must see."

"Is it another of your theorems?" I asked. I tried to sound incurious, but was not in the slightest. Any new creation of Boas's was bound to shake the heavens.

"It will astound you."

"Try me. Right here."

"I cannot simply recite it." He motioned with his thumb, clicking up and down.

I felt at my chest pocket and produced a pen. Boas grabbed it and studied it closely.

"Well?" I said.

He opened a napkin as if it was folded vellum, spread it before himself, and fell to it. He threw down page two, three, and on and on. I watched in silence.

Boas harbored many faults—arrogance, narcissism, and contrariness chief among them—but his mathematical abilities were second to none. Watching him establish a proof was like watching Mozart casually sketch a quartet—no corrections and no hesitations, just a steady script that flowed like oil. The end was reached with a double barline, *fine* and *QED*.

I pinched the work between trembling fingers, sickened, and at the same instant, elated at its divine clarity. Boas had outdone himself. Over drinks, he had crafted an intricacy that humiliated my efforts on last year's dissertation. I stood in Salieri's shoes.

"Good night! Bowie, are you serious?"

"Always." With a wink to the waitress, he accepted a new drink and raised it to his lips.

"If this is true—"

Boas only tasted the rim before lowering it. "What are you implying, *if*?"

"Well, this establishes a theory, but you still must—"

"Ah, your observable proof." He sipped thoughtfully. "I have."

"You have?"

"I've built it. I call it an omniscope."

What awaits us after death? Nothing, claimed academia. Boas thought otherwise. His peers dismissed the question because they feared the answer. Their timid natures denied his own pluck and prodigy. His vindication—their humiliation—would ignite a global revival with Boas himself spitting fire from the pulpit.

All according to Boas, it goes without saying.

"So," I said. I tried to hide my nervousness. "Another universe."

"To measure an eternity, we must first observe it."

"And you can...see it?"

"See? That is...sensually inaccurate. Detect might be a better term. To see through the curtain would require a projection of one plane onto another, which for obvious reasons we can't—well, shouldn't—do."

"An intersection," I said. "A single point."

Boas chuckled.

"And then you can measure... Wait! How big is the aperture between planes?"

"A Planck length."

I laughed. "My dear Boas, I hate to be the harbinger of bad news, but it cannot be done. If you charged a photon with enough energy to measure such a small distance, it would buckle and implode."

"Yes. You know, it really sounds like you want to help."

"You call it an omniscope?"

Boas didn't answer. He stood, albeit with a loose tipsiness, and gathered his jacket. I settled the tab and followed.

* * *

We traveled across town to Boas's lab—machinery, terminals and half-finished projects spread over a warehouse floor. It was as if a clockwork Leviathan had been flayed across the grounds, wiring and mechanisms sliced from its bones. In the middle of the clutter was a large tent, the kind a person staked down at the fairgrounds and filled with turquoise jewelry and feathered trinkets.

"It's in there," he said.

We entered.

I shouldn't hasten to describe too much of the construction. Only Boas truly understood it. Even with my education, only the surface concepts were within my grasp. In essence, Boas had an inverted quantum funnel and was shunting space itself away from a single point. At the same instant, he was burrowing into that point with a focused beam of...I wasn't sure.

"Well?" Boas operated a series of controls on a wide cylindrical tank. It hummed. Something inside of it was spinning.

"A graphene supercapacitor?" My heart sank. I must admit, it was an honor to be shown this arguably historic invention, but my own place in this world was starting to look very small.

"Yes." He smirked. "Attached to the world's most delicate coilgun. Despite its exactitude, it requires an immense jolt to truly sing."

The omniscope was a long, metallic spiral mounted on thick legs. A glass barrel housed its lithium coil. A mass of electrical components sat at the opposite end and connected to the supercapacitor.

"The integument is filled with xenon gas," Boas said. He buffed the coil's glass barrel with his sleeve. "To prevent oxidization of the lithium, naturally. With all the heat, it would otherwise create a quite nasty peroxide." He tapped at the supercapacitor's dials. "And we don't want that."

I could taste it in the air. That much power had a flavor, a little like blood, I suppose. My skin itched horribly.

"But how does it—"

"Simple." Boas threw a lever on the capacitor and its frame began to pulse. The mechanism within must have been spinning at a prodigious rate. "Charge comes through here. Lithium magnetizes."

"Lithium can't—"

"Don't interrupt. It's paramagnetic. It will carry enough for my purposes. I can't have the charge retained or it won't thrum."

"Thrum?"

"Waves of magnetization in the coil cause a resonance in surrounding matter. The effect is quite sublime. You'll see—or rather, hear—very soon. The charge arcs in and compresses to a stream. The lower apparatus syncs everything. It hits this point and then these sensors record it. And we watch it here."

He pointed to a dark screen. "Wear this please." He tossed a mask to me.

"For what?"

"Let's just call it residue. I'm unsure, but it may be carcinogenic."

I started to argue, but Boas put on his own mask and gestured with his fingers. One. Two. Thr—

I slapped my mask in place as he hit the power.

The omniscope jumped to life with a crack like thunder. I staggered back, not stopping until I hit the tent wall. A bluish-green haze haloed the lithium coil. The lower machinery screamed and shook. Boas pulled another switch and I felt it.

"My god," I slipped to my knees.

"I think it may be just that," Boas said through his mask. "This is the frequency of our eternity."

I felt hollow, as if I were skin stretched over chimes of bone. With each pulse from the omniscope my own body answered in kind. It was the thrum Boas had spoken of. Everything answered with a sort of music. The floor, the tent, the air itself. It was a melody, a faultless song.

Boas shouted over the strains. "The neighbors are complaining, as you can imagine." He pulled me up with a proffered hand. "The effect is far-reaching, so we must turn it off soon. They don't have proof that it's my doing, but I must be a suspicious character."

There was a pop and the vibration ceased. The music faded. Boas could once again speak without shouting.

"No, don't remove it." He reached up to my mask. "Look."

The screen showed a multi-colored mesh spider webbed out of a central point. An oddly-spaced pattern within the web glowed.

"Start from zero and go clockwise."

"What?"

"Like a polar graph, but clockwise."

I did so and noticed the pattern. "The brighter webs are primes?"

"Exactly! We are at 2 and 191. That's our melody. Then, 439, 709, 1,009 and so on. Our parallel universes, I believe. The set of primes indexed at modulo 42. Isn't that amusing?"

I didn't know what to say.

"What interests me though," Boas touched the screen, "is our neighbor at 3. Now, I'm going to see if anyone's home, maybe borrow a cup of sugar. Watch the core."

A black thread flowed through the omniscope's coil. It hung in the air, spinning out of nothingness in a hair-fine corkscrew. At the tip of the coil it disappeared.

"What is that?" I whispered.

Boas laughed. "Do you feel it?"

I did. The air was humid, sticky. Everything was shining. How was it getting out of that sealed glass barrel?

"Bowie, what the hell is it?"

"Guess."

"Quit being so damned impudent."

"No, really. I want your professional assessment."

I peered at the coil, still glowing with a faint aura. That hair, coming from nowhere and going to nowhere. No, that wasn't right at all. It was being spun from the world. If what Boas said was true—

"The thread is dense matter," I said.

"Now there's an understatement. It's our thread, from the web, as you say. Matter, gravity, time. At a level where they're closely related."

"Bowie, you are insane!"

"Yes! But, no. You do understand."

It was a string wheedled out of that battery's current. Micro black holes. I shouldn't even be able to see such a thing. They should collapse instantly. I argued the point.

Boas answered. "Another grows in the femtosecond in which its neighbor dies."

"But at that interval, the gravity wave would travel a micron. That would be enough to—"

"Don't agonize over it. We're absolutely safe, relatively, more or less."

The air sparkled with mist. Whatever the substance was that was flattening my hair, dripping down my cheeks, it was forming from the point of the corkscrew and spraying outward, straight through the glass. I held up my hand. Straight through me. Most of the mist caught on the surface, but some drifted through.

My clothes and mask were soaked with it. I could even taste it, popping like static on my tongue. I knew what it was, because it couldn't be forgotten. It had been so long—a lifetime, plus a little.

"Archimedes asked for a suitably long lever," Boas said, "but I'll settle for a sharp enough edge." He rubbed his fingers together in the air. He wanted me to name it. "Give up?"

I couldn't bring myself to say it. "I...I don't—"

"It's a coagulant."

I felt queasy. "Please turn it off."

"Do you know what that implies?"

"Turn it off."

He scoffed and flipped the power. The aura faded. That dark thread, the most destructive force man has ever created, faded to gray and wisped away, appropriately, like a spider web.

"Come," Boas said. "I'm famished. We'll get something to eat."

* * *

Boas gave me a change a clothes, for which I was grateful. I discarded my own, unwilling to even contemplate donning them again. We caught a taxi to an all-night diner—one of those establishments that sells nothing but breakfast—and sat at a corner booth. There were a few other fellows here: mailmen, truckers, possibly a drug dealer. I wasn't sure, but he did keep eyeing us with malice.

"The universe is alive," Boas said. "It is cellular, in a membrane of time."

I shook my head and chewed down a slice of bacon.

"Think of it," he continued. "The boundaries aren't physical. They exist at all points as a quantum skin."

"It was trying to heal itself?"

"Yes, with platelets, primordial ooze, manna. It has many names."

I couldn't even grasp where he was going with this.

"So now what?" I asked.

"I need your help."

"What could you possibly need from me?" I asked. "Bowie, the things you have in there are... Why don't you patent them, sell them, something?"

"Money?" Bowie rolled his eyes. "How trite. Finances do not concern me. This is so much more important." He fixed his gaze on me. "I'm going to make contact."

"Contact? With what?"

"I probably should have asked you first." He scratched at his neck and shrugged. "I'm sorry."

"For what?"

"Look. There are...how should I put this?" Boas picked up his fork and chased a link around his plate. He speared it. "Side effects."

If I hadn't been sitting, I would have fallen over.

"Not lethal. Well, um..."

"Bowie, what did you—"

"Stay calm. It's not like you're thinking. You are quite safe."

I shoved my plate away and squeezed the edge of the table.

"Relax," he said. "Look around the room. What do you see?"

I couldn't take my eyes off him. He'd exposed me to something, knowing that there were dangers.

"It was that…that mist."

"Ylem is the archaic term for it, but ectoplasm is more accurate, mirroring the cellular aspect as well as the metaphysical. Now, look around the room. How many others are here?"

What an inane question. I made a cursory appraisal. "Seven."

"I count eight, but I've had more exposures."

We made a quick comparison, marking off each person in turn, verifying what the other saw. We both saw the truckers, the delivery man, the security guard and others.

"The man at the counter," I said. "Purple suit."

"Purple?" Boas looked confused.

"Yes, strangely outdated."

"Interesting. I don't see him at all. And you don't see the old woman two tables to the left?"

"No."

"What about the child wandering about? He can barely walk. See, he just fell again."

I chewed at my lip and again surveyed the room.

"No," I said weakly, "there's no one."

"Don't move," Boas said. "He's coming this way."

I still didn't see any toddler.

"You should probably keep looking at me," Boas said, looking uncharacteristically nervous. He laughed lightly.

"What?" I asked.

"You didn't feel that?"

"Feel what?"

"He bit you."

"You are a liar if you expect me to believe…"

There was a dull pain from my left shin.

"And now he's—" Boas grimaced. I winced and jerked my right leg hard, jamming it into the table with enough force to upset the creamer. "Davis, you should leave. Go outside. I'll pay and meet you."

I did so, letting the diner door swing shut behind me. I limped away from the building. Sitting on a nearby bench, I checked my right ankle. A ring of tiny marks bent around it. I rubbed at them with my thumb. Indentations were palpably grooved into my skin.

I waited a long while for Boas to join me outside. He never did.

* * *

The next morning I awoke at my apartment and went through the normal routine of gathering the paper, watering the plants and checking the news. I even picked up the phone and called Boas. He didn't answer. He rarely did, so it was hard to read anything into it.

I didn't understand why he left last night, but I didn't understand a lot of things, not in the way that he did. I really needed to speak with him. I called again without success. That's when I saw her.

She was in the living room, sitting quietly and staring at my potted ivy. At first I didn't recognize her. I hadn't seen her since she vacated the apartment nearly a decade ago. The left side of her face hung loosely, like it had slipped from the bone. Her eye was completely covered by her sagging brow, and the corner of her mouth curled wetly downward.

"Mrs. Carmichael?"

She twitched.

"What are you doing here?" I asked. "How did…"

She rose and turned slowly, pivoting on her heels in a manner that was less than pleasing. She stopped, with her toes pointing at me.

Half of her face ran like wax, even its wrinkles drooped smooth and slack. The right side was focused and feral, with a glaring, pin-prick eye and lips drawn back from empty gums. She hissed.

"Did you keep your key? You shouldn't have, though I'd be happy to—"

She moved in the most perplexing manner. Her limbs pedaled backward, but she skated forward with each motion. She fell once, sprawling forward through the coffee table. Its glass surface cracked but didn't shatter. She sank downward and in so doing rose back up.

It was an affront to Newtonian motion. My insides seized at the thought of it. She was following physical laws that were alien here. Blasphemy. Her good eye wobbled in all directions before locking on me again. I ran.

* * *

After a frantic trip via cab, I arrived at the university. The grounds were mostly empty. Maintenance crews were occupied with ambitious projects as department colleagues made their last min-ute rounds. A handful of students looked strangely out of place. A young woman sat in the middle of the walkway, staring at her knees. Another was perched on the edge of a high balcony. An emaciated youth lay face down in the sodden grass. I pressed on without pause, ignoring his muffled sobs.

The Physics offices were deserted and, even more opportune, the labs as well. I'd formed some working theories on the ride over. Boas claimed the mist was from a cellular boundary. If it was still on me, then that meant I was now some sort of boundary too, a human buoy.

I tested a film sample under a microscope. It was confounding. I could feel the substance, but couldn't see it. A nervous test for radioactivity proved negative. Hours went by. I tried every method of detection available: solvents, dyes and reactants chosen with increasingly jittery disconnection. Finally, it dawned on me.

The substance had a sheen, which implied refraction. A simple UV test and the evidence was plain. From fingertips to wrists, my hands crawled with them, by the hundreds, if not thousands. With glassy bodies like string and a thousand legs of thread, they coiled over and around each other, biting and scrabbling to reach my skin and dig into my pores. Under the UV light, they rolled about in an iridescent ecstasy.

My hands shook. My whole body seized. Scores of the creatures slipped from my hands, tumbled loose, and fought on the flooring. The victors raced up over my shoes and disappeared under the legs of my slacks.

I cried out and whipped my fingers in the air. The creatures fell like rain, over the tables and the floor. They bounced about noiselessly, cartwheeling, but always skittered back toward me.

I'm not an easily unsettled man, but I stood there and unabashedly wept. I pulled my shirt loose and watched them squeeze up from under my beltline. I tried to grab them, but couldn't. They were ethereal. An awful realization was dawning. They favored my hands because of the exposure, but that wasn't the only part of me that had been affected.

I somehow steered myself to a mirror without tripping. Several times I was light-headed from the expectation—no, the knowledge—of my dire state. I didn't want to see, but I had to. I needed to know what they were doing. I aimed the UV light at my face.

The world was instantly obscured behind a seething froth of legs and segmented bodies. Glimpses through the mass showed it all too clearly. They had cocooned themselves about my head to spill over my mouth and lap at the corners of my eyes. My nose and ears were clogged. My hair was a nest of them, and others: a spider with legs like darning needles, creatures that were a fusion of wasps and sparrows, a fist-sized beetle covered in eyes that even now deposited its brood.

I dropped the light and retched.

* * *

It took a long while to gather my wits and stagger upright. I moved in a dreamlike stupor, grasping for equipment with numb fingers. More than a few items slipped from my fingers and shattered against the floor.

There had to be a way to neutralize the condition. I had dozens of theoretical cures, from weak acid washes, to infrared exposure, to iodine baths. My mind raced to form new approaches.

"Davis."

In all of this, I'd forgotten about him. I spun about.

"Bowie!" I exclaimed. "Do you know what you've done?"

Boas leaned in the doorway, looking like he'd awoken in an alleyway. He came forward and examined my work.

"I knew I'd find you eventually. See, you *do* have a new perspective. I could have used you."

"I've been calling you all day."

"I couldn't answer."

"Why didn't you just ask? This…this…contamination didn't need to be spread."

"I didn't know, at the time."

"I thought we were friends."

"We were."

I narrowed my eyes at this pronouncement and set the equipment back on the table.

"I'm covered in these…things."

"Yes, I'm aware. Insects. Myriapods. And many new subphyla, I'm certain. They may have lived here once, though they could very well be extra-terrestrial. In fact," he stared at the ceiling, "assume that they are."

I shook my hands and imagined the creatures slinging away. I'd turned off the UV light, but my mind was morbidly eager to fill in the missing details. I reached to my face but stopped. All that would accomplish was to smear them about, agitate them.

"But, why?"

Boas sat on a lab stool and slumped over the table. "Insects outnumber all other living forms, and hence all other spirit forms. Probabilistically, they're the most likely to find you. They have the best sense of smell too. The ectoplasm is like nectar to them."

"I'm getting rid of them. You must help."

"No."

My mouth hung open. Imagining those creatures pouring into me, I clamped my lips shut. I sputtered in frustration, in disgust. "Boas, this isn't a joke. They reflect UV—"

"No, the ectoplasm reflects it. I think they get it inside, or on, themselves. Even if you could remove it—"

"A UV table at a tanning salon, or a sub-dermal laser, for tattoo removal. I will burn my skin off before I accept this."

"It wouldn't do any good."

I marched up to him and glared. Something about what he just said didn't make sense. "Wait. They're gathering it?"

"Yes?" He grinned and flashed that expectant figure-out-what-I-know look of his.

"They should remove it all on their own."

"Like ants after a sugar cube."

"Then this will end."

"No."

"What? Why not?"

"Well..." Boas pushed himself to his feet. "This is a first-aid station?"

"Clearly."

"Have you listened to your pulse?"

I didn't answer. I flew to the nurse's cabinet and dug through the bandages and saline washes. After finding a stethoscope, I put the plugs in my ears, wincing as I imagined those insects crawling inside them. I held the microphone against my wrist.

Music. Brittle precision. I'd heard this before, when the omniscope started.

"Are you familiar with string theory?" Boas asked.

"Balderdash! I don't subscribe to that."

"No matter. It subscribes to you. Parts of it, anyhow."

"You're mad. Quantum vibrations don't operate—"

"No, that would change your structure. Your condition is at the cellular level. That's why the insects are so excited."

I shook.

"They'll get inside you, fill you up like some sort of ghastly piñata. If they haven't already."

I clenched my fists. "We can reverse it. We'll use your omniscope and dial in to a different frequency. Something to cancel it out. Some sort of white noise."

"Ingenious, Davis! I salute you. It would work, but…this is hard for me to say." Boas rubbed at the back of his neck and laughed. "You never asked what happened to me last night."

"I waited for you, but I couldn't find you."

"I know. I understand a few things now. Such as that child, the one who bit you? He attacked you because you doubted him. You were told specifically that he was there and you disbelieved. That is impossibly insulting. But I didn't believe either," Boas said, "so they took me."

"They? Bowie, you're not making—"

I thought Boas had looked the worse for wear, and now that I was able to study him without preoccupation, it was clear. That dark stain at his abdomen. His punctured jacket. I took a step back.

"Please, don't waste the effort."

I rubbed at my mouth, but remembered the insects and fell to the floor convulsing. Boas laughed heartily as I knocked over chairs and banged into tables.

"Enough," he said. "Listen. I've always wanted to make my mark. You know that."

I spit and choked and flapped my fingers.

"It would have been so nice to have my own place, here." Boas walked to the window and stared outside. "Didn't realize we'd lost so many students. Sad, in a way, but not really." He watched through the glass for a long while before turning. "I cast away my regrets. I embrace a new purpose."

I picked myself up and eyed him warily.

"I wanted to prove…well, you know. It would have been fascinating, but nothing compared to this. You see, I was the only one who wanted to knock at the door. But, you've already seen how eager the tenants are to get out."

"Wait, Boas, you can't mean—"

"Yes!" He beamed. "Think of it. Every being in human history knowing what I've done. Universal adulation. Every sentient mind that's ever existed will know my work. That's so much greater than anything I can do here. I conquered eternity. Not our eternity, but *theirs.*"

I searched his face. There was no trace of jest. "You can't."

"Can't? I already have. My equipment was lacquered with it, ambrosia. It was quite easy to manipulate."

Boas leaned back with a look of smug satisfaction. I picked up my UV light and turned my back to him. Forcing my feet to move slowly wasn't easy. After closing the door behind me, I took off at a full sprint down the hall.

* * *

"Hey, you hear that?" the cab driver asked. We were still miles away from the lab.

"I do," I said. "The end is nigh."

"Maybe so. Damned strange thing for kids to play. You see where it's coming from?"

"Up ahead, I believe."

"Catchy little tune."

The lights were off at Boas's warehouse, but the racket within was stunning. I flipped the power on knowing what I'd find.

The tent was still in place. A pale bluish light bled from its seams. I moved as close as I dared. If I had soaked up a lot of that ectoplasm, imagine what that tent held. I flipped on my UV light. It was the last mistake I ever made.

Maybe if I would have charged in, remained oblivious, I could have turned it off. But seeing what squatted around that tent, what coiled around it with a thousand mouths and a million young, what even now turned its ancient gaze toward me, it was too much. I froze. Its children swarmed and tumbled outward, fighting for the prize.

The curtain tore. With the omniscope running at maximum, Boas hadn't just punctured eternity, he'd severed its threads. There was a snap and the spirits crawled out from behind every speck of dust.

* * *

I was there the day it started to rain, here, there, everywhere. I was there as our entire history spilled into the present. As amazing as it seemed, Boas was right. He was the most famous of heroes, the beloved savior. Just ask anyone. They're always in agreement. He'd given them what they wanted most.

ABOUT THE AUTHOR
JOHN F.D. TAFF

John F.D. Taff has published more than seventy short stories during his career that spans more than two decades. His unique brand of dark fiction has been published in *Cemetery Dance*, *Deathrealm*, *Big Pulp*, *Postscripts to Darkness*, *Hot Blood: Fear the Fever*, *Hot Blood: Seeds of Fear* and *Shock Rock II*. Six of his short stories have been given honorable mentions in the *Year's Best Fantasy & Horror*.

His first collection, *Little Deaths*, was published in 2012 and has been well-reviewed by critics and readers alike. The collection appeared on the Bram Stoker Reading List, has been a Number One bestseller and was named the "Number One Horror Collection of 2012" by *HorrorTalk*. Taff's *The Bell Witch* is a historical novel inspired by the events of a real-life haunting and was released in August 2013. His thriller *Kill/Off* was published in December 2013.

Taff's short story "Show Me" is featured in the 2013 Bram Stoker Award®-nominated anthology from Grey Matter Press, *Dark Visions: A Collection of Modern Horror – Volume One*. His tale that breathes new life into the zombie apocalypse, "Angie," appears in the bestselling Grey Matter Press volume *Ominous Realities: The Anthology of Dark Speculative Horrors*. And his second single-author collection of five haunting novellas, *The End in all Beginnings*, received massive critical acclaim when it was published by Grey Matter Press in 2014.

SOME OTHER DAY

JOHN F.D. TAFF

Sometimes the world weeps for us when we cannot. When we will not.

But grief is not a thing that can be stored up or forgotten.

Grief is not a thing that can be pushed aside or ignored.

Grief is not a thing that can be buried or banished like a ghost, even if its causes can.

I know that now, and it's a hard, hard lesson to learn.

* * *

Friday morning. He asked to play catch again today. Nick, my son. *Her* son.

I turned him down...*again*. He came to me, from the silence of his room to the silence of mine. He had his old, beaten Rawlings glove on his left hand, an equally scuffed baseball in the right. The ball didn't move from one to the other; it sat like a stone in his bare hand.

He looked *old*. He was only thirteen, but Christ he looked old.

I stared at the ball's red stitches for a moment. They looked like the dead, crosshatched eyes of a cartoon character.

It had only been a month since she passed away, and her absence left a house full of silent rooms. The only thing with the will to speak was the 60-inch plasma television she hadn't wanted me to buy. I left it on so that there were some voices in the house, happy voices.

Part of me, though, left it on to spite her for leaving us.

So we lived there in our silent house, Nick and I, lived and dealt with the death of the most important woman in both of our lives in the quietest way possible.

We let the TV do the talking.

I heard rain outside, like the hiss of static, pattering the windows and the roof.

I looked at him, his flat, solemn face impassive.

"Raining, Champ," I said, letting the impression of a smile slide across my face. "Maybe some other day."

He sighed, barely audible above the bright chatter of the TV and the white noise of the rain.

"That's what you *always* say." Turning, he made his way back down the darkened hallway to the silence he was more accustomed to these days.

A murky smudge lingered in the doorway like an echo of his presence. My tear-rheumed eyes tried to focus on it, and it seemed to coalesce, as if the air itself were weeping dark, coagulating blood.

I blinked several times and the shadowy fug frayed away, leaving behind a feeling of disappointment and a hint of my wife's perfume.

I heard his door close, just as Sheldon said something funny on TV.

I turned my head back to the flickering lights and descended through waves of canned laughter that washed everything else away.

Still feel guilty about that.

* * *

Monday. I was sitting in the car, listening to a mix CD I'd made a while back for one of our outings. This CD had some stuff by Adele, Tom Petty, Tom Waits. She loved to take short day trips with Nick and me, to farmers markets or state parks or little, out of the way towns filled with diners and antiques and feed stores.

I turned to the passenger seat, and there she was. Her brown hair was gathered in a loose ponytail. She wore a pair of denim shorts and a plain white t-shirt, because she knew that I found this relatively plain outfit sexy.

She turned to me, but for some reason her face was obscured, out of focus. I could see her features, but as if through frosted glass. She smiled, reached over to take my hand. She lifted it to her lips, and I could feel them, smooth and moist, feel her lip balm smack against the back of my hand. I could smell the lotion she used, the shampoo, the body wash.

"It's just a game of catch, you know," she said, her voice sounding as if it were traveling up from great depths.

I closed my eyes, felt the heart within me shudder, and snapped awake in the garage.

I came to, deep into a Guster song. It was dark in the car, lit only by the ghostly dashboard lights. Through the music, I could hear the rumble of thunder and the rain—the incessant rain—patter on the roof of the garage.

I looked in the rearview mirror. The garage door was closed.

The car was running.

Of course, she wasn't there.

What the hell?

Turning again, I jumped at a smeary, pale face in the side window.

Nick.

I shut off the stereo, the engine.

"What are you doing out here?" he asked.

"Just came out to get a CD," I said, smiling as I opened the door, climbed from the car.

Nick looked at me oddly. He had the ball glove on one hand again, the baseball in the other.

"It stinks in here."

I coughed at the thin cloud of exhaust. How long had I been out there?

"Yeah, let's get in the house, Champ," I said, putting my hands on his thin shoulders and leading him away. "I let the car run too long."

He was inside before he realized it. "You forgot your CD," he said.

* * *

Tuesday. Bedtime snack. He chewed on a peanut butter and jelly sandwich. I drank a Coke Zero and crunched distractedly on Fritos straight from the bag.

"When do you have to go back to work?"

I chewed, swallowed. "Next week."

Nick took a drink of milk from the glass before him, wiped away a white mustache. He looked at me with those big, solemn brown eyes. They were so much like his mom's that it seemed for a moment that he wore a Nick mask with the eyes cut out, and she was peeking through.

It was as if he was her ghost, still here, haunting the house. Haunting me.

I thought of the dark, translucent smear he'd left in the hallway a few days before, and for some reason my mind saw her eyes in that mist.

I shivered, but he didn't notice.

"Why so soon?"

"I've been away almost a month, Champ. Gotta get back to work. It's time." I sighed.

He considered this, deciding whether to accept or reject that premise.

"School, too?"

I nodded. "Yep, I go back to work, you go back to school."

"I'm not ready."

"I know, neither am I. But we've got to get on with our lives. Mom wouldn't want us to stop what we're doing. She'd want us to go on and live and be happy."

"I'm happy being out of school," he said, and he smiled, a little smile that curled the corners of his mouth.

"And I'm happy being out of work, but that ain't the way the world rolls."

"*Ain't* isn't a word," he said, his smile growing wider. "Mom says so."

"Well, I'm not arguing with your mom, even now. Now finish up here, brush your teeth, grab a shower and get to bed. Call me when you're done and I'll tuck you in."

I went back into the living room, let the television's droning wash over me.

I must have fallen asleep because I jerked awake on the couch, wide-eyed.

I rubbed my head, yawned.

Shit. I forgot about Nick.

Leaping up, I went to his room. The door was ajar, and it was dark inside, just a *Star Wars* nightlight casting elongated shadows on the floor.

I stepped around toys, discarded clothes, shoes—so many shoes—to see if he was awake.

He wasn't, and I felt bad that I'd fallen asleep. He was a little old to be tucked in, but given the circumstances...

Like all teenagers he sprawled across the mattress, seemingly unable to lay parallel to a bed's rigid lines. The covers were rucked up around his legs, and his feet stuck out, clad in dirty socks. I took each foot, surprised at how big they were getting, and gently peeled the sock away, held it for a moment wondering what to do, cast it into the darkness.

At some point, we'd have to address this room, do some laundry.

I moved closer to the bed. I could smell the mint of his toothpaste on the air. Good, he'd actually brushed his teeth. I could also smell the unmistakable sourness of unwashed boy. So, he hadn't taken a shower. Oh well.

I ruffled his hair, pulled the covers over him.

A book slipped away from the hand that hung over the bed.

I pinched it between finger and thumb, lifted it. It was an oversize, thin hardcover volume of nursery rhymes. I remembered the book vaguely, something she'd bought for him a few years back. He was too old for the book, even when she'd gotten it for him.

Chuckling ruefully, I wondered what possessed him to grab this book and read it.

I flipped through it casually, closed it, set it onto his nightstand, jostling an action figure of some super hero or another, which clattered to the floor.

Nick groaned, stretched, and I retreated quietly toward the hall.

"Mom says to play catch with me tomorrow," he said, his voice sleep fuzzy.

The room became a little colder at that, and I wondered who he was talking to. But I chalked it up to his being not fully awake.

"Okay. Long as the rain stops."

"You mean it? Really?"

I nodded, drew the door mostly closed. "Good night, kiddo."

"Night, Dad."

* * *

Why did I avoid playing catch with my son?

Well, first, I hate baseball. More of a football guy, but Nick was too small and thin to play just yet.

Second, it was his mother who'd played catch with him.

And now—right now—I just couldn't.

I was going to have to take her place in so many other things in his life that I couldn't do *that*.

I knew the rain would stop eventually.

I knew he'd come out of his room, his eyes beseeching mine with hers.

I knew I'd have to play catch.

I just didn't know how soon.

* * *

Wednesday. Breakfast.

He huddled over a bowl of Cap'n Crunch. I slumped over a cup of coffee so strong I considered inhaling its vapors rather than actually drinking it.

She usually made the—

"Catch today?" he asked around a mouthful of cereal.

"Don't ask important questions with your mouth full," I muttered, drawing in a deep breath, taking a drink of the black slurry and grimacing.

He chewed quickly, swallowed, opened his mouth wide, stuck his tongue out.

"Okay, smart guy."

"Can we play catch today? You promised, remember?"

I swiveled my head around to look out the kitchen window. The light that came in was the color of skim milk, hazy and opaque.

"It looks like it might—"

"Dad, don't even say it!" he said. "I'll get dressed fast and meet you outside."

"Okay, okay." I laughed, trying a sip of my coffee. It raced down my throat, hot and bitter and nearly acidic, and my whole body shook with its progress.

Nick spooned the last few soggy morsels of cereal into his mouth, raised the bowl to drink the milk, something his mother had never tolerated. He watched me over the rim of the bowl to see how I'd react, but I just raised an eyebrow, contemplated the advisability of a second sip of coffee.

I rose, dumped the dark liquid into the sink.

"Ten minutes and I'll meet you outside. Dishes in the dishwasher first," I reminded him.

Nick leapt up, slid to a stop, raced back to put the bowl and spoon away, then shot off down the hallway.

I honestly thought I was safe. Honestly thought that the rain was just moments away from starting up again.

Now, three months later, I think, I really do believe that it probably was.

* * *

Nick raced out the front of the house, let the screen door slap shut. Another of his mother's pet peeves.

"What took you so long?" I asked, showing a little more irritation than I should have. I'd been outside on the front lawn for about fifteen minutes. In that time, he'd changed from his pajamas into last year's little league uniform, cleats and all.

And the sky had changed, too, from a uniform pale grey to an almost cloudless deep blue.

He came to a stop right before me, and I saw that his face was red, flushed. His eyes were wide and bright, and he took in the suddenly sunny, rainless day.

I thought he was excited about playing catch, excited to get outside and play in the sun with his old man.

I reached out, took the spare glove from him.

His mother's glove, a little snug for me, but it would work.

Nick stepped back about a dozen paces, crouched a little.

I jammed the glove on my hand, popped the ball into it a few times to loosen the leather, loosen my wrists.

So we played catch that early spring morning, just a few weeks after she'd died.

And it was good.

The air was cool and just a little damp. The sun sparkled on the emerald grass, and the wind played with the leaves, the little cowlick of hair at the top of Nick's head. I could hear the distant putter of a lawnmower, could smell the green smell of freshly clipped grass, that clean, indefinable smell of spring air.

And it was good.

* * *

We played catch all that week, every morning, sometimes in the afternoon or early evening, too. It was like a proverbial cloud had lifted and not just the real ones overhead. Nick was as happy as I'd seen him, almost as happy as before. It made it easier for both of us to go back, him to school, me to work.

Both of us to our regularly scheduled lives.

I slept better. Well, actually slept, period. I still saw her in the house, out of the corner of my eye. A smudge in the mirror as I brushed my teeth. Standing in the doorway of the bedroom as I fell asleep.

Nick and I ate real meals together, went out a little, to the movies, the mall, a ballgame or two. We started building a new life, a life without her.

And the darkness that circulated through the house like a miasma? That presence of *her* that lingered, coloring the air with its sadness and disappointment? It lifted, too.

We even turned the television off, and it stayed off most days.

That's why it took so long for me to even hear about it.

* * *

What is grief, really?

Is it just existential? The loss, the physical absence of a loved one?

Is it just chemical? An emotion secreted by the glands to fill the void?

Is it just physics? Some force between two bodies that grows stronger with separation?

Or is it alive? Something that has to be nurtured, tended? Like a garden?

It could be all of these things, and none of them.

These days, though, I think it's like a bomb, a bomb that you hold in one hand while the other holds the tinder. The longer you hold the tinder, the longer it takes for you to light the bomb, the more powerful the bomb becomes.

Not that it matters, really.

In the end, the bomb blows you up just the same.

In the end, it's just a matter of how much of your world you want it to take with you when it explodes.

Nick and I?

We waited too long.

* * *

I stood outside on a Saturday morning late in June. It was only about ten o'clock, but it was already hot. I wiped sweat from my forehead as I walked across the front lawn.

Restless and edgy, I paced back and forth, growing impatient.

I knew Nick was inside, dressing in his baseball uniform. Not just for the game of catch we were going to play, but also to visit his mother.

Her stone had finally been placed at the cemetery, and we were headed out to see it. It was special ordered, cost a small fortune and took several months to make. But I had seen pictures emailed to me throughout the process of its creation by the stonemason, and it was worth it.

Today, after catch, of course, we'd go out and see it in person.

See her.

Nick came bounding out the house, across the porch and down the steps, just as I noticed the grass.

It was sere and brown, crackling under foot.

Dead.

I looked up, saw that my neighbors' lawns, too, were a more or less uniform crispy brown.

"I guess we should water the lawn," I muttered, snugging the glove down onto my hand.

Nick looked at me quizzically.

"And get arrested?"

My face said it all.

"Water rationing, Dad. Duh. Do you even watch the news? They talk about it every day in school.

I considered that for a moment, shrugged. "Huh, I guess I haven't been paying attention."

"To the drought?" Nick laughed.

I caught the ball he snapped at me, held it for a second.

Yeah, I guess it hadn't rained in a while, but *drought*?

"Well, yeah," I offered gamely.

Nick snorted. "Well, at least it stopped raining. A few months ago, it rained all the time. It ruined everything. It…"

He trailed off, looked at his cleats.

Sighing, I popped the ball into my glove, closed it tight, walked over to him.

"Dad, is it okay if I don't go to the…to see the stone today? I'm really not feeling like it."

I considered this, embarrassed that I thought about making him come because I didn't want to go alone.

"Sure. I understand. I'll just be gone an hour or so. Stop by and pick up flowers to leave for her. You know…"

"Yeah," he said. "Can we throw a couple more before you leave?"

* * *

Nick and I had a great time that summer.

We never once talked about what was really on our minds, though. *Her.*

Or rather, her absence.

We each held our bomb in one hand, our tinder in the other, and pretended not to notice either.

* * *

The months went by, and things got worse. Now there were bans on lawn watering, car washing, swimming pools and water parks. Rolling "water blackouts" were enforced. Nick and I made the most of it, in a manly way, seeing how long we could go without showers or flushing the toilet. "If it's yellow, let it mellow. If it's brown, flush it down," became a mantra.

But we played catch every day, though it was so breathtakingly hot most days that we only played in the early morning or at twilight.

Playing catch was beginning to be *our* thing, finally.

I think we both felt as if we'd banished her ghost.

* * *

I was inside after one late game, watching the news. It was now going on about five months without rain. Five months with 100-degree-plus temperatures.

The National Guard was airlifting in tankers to ensure vital facilities—hospitals, schools, food banks—had water. Crops were withering in the ground. Prices for meat, vegetables, milk, butter, eggs were all skyrocketing. Bottled water was disappearing from store shelves almost the minute it was put out. People were dying.

Nick came in, freshly showered. It was the first one he'd taken in almost a week. I had insisted. His room was beginning to smell like an animal's den.

"What's up?"

"More bad news," I said.

"Water?"

"Yep. It'll be more expensive than gas pretty soon."

I looked over and saw him, gangly arms on bony knees, leaning in towards the TV, watching it intently.

His face was grave, tight, lit by the flashing television. His lips compressed into a thin band.

"Selfish," he whispered, then he stood and left the room.

I checked on him later, but he was asleep. The real talent of teenagers is to fall asleep anytime, anywhere, under any circumstances. He was splayed atop the covers, already breathing slowly, regularly.

I brushed his head with the tips of my fingers. His hair was still wet.

Doing my usual tiptoe out of the room to avoid toys—particularly those damn Lego pieces—I caught something out of the corner of my eye.

It was the book she'd bought him, the book of nursery rhymes.

It was jammed at an odd angle against the wall across from his bed, upside down, the pages rifled and bent as if he'd flung it there.

I pursed my lips.

I thought, I really did, that this was misdirected anger, that he'd thrown the book across the room because of grief, because somewhere over the last few weeks he'd brought the unseen bomb and the unseen tinder together in his hands.

I paused there in the cluttered darkness, thought about what to do, what I *should* do.

I left it there, left it where he'd thrown it, where it had landed like some stricken bird.

I didn't want to pick it up, replace it on his nightstand.

Didn't want him to know that I'd glimpsed a very private expression of rage at his mother.

So, I crept from the room, forgot it.

* * *

Saturday morning. There was a knock at the door while we ate breakfast. We exchanged looks, and I got up from my coffee and toast to answer the door.

It was a uniformed man from the water company. Behind him stood a uniformed police officer. The water company employee explained that we were required by law to let him in to search the house and install locks on certain faucets, low-flow valves on others. Newly enacted crisis legislation, no choice. All at my cost, of course.

I let them in. The water worker seemed edgy, nervous. The cop was grim but detached.

Nick watched the pair descend into the basement.

He flashed me a look that was worry, fear and guilt somehow all rolled into one.

"It's okay, kiddo," I said, smiling. "Our showers are probably going to get pretty dribbly from here on out. You want to go outside, throw a little while they're working?"

He stared at the basement door for a moment, shrugged, left the kitchen to go to his room. It was too hot outside to wear baseball gear, so I imagined he was just swapping his pajamas for shorts and a t-shirt.

Sniffing my own fairly gamey clothes, I thought that might not be such a bad idea.

I passed the basement door on my way to my room, heard the clunking of tools on pipes. Nick's room was right down from the door to the master bedroom, and as I started to go into my room to change clothes, I heard voices.

Correction. I heard *a* voice talking, almost chanting.

I paused in the hallway. His door was open just a crack. We hadn't gotten him a cell phone yet, so was he on mine, talking to someone?

Leaning in closer, I peeked into the room.

Nick was curled up atop his rumpled bed, his legs drawn up, his arms wrapped around his knees. His eyes were tightly closed, and he was clearly upset.

But that wasn't what stopped me, what made the air in my lungs evaporate.

It was her, her form, standing there between us, her back to me.

I knew it was her, the fall of her hair across her neck, the dark dress we'd buried her in, the smooth skin of her shoulders, her arms.

But she was insubstantial there in the darkness, a ghost. I could see Nick clearly through her form.

She didn't turn to me at all, didn't acknowledge my presence.

Rather, she focused on Nick, on what he was saying.

I could just make out words.

…some other day.

I hesitated, still not sure what he was saying, who he was talking to.

As I stood there, silent as I could be, I heard all the words he was saying, and my blood chilled faster than my brain could figure out their implication.

My mouth dried as thoroughly as if I'd stood outside and held it open to the midday sun.

Nursery rhymes?

Why would he—

A 13-year-old boy reciting nursery rhymes can't—

Of course not.

That's crazy.

Inside his room, he whispered the words again.

Not knowing what else to do, I held my breath, backed away from the door, went into my own room.

I think I held my breath the entire time I dressed, only breathing again as I stepped outside to play catch, when the hot, dry air sucked it from me.

* * *

Saturday night. I was sitting on the edge of the bed when he came back from brushing his teeth.

He cut his eyes at me as he pulled off his socks, threw them on the floor. We still hadn't dealt with the room, and laundry was still haphazard because of the water restrictions.

"Let's talk," I said, scooting over to make room for him.

"What's up?" he asked, and right there, *right there* I knew.

"We haven't talked much about your mom."

"What's there to talk about?"

"She's dead."

"Duh. Why do we need to talk about that?" he asked, his tone becoming petulant. He sidled around me, stretched out on the bed, covered his face with a pillow.

"Because she's still here, everywhere. I see her here in the house every day, in every room. I see her in you. But she's not here, not really. And we haven't talked about how we feel about that."

He made no response, but I could see his thin chest hitching up and down.

I reached over gently, tried to remove the pillow. His arms clenched reflexively over it, clamped it down.

"Nick…"

I pulled at the pillow again, and he let it loose—slowly, grudgingly—exposing the red, tear-streaked face he was trying to hide.

For a moment he just glared at me, his chest rising and falling so quickly that he could scarcely catch his breath much less talk. Tears welled from his eyes, snaked down his cheeks, fell onto the pillow beneath his head. *Plip-plip-plip.*

The bomb was finally exploding—his, at least.

There's no need to go into the scene that followed because grief is reduced somehow in the telling. Grief, in all its forms, has a certain triteness when expressed second-hand, a certain banality.

I don't want to lessen what he felt by trying to express it here.

I comforted him as he allowed me, what with him being a teenager and all, trying to mourn yet also trying to hold onto some of his recent, hard-won masculinity.

When he'd calmed somewhat I stood, picked up the book of nursery rhymes, sat back on the bed with it.

"Want to tell me about this?"

He flushed, wiped tears from his eyes.

"It's just a stupid book, just baby rhymes. But…"

"Go ahead."

"I wanted mom back so badly, just part of her. And you wouldn't…
I couldn't say…couldn't…"

The tears started again, so I risked reaching over and wiping his
eyes for him, something I had done dozens of times when he was
younger. He let me, sniffled and smiled a little.

"I wanted that part of her back, and you wouldn't give that to
me…so…"

I swallowed. My throat was dry. "You know I missed—*miss*—her,
too. I'm sorry if I closed you out, Nick, I really am. But I didn't know
what to do. I know you don't want to hear this from your dad, but I
was just as lost as you."

"Dad, it's okay. I understand. It's…well, now I feel stupid and
selfish."

"No, kiddo, no. You don't have to feel that way at all. I forgot I can't
just stop being a dad, whatever the reason."

Nick sat up a little in the bed, took the book from me, flipped
through its pages quickly.

Even upside down, I saw a dish running away with a spoon, a
house-sized shoe surrounded by children, a cat with a fiddle.

He found the page he was looking for, passed it to me.

The watercolor illustration showed a young boy looking from a
window. Outside, the rain fell in sheets. His face was ridiculously
sad, and he held a baseball and glove.

Rain, rain go away.

Come again some other day.

I held the page with shaking hands.

"Mom used to read it to me. I read it to see if it worked."

I licked my lips, lowered the book.

"Every day I came in here and read the rhyme out loud, and I can
feel her here with me. Sometimes…sometimes I even think I can see
her, standing in my doorway, looking in on me."

My breathing hitched. I remembered the dark cloud in the hallway, my experience in the garage. I remembered her standing here in this room, beside his bed.

And I could feel her presence here, around us, unseen, urging us on.

"I didn't think it would work, but it *did*. Dad, it did! That very first day. Remember? We played catch. So, I did it the next morning and the next and the next. And it worked every day. It's worked all this time."

"Nick—"

"You don't believe me, but it's true. I just wanted...I just wanted you to play catch. I wanted you to notice me, like she used to."

I pulled him to me, pressed my lips to his cheek and apologized, over and over.

I felt tears slip from my cheek to his, fall to the bed. *Plip-plip-plip.*

"I caused this. It's my fault. The drought, the water rationing."

I pulled away, cupped his face with my hands, shushed him.

"It doesn't matter anymore, Nick."

"But Dad, the water...?"

I shrugged. "You've said the rhyme every day? Well, not that I believe it's anything more than coincidence, but if it makes you feel better, just don't say it tomorrow. Don't say it anymore."

His eyes narrowed. "Will that work?"

"If saying it worked, not saying it should work, too."

And I believed that.

* * *

Sunday. Early in the morning.

It was late when I finally went to my bed, threw myself on it, hunkered down into the pillows. Even though I hadn't seen her recently, hadn't even dreamed about her, I could still smell her on the linens, despite the scented laundry detergent, the fabric softener. I supposed her ghost would linger here the longest.

But even with that thought, I still felt as if an enormous weight had been lifted from my shoulders, my heart, and I fell into a deep sleep fairly quickly.

There were no dreams, and I floated easily through the night.

I was awakened by the sound of the wind outside, whistling, whining; tree limbs raking the sides of the house.

There was a flash of lightning, a tremendous rumble of thunder.

And then a sound, loud, from above.

Something heavy hit the roof, thudded through the house's bones.

Then another, and another.

I got out of bed, went to the window, yanked open the blinds.

It wasn't dawn yet, but the sky was a nauseous shade of grey-green. Clouds roiled high in the sky, churned, boiled with lightning.

Something struck the lawn, left a crater in the dry dirt.

It took me a moment to figure out what it was.

A raindrop.

A raindrop the size of a bowling ball.

More hit. One struck the branch of a tree, snapped it off.

I thought about running into Nick's room, grabbing the book.

I thought about having Nick recite the nursery rhyme just one more day.

But I knew we had waited too long.

Sometimes the world weeps for us when we cannot.

Eventually, though, the world weeps on its own.

ABOUT THE AUTHOR
HANK SCHWAEBLE

Hank Schwaeble is a World Fantasy Award nominee and the two-time Bram Stoker Award® winner of horror fiction that includes his first novel *Damnable*. Schwaeble is both a writer and an attorney who lives in Houston, Texas.

Schwaeble's short fiction has appeared in anthologies that include *Alone on the Darkside*, *Five Strokes to Midnight*, *Horror Library - Volume IV* and *ZVR: No Man's Land*.

In 2011 he released his second novel, *Diabolical*, and followed that up with his most recent, *Angel of the Abyss*, in December 2014.

HAUNTER

HANK SCHWAEBLE

She would not be easy to find, but Matthew knew she was in there. Somewhere deep. Somewhere hidden. But definitely there.

"And now, for word on a developing situation in Cobb County, Georgia, we go to Atlanta where Jane Riley has been following events and is live on-scene. Jane?"

The plantation-style house loomed large before him as he made his way down the hillside path. Its white clapboard façade, double portico porch, pitched-roof dormer and fanlight entryway were exactly as he had envisioned them. The structure looked very old, almost part of the natural landscape. Very old, but recently built.

Just as he'd expected. Just as he'd told himself.

"Thanks, Ted. Years ago, a quiet, residential community, similar to the one whose homes line the street behind me now, was stunned by the bizarre slayings of two of its residents."

Matthew heard his own reassuring voice, a running narrative instructing him, giving him directions, telling him to remain relaxed, that he was in control, that there was no reason to be afraid. He was safe in these surroundings. They were his creation; familiar, comforting, known to him. He took a moment to study the features of the house, to concentrate on its details. Details meant focus. Focus was the key to success. Focus was *always* the key to success.

The edifice was precisely as he'd envisioned it. The roof's split-wood shingles cascaded uniformly in valleys that straddled the dormers. The two-story portico rose high beneath the majestic pediment, protruding forward on columns set one atop another, Ionic over Doric, separated by a balcony. Nine-over-nine, double-hung sash windows stared outward, unblinking eyes cocked sideways between louvered-shutter lids.

Everything was just as it was supposed to be.

Matthew walked forward and stepped onto the porch. Glass side-lights with lead dividers separated pairs of colonettes, framing an exquisite set of fielded panel double doors beneath the arching fan-light. He hesitated as he reached for the door handle, his disembod-ied voice telling him to be calm. Breathing deeply, he listened to it. *This was why you came,* it said. *Go inside and find her. This is where she would be.*

The door opened as he touched it, swinging inward, revealing the foyer and beckoning him across the threshold. Vague light from un-certain sources illuminated dark walls and darker floors. Just past the entryway, a huge staircase wound upward to the second floor, carpeted in red, with scrolled face-string paneling and ornately carved balusters. To his right was an open dining room, simply but tastefully furnished. To his left, a library. The books in the library were aligned in tight rows from floor to ceiling, packed around a marble-faced fireplace with a mahogany mantle and Doric pilasters.

> *"When police arrived at the Chambers' home in response to a domestic disturbance complaint, they found twenty-six-year-old Melody Chambers sprawled on her living room floor, the apparent victim of a strangulation. The police didn't need to wait for the autopsy to realize she had been, in the responding officers' words, 'throttled.' The imprint of her killer's hands was still clearly visible on her throat."*

Matthew told himself to ignore the upstairs. He needed to descend deep, to travel far into the recesses of the house, the house he had so painstakingly designed, the house he had built piece by piece for this very purpose. That's where she would be—deep, deep, deep—pressed back into some distant crevice, dug in like a tick.

He took a moment to take in his surroundings, to smell the leather of the library, to feel the wood of the floor beneath him. Only after immersing himself in the details of the place, testing the reality of it, did he continue forward. With calm, measured breaths and steady steps he moved past the staircase, looking for the opening to the basement.

She had been making her presence known to him for some time now. Sleep was her invitation, her opening. She insinuated herself into his dreams like a virus. More of the computer variety than the biological kind, a piece of malware bent on shutting down his operating system. If he was dreaming of making love to his wife, he might feel a tap on his shoulder, then turn to see her standing there, mere inches away, that rictus smile on her face, baring jagged teeth. If the dream was the product of generalized stress, the type where he'd find himself all but naked as he rushed to meet a crucial deadline, she would pop out of nowhere, taunting him, laughing at him, warning him that eventually there would come a dream from which he would never wake up, because it wouldn't be a dream at all.

Sometimes, he didn't even need to be asleep.

It would start with that voice. Cloyingly sweet, a cocktail of seduction and spite, calling his name. Then, once it got his attention, not sweet at all, just shrill and abrasive as it grated against his brain, vocal fingernails on a chalkboard. He might be in a meeting, discussing the latest marketing campaign, or in an elevator, surrounded by co-workers. "*Matthew*," would come the scrape. "*Maaaaaath-yew.*" No one else ever seemed to hear it. Everyone seemed to notice that he did.

But the dreams were even worse. He often woke in a start, bolting upright in bed, his t-shirt damp and clinging, her lingering presence so real, so tangible. He could smell her, taste her. Feel her.

The rude awakenings, the panic attacks in the middle of the night, the exhaustion that defined so many days that followed so many restless nights—those things were bad enough. Lately, however, he had begun to wake up having left his bed.

The sleepwalking seemed almost planned, controlled, and if that was the case, Matthew knew she was more powerful than before and would have to be dealt with. The evidence was impossible to ignore.

A week earlier he awoke in the kitchen, having grabbed a knife as she leapt toward him, her eyes blazing, her jaws set wide, her wiry body springing like a leopard. But when consciousness hit him, jolting through him like electricity, the knife in his hand was poised at his own throat, its point depressing the flesh near his jugular. This last time, rather than fending off an attack, he found himself standing beside his bed, wielding a large hammer, his arm cocked high above his head, ready to bring the head of it down on the skull of his sleeping wife.

She was building up to something.

Something bad.

"What police found next would shock the sleepy bedroom community and make headlines for months to come. The controversy would ignite a debate that dominated local talk radio and raised questions no one seemed able to answer."

Beyond the staircase, the house stretched back in a long corridor, gradually narrowing into darkness. Photos lined the walls of the hall as far as sight could take him. Matthew had seen the images all before. Photos of him. Photos of his new wife, Jill. Stills of the two of them at the beach. In the park. At a dinner party. On their wedding day. There were many doors along the hall. One for every handful of photos. But he knew she wouldn't be behind any of them.

She would be in the basement.

Her space would be dark. Out of the way. Hidden. Buried. Deep, deep, deep. He was certain that's where he'd find her, if she was there at all.

She's there, he told himself. She had to be. The alternative was that he was crazy, and he wasn't crazy.

Matthew paused a moment to remind himself of that. It was something he needed to hear again and again, and he indulged the part of him that demanded it. But such reassurance only went so far. The doubts preyed on his mind almost as much as she did. It was no longer enough to tell himself this was her doing, he needed to prove it—prove it and do something about it. He could live with the voices, her hellish vocals interrupting his day, disrupting his conversations, intruding on his most intimate moments. It was maddening, but he could handle it.

Those dreams were another matter. He couldn't let himself sleepwalk while she was manipulating him like that. It was only a matter of time before she succeeded in making him do something horrible.

He had to confront her.

This had to end.

"Young Steven Chambers, a two-year old known to friends and neighbors as "Boo-Bear," lay on his parents' bed, his lungs filled with water. Drowned, the evidence would show, in his own bath."

Matthew walked around the staircase, opening a door in the wood-paneled wall beneath it. Something was wrong. The entry to the basement should have been there. The door was properly positioned, but it opened to reveal only a closet filled with boxes. The layout of the house had been altered. Matthew wasn't certain what to make of it, but he doubted it could mean anything good. The prospect of not being as familiar with the interior recesses as he had thought was more than disturbing.

Another series of breaths, another pep talk about focus. He was not about to turn back. No way. The entry had to be somewhere down the hall. Somewhere deeper.

Matthew entered the blackened corridor, heading deeper into the house, surveying the pictures astride him on the walls. So many pictures, each joined in some way to another until a larger picture seemed to emerge from the pieces. A happy couple, surrounded by bright colors, beaming smiles on their faces. Then the larger picture receded. With each passing door the photos showed Jill less and less, until she no longer appeared in them at all, conspicuous in her absence. The scenes that followed were somber, solitary portraits, colors washed out. Most depicted alcohol in some form. There were women in some of them. None of them smiling, and never the same one twice.

The light became dimmer as he progressed. Concentrate, he told himself. The hall seemed to extend interminably, stretching forward into the distance like tracks into a tunnel. But he continued to walk. Continued to instruct himself. Continued to focus.

The gathering blackness seemed to embrace him as he moved forward. He could feel it enveloping him, felt it taking his hand, caressing him with unspoken promises, urging him to give in to it.

He struggled to maintain his concentration, forced himself to perceive the images around him despite the dearth of light. The photos were faded now, and the few scenes he could make out were austere. Sitting alone in a one-bedroom apartment. Drinking himself to sleep. Crying. A few more steps and they were completely colorless, limited to shades of gray, making them even harder to discern.

Ten yards further and the photos were all empty sheets tinged the hue of an overcast sky held deep in the grip of the shadows. Ahead he saw a door.

> "*Sitting next to Steven on the bed was Matthew Chambers, a prominent, young Atlanta architect. Police described him as all but oblivious to their presence as he stared at his son, stroking his wet hair. "I had to do it," was all the officers recalled Matthew Chambers saying when they covered him with their revolvers, instructed him to step away from the child and place his hands on his head. Police testimony would later describe the scene as containing ritualistic elements, a bizarre arrangement of crystals and herbs and burning incense.*"

Behind the door a steep flight of stairs descended into an inky darkness. Once again there were photos and doors along each side, barely visible, but he avoided looking at them. Down, down, down, stopping at small landings, forcing himself to keep his surroundings in focus. After several flights the stairs terminated at another door. He opened it and stepped inside.

The room swallowed him. He was standing in the center of it. A shadowy, windowless dungeon of a suite, one he knew very well. Everything was strangely visible, despite the surrounding shadow and no obvious source of light. The recognition that it was the bedroom from his old house, the place where his world was ripped out from beneath him, was immediate. As was the realization he was not alone.

"I knew you'd be here," Matthew said.

She was sitting on the bed, Steven's head resting in her lap, his eyes closed. She was looking down at the boy, petting his forehead.

The sight caused his throat to tighten, making it difficult for him to breathe. Tears welled up, spilled over his lids and down his cheeks. The child was just as Matthew remembered him. Rosy cheeks and blonde hair. That tiny body prone to marathon sessions of horse-play as if it were powered by a compact dynamo. At that moment all Matthew could think of was how energetic his son had been, how he had always been running or jumping or climbing.

Laying there now, the boy looked peaceful. Angelic.

Melody did not.

"Hello, Matthew." Her voice was raspy, straddling some tonal line it had found between menacing and titillating. Her eyes locked onto his like the jaws of a pit bull. "I've been expecting you."

> "Matthew Chambers—a man neighbors would describe as a loving father and pillar of the community—was arrested for murder. If that wasn't shocking enough for the residents of the idyllic neighborhood that the Chambers' called home, Matthew Chambers' defense would certainly prove to be. Chambers' lawyer was to plead the affirmative defense of justification."

She was just as she had appeared in his dreams, only more so in every way. Her face was a death mask, withered, mummified, her skin shriveled and desiccated, her lips peeled back in a constant grimace, displaying a rapacious set of teeth. Her body was thin, angular; leathery gray skin wrapped around long bones that were unsettlingly close to the surface. But none of those features could compete with her eyes. They were wide, round, piercing, with pupils that cut into the bright green of her irises like violent stab wounds. She was almost naked, with only a thin stretch of cloth—decayed and earthen—pasted around her torso. A wild mane of jet black hair framed her face. Every bit of her seemed feral. Predatory.

"He was a beautiful child, wasn't he?" she asked, dropping her head to gaze at the boy again. "You shouldn't have caused his death."

Matthew felt his heart stomping against his ribcage. Surges of adrenaline and pangs of anxiety shot through his chest, each feeding off the other. He bit down and forced himself to focus, reminding himself of why he was there. What he came to do.

"I didn't kill him," Matthew said, clipping his words. His breath hissed through clenched teeth as he tried to retain control. "I didn't drown my son."

"Oh, you may not have physically held him under the water, but you most certainly were responsible for his death." Melody leaned her face close to Steven's, gently pinching a section of the boy's cheek. "For both our deaths."

> "The story Matthew Chambers told police caused almost as much controversy as the murders themselves. Chambers, the handsome, up-and-coming architect, admitted to killing his wife—but swore he had done it because she, not he, had drowned their son. Investigators initially dismissed his story, but the investigation became more complicated when Chambers passed an FBI polygraph—administered at the request of his defense team—and when forensic reconstructions seemed to support his version of events."

"You killed him, you sick bitch. You sent me outside, murdered him, then waited in the living room to tell me about it. How the hell did you expect me to react? I... *You* deserved what you got."

"Did I? Did I deserve for you to tell me you wanted a divorce? Did I deserve to be traded-in like a used car? Did I, Matthew? Did I deserve to bear your child, only to have you fuck that sleazy receptionist? Is that what I deserved?"

"We were through, Melody. Finished. You knew that. Why did you make me go through the motions, let yourself get pregnant? And Steven... God, Steven. Why did you—"

"Because I wanted you, Matthew. I was never going to leave you. Never. Once we had a child, I thought you would see. I thought you would realize we were meant to be together. I loved you, Matthew. I've always loved you."

Without noticing exactly how it happened, Matthew saw that her appearance had changed. At some point she had transformed into the trim, shapely brunette who'd caught his eye at the gym, the one he had married after a torrid fling. Instead of the tattered cloth, she was wearing a white cotton dress that gently clung to her at the breasts and hips.

"I remember when it was me you wanted to fuck," she said, lifting a leg beneath her son's body and crossing it slowly, revealing the smooth, tan flesh of her calf and thigh. "All night, sometimes. Long lunch hours, mornings in the shower. Every chance we got. Do you remember, Matthew?"

He remembered. He remembered the desperate feeling of needing to take a breath that wouldn't come, of wanting out, of wanting away from the exhaustive weight of their marriage. Two weeks of unending sex culminating in a hop to Vegas, and he suddenly found himself with a wife. He wondered what he could have been thinking, how he could have been so moronic. Maybe his sanity deserved to be questioned, after all.

"That didn't last very long, Melody. You became more obsessive every day, smothering me, calling me at the office a dozen times before lunch, questioning every place I went, every move I made. You drove me away. We weren't meant for each other. Whatever spark there was quickly died out."

"Not for me, you son of a bitch! What happened to love, honor and cherish, Matthew? Huh? What about that? All I ever wanted—all I ever demanded—was for us to be together." Her voice softened as she looked down at the boy again, gently touching her forefinger to his nose. "You know, before Steven was born, when we were starting to have trouble, I even sought out a Wiccan. I learned what I could about love spells. I found one that was supposed to link our souls, that was supposed to ensure I'd always be a part of you. But still, you pulled away. So I tried a stronger one, one that required I sacrifice a part of me. A part of us. I put off doing it for a long time, Matthew, I agonized over it. But you gave me no choice." She slowly lifted her head and hitched her shoulders, smiling. "I guess it worked, huh?"

Matthew clenched his eyelids, pressing them tight.

It wasn't my fault, it wasn't my fault, it wasn't my fault. Oh, God, don't let her do this to you. Get a grip. Remember why you came here. This was not unexpected. You have an objective. Focus, man, focus.

When he opened his eyes, Melody was the cadaverous creature she had been before, grinning like a hyena.

"I'm not insane," Matthew said.

"No, Matthew, you're not."

"Matthew Chambers was charged with second-degree murder. Women's rights advocates were outraged that a man would attempt to justify the murder of his wife by blaming the victim for her child's death. Protesters carried signs and marched in front of the courthouse every day of the trial. The controversy only intensified when a plea

bargain was struck before the verdict. Matthew Chambers would plead guilty to manslaughter, a deal that infuriated the many groups following the trial. Under state sentencing guidelines, he would be eligible for parole in three to five years. As part of the deal, he would also receive psychiatric counseling, despite having rejected an insanity defense. Court documents revealed his lawyers often heard him complain that his dead wife was somehow inside his head."

"Did you really think you could get rid of me so easily? All those sessions with the psychiatrists, all those useless drugs and therapies. After all those things didn't work, couldn't work, you really thought you could just push me away on your own, shove me deeper and deeper into the dark? Really, Matthew, bury me with willpower? You actually thought I would never come back? I was just biding my time, *dearest husband*. Waiting."

"Waiting? For what?"

"Your new life, of course. To steal from you what you stole from me. Your marriage. Your family."

Jill.

The thought sent a tremor though his body. Not Jill, the woman who had befriended him when he was at his lowest. The woman who heard him crying through the paper-thin walls of his tiny apartment, who wouldn't stop checking on him. The woman who drew him out of his isolation, who cried with him when he confessed what had happened, what he had done. The woman who believed him, who believed in him, who restored his confidence, who straightened his tie before interviews and never let him give up. The woman he loved in so many ways, for so many reasons.

The entire structure of the house seemed to shake as he trembled with rage.

"You leave her out of this. Don't you dare touch her."

"Oh, I won't lay a hand on her."

"I'm serious, you psychopathic cunt! Stay away from her."

"Really, Matthew, such language. You must learn to control your temper. I haven't seen you this angry since, well, you know."

"If you so much as—"

"Come now. How do you suppose *I* would do anything to her? You're the one who is going to do it."

"Me?"

"Yes, Matthew. You. And once you do it, you'll have atoned, and then we can be together forever. You can't avoid it. I will make you do it, drive you to do it. Just like you drove me to do this." She gestured down to Steven's body, which no longer appeared angelic, but was instead now rotted and decayed, with patches of flesh the color of sewer water clinging to its bones. Then she gently lifted the boy's skull off her lap, and Matthew saw she was now holding a baby. A tiny baby, hardly bigger than her hand.

"Your unborn son, Matthew. Carried inside that slut you married." She stretched her smile even wider as she placed a hand over the baby's nose and mouth. "It is every woman's choice."

"No!"

Matthew lunged at her, his arms thrust forward. His hands found her throat, thumbs hooking it. She was laughing as he did it, the same screeching laughter he'd heard mocking him for so many months. Her face was grotesquely contorted, teeth jutting forward in a snarl. Mummified cheeks, putrescent lips and savage, feline eyes all now just inches away.

This is why you came, he told himself. *This is what you are here to do.*

He squeezed with all his might, digging his thumbs into her larynx, feeling the snap of bone and hearing the choking, gasping sound that he had heard only once before in his life and had tried so hard, for so many years, to forget. Then the death mask faded away.

The skin became creamy smooth, with a pinkish hue. Everything else melted away, too, including his dreams. All of them, forever.

"Oh. God," Matthew said, releasing his grip. "Oh God no…"

"That was close to nine years ago. Nine long years, and history has apparently—tragically—repeated itself. Inside the home behind me, police have just arrested Matthew Chambers once again, this time, incredibly, for the murder of his second wife. Officials report that police responded to a neighbor's call concerning this house. Sources close to the investigation have told Eyewitness News *that when police entered, they found Matthew Chambers with his hands still around the neck of his dead wife. Details remain sketchy, but the detective in charge has confirmed that paramedics pronounced Jill Chambers dead at the scene… Chambers, age thirty-four, the apparent victim of a strangulation.*

"A police spokesperson refused to comment on the rumor that, at the time of his arrest, Matthew Chambers had earbuds in his ears connected to a smartphone in his pocket, and that playing on his phone was what the responding officer described as a self-hypnosis audio. Police have also refused to comment on other rumors that the victim was approximately three months pregnant. There are indications she may have just returned from a doctor's appointment when the murder took place, but again, none of this has been confirmed.

"Witnesses did, however, observe a visibly agitated Matthew Chambers shouting hysterically for someone to "stop laughing" as he was led by police from his home. They also report that he was screaming things like, 'she's inside' and 'someone get her out of my head.'

"One thing is for certain: no matter how he pleads, Matthew Chambers is unlikely to escape punishment this time.

"Back to you, Ted."

ABOUT THE AUTHOR
JOHN C. FOSTER

John C. Foster credits his love of horror to his haunted birthplace, the historic town of Sleepy Hollow, New York. As a result, Foster has been afraid of the dark, and writing about it, for as long as he can remember.

An author of both taut thrillers and dark fiction, often mixing the two genres into a dread-filled stew, Foster spent many years during his early career in the ersatz glow of Los Angeles, California where he worked in the entertainment and marketing industries before relocating to the relative sanity of New York City where he now lives with his lady, Linda, and their dog, Coraline.

Foster's short stories can be found in *Shock Totem #8* as well as the anthologies *Under the Stairs* and *Big Book of New Short Horror*. His dark tale of horror and espionage, "Mister White," is featured in *Dark Visions: A Collection of Modern Horror - Volume Two*, published by Grey Matter Press. He has written two novels, *Dead Men* and *The Isle*.

BURIAL SUIT

JOHN C. FOSTER

You know my father's name.

I took the suit out of the box where it had rested for three years. I had used it once for an interview that didn't go well, then never returned it. It was my father's lucky suit.

The suit was black wool with narrow pinstripes, the fabric a bit shiny at the seat and elbows. As a kid I called it my father's gangster suit, and he'd laugh. When he lent it to me as an adult he didn't laugh. He just put a hand on my shoulder—because he wasn't good with emotion—and said, "Good luck."

I picked a couple shirts from my closet and carefully folded them before adding them to my overnight case. One shirt was a green color that I thought looked good. The other was white, just to be safe.

The tie was easy. Black.

I put a cat carrier on the bed and scooped up The Loose from the animal puddle she made at my feet, too aware of the bones beneath her fur and the cruel outline of her hips.

The doctors told me The Loose had only weeks. Talked about peaceful options. Peaceful, my ass. I took her home and gave her food she wouldn't eat, except ice cream, she would still steal my ice cream when she had energy.

When I took her to the vet she had howled at me from inside the carrier. Now she didn't talk to me at all.

I unwrapped the yellowed handkerchief, revealing a greasy, black .45 revolver. Shiny brass winked up at me from the cylinders like they meant business. Even so, I stuck a claw hammer and a pearl-handled straight razor into the suitcase before I closed it up. Opened it again and added a roll of black electrical tape.

I got as far as "G'bye babe," on the postcard before I froze. So I added, "Love," and my name and stuck it in a mailbox. Screw it, words were never my thing and she'd understand.

Besides, I was sure she'd be able to read about it all before too long.

* * *

The windows were small with no light shining behind them, and the wooden sign hung crookedly on the bricks. If there was more than one funeral home in town, then this was the shitty one.

I parked next to an abandoned factory on the next block and walked back, boots clacking on the cracked sidewalk. Occasionally I'd hear the low tone of a motor in the distance or the scratch of a newspaper against the road as it danced with a breeze. The Loose still wasn't talking to me from inside her carrier.

The fence sagged but held under my weight, and I slipped between the funeral parlor and the building next door, hunting around until I found some boards I could lean against the back wall beneath a window. A couple of short jabs with my elbow spider-webbed a pane of glass, and with a bit of reaching and wriggling The Loose and I were inside.

I flicked on my lighter and looked around the room. Some sort of records storage, littered with dusty piles of paper. Mold streaked the walls and I wondered when the window I'd used had last been opened.

Floorboards creaked under each step as I eased into a narrow hall. The flickering light in my hand picked out tiny details as I passed. Framed newspaper obituaries hung on the walls alongside a state mortician's license, and a nearby shelf was stacked with takeout menus.

When I reached the cellar door I grasped the knob and turned it quietly in case some apprentice had a room upstairs. The knob turned easily, and a draft of cool, medicinal air wafted out. Wooden stairs dropped into the dark, and I descended behind my small flame until I found a dangling cord. The bare bulb hanging from the ceiling threw a white, actinic light across the square cellar with its shelves of equipment, machines and coiled hoses mounted on one wall. The floor itself was cement and sloped gently towards a drain set dead center in the room.

* * *

I stuck a lit cigarette in the dead man's mouth and rolled one for myself as a thin spiral of smoke rose to caress the dangling bulb. The smoke was the same color as his skin, milky and lifeless. Another man might have wondered at the symbolism of the rising vapor.

A cone of light shone down from overhead, isolating the steel table with all the class of a cheap pool hall. Everything beyond was darkness, and the only sound was the scrape of a bowl as The Loose drank from it. It was a metal thing shaped like a kidney, and she was dragging it around the floor with her front paws. She could still do that.

The dead man was naked on the cold table and smaller than I remembered. The light made his hair seem wispier, his crotch more pathetically shriveled. It deepened every wrinkle with shadows and delineated each rib, making me wonder what he had been eating near the end.

I took it all in.

The cigarette in the corpse's mouth was a solid inch of ash when a breeze I didn't feel powdered it along one pale cheek. I wiped it away from a face that felt like plastic and plucked the butt free, sticking it in my mouth to relight it, dragging deep, tasting embalming chemicals on top of the smoke. When it was going, I wedged it back between his stiff lips, braced against teeth and gums that had been sewn together.

"You said we'd smoke one when I got out," I said.

When our cigarettes were finished I kicked them toward the drain and lifted my bag onto the table, removing the pinstripe jacket and slacks.

"Brought your favorite suit," I said, pulling out a pair of wingtip shoes and socks. "Your lucky suit."

Then I dressed my father.

* * *

O'Malley. That was the name I had in Garfield Heights, a shithole east of Cleveland. There were four of them listed in the phone book.

"Fuck," I said around my cigarette, the orange tip bobbing as I carefully dragged a pen through the third O'Malley.

I glanced at my father stretched out on the other bed, old pennies on his eyelids. After a week, the motel room stank of chemicals and something ugly even with the window open. But at least he didn't talk, and after three years with the Egyptian as a cellmate, I was done with talking. The Egyptian had talked through the day. He had talked through the night. He was insane.

"Don't eat Dad," I told The Loose. "That embalming stuff is poisonous." She had no appetite so I wasn't really worried. Just looking for something to say.

I lit a new cigarette from the tip of the old one and dropped the butt onto the rug. Ground it out with my boot and made a new stain. My knee was stiff where I'd wrapped it with what was left of the electrical tape. I gingerly probed at the shiner beneath my eye, a little concerned. I couldn't afford to get seriously hurt before I finished the job.

Garfield Heights.

I stuck the gun in the back of my belt and pocketed the straight razor.

O'Malley.

* * *

The first and last few characters on the neon sign were dead, so only a green MAL reflected off the oily puddles in the street. The potholes were big enough to eat a foreign car, and I figured the garage on the corner did a lot of suspension work.

People walked in and staggered out. The walls on either side of the graffiti-covered door were stained with fresh piss, and no one seemed to mind. I hated to think of my father in this kind of place but couldn't erase the image from my mind. A hunched, skinny old guy sitting at the bar with a pack of cigarettes and a diminishing pitcher of beer. Doing anything to avoid being at home alone.

Two in the morning came and went, and I saw a cluster of men leave, talking more or less sober, as they locked up. There was a big guy with a face like a baked potato, another guy helping him put on an expensive raincoat—London Fog, maybe. He looked sick in the green neon light and had potholes in his cheeks that matched the street.

After the backslapping and bullshitting, the group split up. O'Malley got into a big white car—maybe a Cadillac—with two other guys. He sat in the back while they took the front.

I followed but got stuck at the first red light. They were long gone by the time it turned green.

* * *

"Lady next to you complained about a smell," the tweaker at the motel desk said. His pupils were fat, black things that ate the whites of his eyes.

"Gonna need the room for tomorrow," I said, sliding a little more than the room warranted across the sticky counter.

Upstairs I found The Loose sitting on my father's chest. The bathroom smelled horrendous, so I hung up a few more air fresheners shaped like pine trees, disturbing a cloud of blowflies.

I made six trips back and forth to the ice machine, dumping the cubes into the tub where I stuck in a couple of 40s to chill alongside the three severed heads and the hand. The heads were ballooning up in a funny way and it was hard to look at them. I saw movement in the nostrils of one but decided it didn't bear investigating.

The detached hand had curled like a smacked spider, and I wasn't sure why I had taken it. I should have just kicked it down into the hole beneath the hydraulic lift with the rest of that dead O'Malley. It had become a white thing in the water, fingers bloated like sausages, crescents of black grease under the fingernails. A mechanic's hand. Useless, but I took it anyway, like a kid gunning for extra credit.

People act funny under stress.

I carved my father's name in each forehead with the straight razor, the cuts parting like lipless mouths as I sliced. Wriggling things slid from one, but I grabbed it by the ear and continued working until the job was done.

"Enough then."

My bed squeaked when I sat down and knocked the cap off a Miller High Life, the champagne of beers. I swigged and belched and thumbed the remote, but the color on the TV was screwy, and the actors looked like painted clowns. A brown stain was spreading on the wall across from the bed.

"What a dump," I said, my voice hoarse.

I stared at The Loose until I saw her ribs moving, afraid that she'd caught what my father had by laying on top of him. You know, catch a little death.

Heat grew behind my eyes. Pressure.

I looked at the shiny insects on the fly strip hanging by the window.

"One more, Dad."

* * *

I woke up at a clatter from the bathroom. Sat up in the dark, confused, a crazy image of my father in there giving his old man's bladder some midnight relief.

I heard a sloshing sound, and the hair on my arms stood on end as I slid my bare feet onto the sticky carpet. The .45 had already migrated from beneath my pillow and I thumbed back the hammer, the metallic click loud in the small space.

"Who is it?" I whispered.

My knees cracked like rifle shots as I rose, glancing at my father's bed and into glowing green eyes.

"Loose," I whispered and the eyes vanished.

The dark rectangle of the bathroom doorway held a deeper blackness than the bedroom itself. Again came the sloshing. Goose bumps fanned across my naked torso as I crossed the room on the balls of my feet. The doorway ate my vision and revealed nothing.

Behind me, the television suddenly sprang to life, and I spun around holding the revolver in both hands, tracking the shadow moving across my bed. Rationality was already insisting that The Loose must have stepped on the remote and hit the power button. My father had not sat up in the dark to take in a little TV.

I stepped inside the bathroom, slapping at the wall with my free hand until I found the light switch, squinting against the fluorescent glare. The melting ice in the bathtub shifted, and a Miller High Life rolled over with an audible clink. The heads swayed from side to side in the brief current as if they disapproved.

I let out a breath I hadn't realized I was holding and turned toward the sink.

"You didn't get him!" I recoiled from my father's furious face in the mirror. A pale face. A dead face. The sour-milk eyes bulging in fury. "Get him, boy! Get him!" He grabbed the edges of the mirror on his side as if to drag himself through. Staples in the black autopsy scar on his chest pulled, stretching puckered flesh.

I shrieked and stumbled back, arms wind-milling as I sat down hard in the tub, banging my skull against the tiled wall. The .45 tumbled into the water and I grabbed for it, my hand jerking back as it brushed against teeth.

"No, no, no," I repeated as I pushed myself from the cold water and snatched up the gun from between two rocking orbs of bone and flesh.

In the mirror I saw my father's retreating back as he walked away from me, the lumps of his spine visible over his withered flanks. I smashed the butt of the revolver into the glass and cracks raced across its surface, splitting my father's naked figure. He turned and stared back at me over one shoulder until I looked away.

Back in the bedroom I sat on my bed and listened to the buzzing of the flies, watching the unmoving form of my father's dead body until sunlight seeped beneath the shade and spilled across the floor.

* * *

The bar's interior was windowless, dark and stuffy, and the red Christmas lights strung about the place served as a reminder of what your life didn't have, so have a drink. A corner television flipped between boxing and horse racing as the remote was passed around, and a broken video poker machine squatted at one end of the counter. Neon signs for beers you wouldn't drink hung on the walls, and phantoms danced in the mirror behind the bar like fish in muddy water, half seen in the murk. Bottles caught the weak light and invited themselves over with a shimmering of gold and red and blue, depending on the poison. Have a drink.

I took the suggestion. "What's on tap?" I asked the albino tending bar.

A can of Busch smacked against the countertop. "Two fifty, tap's busted," the charmer said, turning his head to cough

"Cover your mouth," a fat man said.

"Fuck you," the bartender replied with the conversational rhythm of a couple married fifty years.

I peeled my sleeve off the bar and dropped three singles in the wet ring left by the can.

"Get him, get him!" The old man next to me was whispering at the fighters on TV. He looked at me and dropped his eyes to his near empty pitcher, adjusting his trucker hat.

"Spot me one?"

"Tits aren't big enough," I said and shied away from the light like everyone else when the door opened. Somewhere on the street a car backfired and exhaust billowed inside, improving the atmosphere.

"You'll be here soon enough," the old man said.

"No I won't."

He moved to put a barstool between us, herding his pitcher and smashed pack of Winstons over to the new pasture.

"Get him!" A ragged voice hissed. I looked up, confused, but the old man had his glass to his lips. "Get him!" I searched for the bartender and saw a glaring face in the mirror, lips pulled back from long, yellow teeth.

I flinched away, knocking over my barstool, but the seat next to me was empty. Trucker Hat looked at me and his eyes twinkled with dark knowledge, smiling at the decay he thought he saw.

Snatching up my beer and the empty glass, I moved away from the mirror to a small table by the wall, where the reflections were too soupy to pose much threat. Any time the door opened I was careful to concentrate on pouring beer into my glass.

"Get him." I could hear it underneath the hum and clank of the bar, the non-stop whisper of insect wings. A red eye hovered in the middle of the bubbling liquid in my glass, and I told myself it was a reflection from the damned Christmas lights. Something brushed my ankle. Looking down I saw nothing but floor.

I put a coaster on top of my glass and hit the men's room, standing in a puddle as I braced my hands on the stained sink to gather myself. I lifted my chin.

"You didn't get him!" The bony palms slapped against the mirror from the other side, held back by spray painted black swirls that read MARY HAS A DICK on my side, maybe something else on his.

"Stop it," I said to the glass.

"Useless," the old face hissed, wormlike lips rippling with disdain. "Failure!"

"No more!" I said, barely avoiding a shout. I banged out of the bathroom and ordered another beer. Retreated to my table and lifted a toast to Mary.

The place slowly filled up as second shift ended, and I nursed three beers and pissed twice while I waited, avoiding the mirror no matter what the whispers said. On TV a horse named Prodigal

Son had won, and a buzz cut guy was slapping everybody five when O'Malley finally walked through the door.

* * *

O'Malley was never alone. People went over to his table all night. If the guy was well dressed a thick neck in a brown suit would stroll over to the bar and chat with the albino while the supplicant sat down and had his five minutes. If the guy looked broke, beaten down—like me, in other words—he stood while he talked to O'Malley, and the thick neck gave him a look, the kind a guy who wears brown suits thinks is intimidating.

Sometimes money changed hands. Nobody tried to hide it.

Trucker Hat took his turn to stand in judgment, twisting his hat while O'Malley smiled and Brown Suit silently eye fucked him.

It was impossible not to see my father in that same position, the same posture, the same beaten down place where he wasn't allowed even his pride. I wondered if what I saw in the mirror was all that remained of him, the stale hate left over from standing like that as the whole bar watched him get stripped down.

I thought about the razor in my boot. The gun in my waistband. Egyptian magic.

I drank and pissed and O'Malley was never alone. When two in the morning came I was herded out onto the cold sidewalk with the barflies. We stood in a confused clump, breath gathering in a poisonous cloud over our heads until we each shuffled off to whatever hole awaited.

I had to try twice to get the key in the car door and leaned close enough to fog the glass as I watched the lock pop up. I didn't register the footsteps behind me until the revolver was jerked from the back of my pants. I spun around and had just enough time to register that ugly brown suit before a fist the size of Detroit turned my lights out.

* * *

Creedence was singing about a bad moon rising when I woke up in the back seat of a moving car. I shifted my lower jaw from side to side and felt a jagged bolt of pain, heard a click. The inside of my mouth was swollen and the outside felt like it was shaped wrong. I tried to spit out the coppery taste and dribbled blood down my chin.

"He's awake." The driver's fat neck was wider than his head.

"No shit," I said, sounding like I had a mouth full of marbles. I tried to touch my face and noticed my wrists were taped together.

O'Malley turned around in the passenger's seat and looked at me. Mildly curious. Like how-did-this-red-sock-wind-up-in-my-drawer curious.

"Who are you?" he asked.

"You know my father's name," I said. When he didn't react I told him the name.

"Who?"

I stared at him, the pain growing as my drunk wore away. I blinked as headlights from a cross street flooded the interior. Rain pocked against the windshield and beat a tattoo on the roof. The wipers went on.

"The gun for me?"

"Maybe."

"How's that working out for you?" O'Malley said, and the driver laughed.

"Laugh it up, asshole. Your suit looks like a diaper stain."

"What's that?" Brown Suit said. I saw his eyes shift my way in the rearview mirror. "Sounds like someone busted your jaw."

"You bring that gun for me?" O'Malley asked again, but I didn't answer, just looked out the window at the empty storefronts and occasional bit of neon. O'Malley asked a few more questions. Did I owe him money? My father, did he owe some dough? My jaw hurt too much to talk.

"River?" I heard Brown Suit ask, and O'Malley sighed, the vinyl seat squeaking as he settled back in and looked out the rainy windshield. He nodded. "Cuyahoga River is the dirtiest river in the country," he said, I guess for me. "You'll be with your own kind."

The *schwick-schwick* of the windshield wipers sounded like an insect rubbing its hind legs together, and I had a thought. I think I smiled, but with my mouth the way it was, who could tell?

"Hey, Dad," I whispered.

"Something to say, dead man?" O'Malley spoke to the windshield, to my father, to me. I laughed.

"Diaper stain, I'm talking to you," I said, watching the rearview mirror until his eyes shifted over to meet mine and instead met my father's.

The driver screamed and so did the brakes, and the crash rattled my bones.

* * *

Brown Suit was halfway through the windshield, big arms spread across the crumpled hood like he was hugging the car. I felt the rain cleansing me as I grabbed his wet hair in my left hand and cut his throat with my right. Low rent asshole hadn't looked for the razor in my boot.

Steam was billowing from under the hood and I imagined it carrying his soul heavenward. I made the sign of the cross with the razor and smirked. No one was going to heaven.

I glanced into the front seat and saw my .45 in the foot well, but no O'Malley. I took my gun and limped around the back of the car since the front was piled against the bricks of a corner store. There was a bright flash and clap of thunder as something punched me in the ribs. Then I was sitting down, lifting my own thousand-pound weapon to fire at the weaving back of O'Malley as he made his staggering getaway. His London Fog billowed like a balloon injected with hot air and he went down, skidding on his face, ass high.

The rain was cool on my face as I stood, but the blood running down my belly beneath my shirt was warm. Hot. It smelled like a soldering iron.

O'Malley was whimpering as he pawed for the bullet hole like a wounded animal. I kicked him in the ribs until he rolled over, crying out, a little more curious now about who and what I was.

"You destroyed my father," I said, and he shook his head.

"I swear I didn't. I don't know him, I don't—"

My bullet took him through the heart and shut him up.

I knelt next to him, not feeling great. It took forever, sawing away with my straight razor as the downpour thickened and wrapped us in privacy. Eventually I had to brace my feet on his collarbones and rear back, pulling with both hands locked onto the fat of his chin.

When it was done I laid there on the sidewalk, panting and bleeding, eyes blinking against the raindrops.

"Get up." I think I said that. So I did and found O'Malley's head had rolled into the gutter, his eyes still open with fright. I picked it up and nearly shit myself when they blinked, so I banged it on the road.

"Enough out of you," I said, staring into his dead eyes. I stole a car and drove back to my motel, what was left of O'Malley face down on the passenger seat.

* * *

We drove out to the empty field I'd selected. My father rested on the back seat with The Loose curled on his chest. All four O'Malleys were banging around in the trunk. I parked and shined my headlights on the dead oak I needed, breathing oddly. It took two tries to get out of the car, and the seat I left behind was soaked with my blood.

I worked under a blue moon and the colder wash from the

headlights, each swing of the pickaxe threatening to tear my ribs apart. I was spitting blood and more ran down my leg as if I had wet myself. The shovel work was harder, and then it was done.

My father was light and The Loose nothing but a twig, but I struggled to carry them to the grave, streaking my face with tears even hotter than my spilling blood. I set my beloved cat on the ground and my beloved father into the hole with care, although he thumped at the bottom. The O'Malleys I threw in like trash, pausing only to carve the name they'd follow on the forehead of the last of them.

The headlights were dimming, and the moon hid its face behind clouds as I shoveled in the dirt, or maybe it was just my eyesight sneaking away. Enough light remained for me to see the cloud of red mist come out with the words I spoke. Not English, not even Egyptian. Even dizzy I could remember them all, so often had my cellmate repeated them. The sound of them hurt my ears, and I sensed the scuttle of beetles fleeing away from me in all directions, the grass bending outward.

When the hole was filled I stretched myself across the soft dirt like a crossbar and pulled The Loose onto my chest, with my .45 and straight razor resting across my mid-section. Her breath was hitching and so was mine, but in a show of strength she opened her eyes, just as the mad Egyptian had predicted.

The night became quiet, its own breath held.

Hoarse and ugly, I said the last awful words and she blinked at the sprayed blood. I added a few more of my own, things I used to say to her, hoping the powers wouldn't mind.

My father's murderer would serve him in the afterlife. The extra O'Malleys could wander lost forever for all I cared. The Egyptian hadn't covered that.

The Loose would guide my father to his new home, because cats can see the Doorway to the Other, even in life. I was going along as muscle.

The clouds parted and I spoke my father's name to the blue moon just as The Loose let out her last breath.

"Good girl," I said, picked up my straight razor, and followed her.

ABOUT THE AUTHOR
AARON POLSON

Aaron Polson is a high school guidance counselor, recovering English teacher and author of weird tales. His stories have featured magic goldfish, monstrous beetles, and a book of lullabies for baby vampires along with other oddities.

Polson's work appears in the anthologies *Blood Lite II: Overbite*, *Shock Totem 3: Curious Tales of the Macabre and Twisted* and *Dead Bait*. His short story "The Thing About Ray's Smile" appeared in *Black Heart Magazine* and "The Summer I Fell in Love" is featured in *Niteblade Fantasy and Horror* magazine.

Born on the Ides of March, Polson currently lives in Lawrence, Kansas with his wife and six children. He's now at full sitcom level. Rumor has it he prefers ketchup with his beans.

NINE

AARON POLSON

The boys, Nate and Gabe, hide small plastic Easter eggs. Or rather, they hide things *in* the eggs. They seal the plastic cages with clear tape and stash them around the house. Finding the eggs becomes a game, like cat and mouse or hide-and-seek.

They are good boys. They play outside with friends and walk through the house like ghosts, quiet and only-sometimes-seen good. They are good even as they start to fill plastic eggs and play a game of fooling each other. Can my brother find the eggs before the prizes rot? What about Mom? Can she? But not everything in the eggs will rot. Some prizes are rotten before they are hidden in the eggs.

Their father, Charlie, died exactly two years, one month, and twelve days before their mother finds the first bones in an egg.

* * *

Nate is eight and Gabe six, well-spaced and timed with logic and precision. Things went as planned with both pregnancies, and the boys arrived in June, each of them, avoiding complications with Beth's university position. Tenure waited for no one's biological clock. Charlie, her now-dead husband, had painted both boys' nurseries to Beth's specifications: pale blue—Summer Sky, eggshell finish, from Home Depot—upon learning the sex in utero. For Beth, these were things to manage, details to sort and for which to prepare.

Charlie had smiled and painted and smoked marijuana in the shed after cleaning his brushes. He continued smoking on occasion until he died. Once, when Nate was five, he caught his father with a tiny stub glowing red between roach-clip pincers. Nate had gone to the shed looking for a lawn sprinkler so he and Gabe could cool off in the sun. He'd never seen his father smoking and wondered for a moment why anyone would use a binder clamp to hold a cigarette.

Charlie had laughed, tussled his hair, and helped him find the sprinkler.

* * *

Beth lectures at the university, three classes a semester including Introduction to Archeology and two sections of Physical Anthropology. She understands bones and knows how to remove them from the earth. She drinks red wine, at least one glass a night, and complains about pain in her lower back. If she drinks three glasses, the headaches derail her the next day. Two glasses bring sadness and bad memories. One is enough.

She killed Charlie with her bad back, indirectly at least. He died in a car accident, a hit-and-run after midnight, early on a Wednesday as he drove to Walgreens. Beth's back was especially bad that night, and she needed more Aleve. The red wine came after his death.

Now she spends half her days on campus, gathers the boys from school and shuts herself in her office for the rest of the afternoon. The boys are free to fill eggs and hide them.

She is the world's foremost expert on the M'busai people, a vanished tribe from the lower Congo. The M'busai are one of those groups you haven't heard about until a story in National Geographic, or a nature documentary on satellite television. Only, there are no stories or documentaries. There are no desert digs in the Congo, no favorable climate to keep human artifacts packed away in sandbox preservation for millennia.

The M'busai are a mystery, a Big Mystery.

During her investigations she learns things people shouldn't remember about the M'busai, like how they cut the little finger from the left hand of each boy when he turned nine. This is a puzzle she's pieced together from bits of folklore—what little remains—and one interview with the great-grandson of a Frenchmen who had direct contact with M'busai tribesmen before their assimilation or extinction. She knows the M'busai, whatever their fate, winked away like the Roanoke Colony but left no "Croatoan" messages to decipher.

They left no plastic eggs with surprises for future generations.

* * *

The boys fill the eggs with things they find in the garage, trinkets and tidbits found in boxes and behind shelves: screws, broken wristwatches, grandpa's service ribbon from Vietnam, a .22 cartridge, an empty rolling paper folder, nail clippers, a small cellophane package filled with candy hearts. They hide items from the refrigerator: grapes, strawberries, bits of cheese and leftover sausage bites. They hoard treasures in the eggs. They play a hide-and-seek game, challenging each other with instructions like "they're all blue this week" or "look for the colors of the rainbow."

Empty eggs wait in a cardboard box in Gabe's bedroom closet. The box dates to the move—shortly after Charlie died—and wears the words "kitchen/dishes" in black marker.

Nate likes the blue eggs, but Gabe prefers green.

Gabe hides eggs under couch cushions, nestled in potted plants, and on high windowsills where they are visible but must be knocked down with a broom handle. Nate is more selective. His eggs sulk behind the couch with clumps of cat hair and dead spiders. He buries them with the houseplants, sweeping away loose dirt afterwards. He pulls back baseboards and sneaks them behind the walls. Nate's eggs become secret things, incredibly hard to find unless he wants them found.

The boys argue about where they find their treasures, especially the bones. Nate scares Gabe one afternoon by saying, "Dad gave them to me." He rattles an egg.

"Stop."

"He did," Nate says.

Gabe blinks. His six-year-old stomach feels like too much marshmallow fluff. "Dad?"

"Yes. In the yard." Nate shakes his egg again. His eyes narrow. "He was with the others."

* * *

When he died, the local paper described Charlie as a "good father" and "caring husband." What's true is this: Charlie always made midnight trips for anything Beth needed. He'd fallen in love with her in undergraduate school because she looked good in jeans and liked to hike. Her blue eyes and the little wrinkles flanking them helped. He stayed in love with her with little notes every Saturday morning, messages detailing what he would do for the house and family that day, not because he needed the reminder or list, but because he knew she did. He loved her. He cooked for the boys four nights a week and any other time Beth's job pulled her away from home. His cheeseburgers were legend.

What the paper printed—"good father" and "caring husband"—rang true, but truth-truth has meat on its bones. It can be broken into pieces, details, things easily hidden inside plastic eggs and buried, but not buried by history. Beth learned about love from Charlie. What Beth has yet to learn is that the M'busai fingers were a sacrifice to ward off evil, and a wish to have full, happy lives. They were a promise to the mother of a M'busai boy's future children that he would make similar sacrifices for them as their father.

When Charlie was alive, Beth slept curled in a ball on the left side of the bed. He would pull his body close to hers and his heartbeat lulled her to sleep. She still sleeps curled in a ball on the left side of the bed, her elbows and knees hanging slightly over the edge. She sleeps but does not sleep well.

Charlie is dead, and Beth tries to solve dead mysteries.

* * *

At first, Beth didn't' realize she was part of the egg game. The boys gave her no formal invitation, only eggs she stumbled across during her routine: blue one on the bathroom counter after a shower, a trail of three—all pastel green and filled with shiny roofing nails from Charlie's workbench in the shed—a pink one in her slippers. The boys, neither talkative, were communicating. She interpreted the eggs as communication, at least.

Now she wants the game to stop. She tires of missing rolls of tape and broken bits of plastic when she steps on an egg, always by accident. She wonders where the boys find their treasures and where they find the eggs. There can't be so many left in the plastic tub marked "Easter" with masking tape and marker in the garage, but Beth doesn't look. Maybe she doesn't really want to know.

What she knows is simple: when she found the bones in a yellow egg—two years, one month, and twelve days after Charlie died—she was scared. She now knows fear tastes like metal. It makes her head feel like it's full of mud. Fear makes her fingers tingle.

That's what they were. Finger bones. Phalanges. Small ones.

* * *

She looks in the mirror each morning and tries to tell herself she is naturally pretty because she is afraid. She's afraid of normal, right-now things: being alone, failing her two sons with no father, never finding the breakthrough magic bullet to put her and the M'busai on the academic map.

Two dates fell flat in the last year. The first was a blind date with a red-faced accountant who drank too much and tried to grope her on the way back to his car after dinner. The evening ended with a cab and ten dollar bonus to the babysitter because she was embarrassed about crying and didn't want to answer questions. The second, coffee with a new instructor in the department, a man named Ben—seven years younger and hair graying in a suave, sophisticated manner—ended with "I'll call you" and he never did. His easy, cool, rumbling voice left her wishing she was prettier.

When her back hurts at night and she can't sleep, thoughts pinging between Charlie and Ben and the red-faced accountant, she sometimes looks from her bedroom window into the yard. On one of these nights, Beth sees them in the yard, like branchless trees in rows. She sees them but doesn't see them like anyone confronted with impossibilities.

Warriors, she thinks.

M'busai warriors.

No lightning comes, no dramatic flash or full moon to see the whites of their eyes or flint-sharpened spear points.

Just shadows. Impossible shadows on which it is impossible to see if the left hand still has five fingers or four.

* * *

Gabe wakes after midnight with his heart careening around his ribcage. He doesn't want to look outside, but he does. His body is frozen, locked in combat, a war against his brain. The fear he feels is real, and what Nate says about the yard, about Dad, can't be. The war continues, but he fights his way out of his bed. He stands next to the window and peeks through the blinds. What he sees sends him to his mother, his face pale and *Mario Kart* pajamas soaked with sweat.

Her light is on. She's at the window, too.

"What's the matter?"

He mutters and stumbles over words. She hears "outside" and knows.

She holds her son for the first time in over a year and tries to whisper sweet, mothering things, but her voice no longer sounds pretty to her ears. She wishes it did.

* * *

Nate keeps the bag of human fingers under his bed. The fingers are just bones and look like they could be made of plastic, but when he holds them, when he feels how light they are and how the smooth surface feels, he knows. His father brought the fingers in a cotton sack, small and stained like an old pillowcase. The ghost left the bone fingers on the back porch and then woke Nate to let him know.

The porch light hadn't worked when Nate stepped outside to grab the bag, and he'd felt the cold, dark strangeness of the world.

Nate wonders why his dad chose to come back to him and not

Beth. Why did he get the bag of fingers and not Gabe? The second question is easier because Nate is eight and ready to take on responsibility. He's eight going on nine and needs to think about getting older and taking care of his mother. He thinks about how sad she seems most of the time and wishes he could make her smile. These thoughts make his head hurt. He stays in bed even when he can't sleep and watches car headlights from the street play with shadows on his ceiling. He thinks about the dark strangeness of the world and the pain in his head. He stays in bed and thinks about the things ghost-Charlie whispers to him.

Did you hide them well?

I'm proud of you.

I love you.

Nate wonders and worries a little about things like responsibility and what his father would want him to do. Sometimes he dreams of dead M'busai warriors with nine fingers and flint-sharpened spears. Of course, he's never seen a M'busai warrior, no living person has. The dreams flash like lightning, and he always wakes sweat-dampened and heaving. His room is opposite Gabe's, so they don't share a wall. No one hears him gasp.

It's on those nights, the nightmare nights, that Nate lies in bed thinking as sweat cools and causes thick, gooseflesh puckers on his skin. He thinks through everything like a puzzle, like a jigsaw without a picture, and imagines places to hide the eggs. He calculates crevices and shadows and things about which his father might be proud. There's a delicate balance to the game he plays with his mother, certain rules to hide-and-seek.

She should find all the eggs and the fingers inside.

But not too easily. Never too easily.

And maybe, just maybe, it might make her smile.

* * *

Beth only sleeps two or three hours most nights. The good sleep is gone, lost with the end of her Lunesta prescription and the discovery of human remains in plastic eggs. Of course, for Beth, good sleep meant four, maybe five hours a night. She lies awake thinking of the boys. She imagines she should tell them how wrong their little game is. She can't imagine where they found the bones. She doesn't want to believe the bones are real. They are, in a way, exactly what she needs: evidence of the M'busai and their rituals. But these bones can't be M'busai bones, not here, not halfway around the world in her comfortable house on a quiet street.

She knows her imagination conjured the figures in the yard, but wonders why Gabe saw them too.

Thinking about these questions draws extra lines on Beth's face. It wears on her and hangs black rags under her eyes. She wants to be pretty and a good mother and everything she never was but wishes she could have been for Charlie.

Charlie is dead. The M'busai are dead.

Dead, dead, dead.

The words ping in her skull like old typewriter hammers.

Dead, dead, dead.

She can't sleep so she searches the house, trying to find plastic eggs in the dark. It's a game. Their pastel colors mute to grey in the midnight house, but she won't switch on the light. She won't enter the boys' rooms, either. They're asleep, she thinks, or should be, but Nate lies awake staring at the ceiling and wondering.

* * *

Nate continues to tell Gabe about Charlie, about Dad and how he's come back and how he brought the bones. Gabe nibbles his lip and whimpers and his eyes swell with tears.

When Gabe tells Beth, Nate and Beth have the Big Conversation. "Your little brother doesn't need this from you," she says.

Nate shrugs his shoulders. He's sitting on his bed, knees pulled to his chest, staring at the wall behind his mother. Her mouth continues to open and close, words falling out, but they're lost in the carpet. Her tired eyes pinch shut. Her head wags from side to side. She looks unreal, standing there. Nate imagines his father and tries to put the puzzle together. Maybe the ghost was warning him, telling him about his mother and how she was.

Maybe Dad chose to die, he thinks. Maybe he wants me to join him.

"Do you understand?" Beth asks.

"I think so," Nate says. His voice is cold and low and hurts his throat a little.

"Good." She smiles. Her lips struggle with the smile, up then down. "I need you to be responsible. I need you to help."

Nate hears the word "need" and it feels like a stone tied to an itchy rope around his neck. He scratches involuntarily and says, "Sure."

When she leaves, he lies in bed and thinks about all of it, the bones and eggs, his father and mother, the little game he invented with his chicken-shit little brother... He thinks about all of it and wants to know something other than plastic eggs and clear tape. He wants to imagine something bigger than hunting for dead mysteries like his mother and the cold grey stone marking his father's grave. He doesn't want to cry—his mother hadn't at his father's funeral—but the tears come, warm and heavy.

And that's when he decides to leave.

* * *

The police can't solve Nate's puzzle. He's left no plastic eggs behind as a trail. He's left nothing except a bag of human bones under his bed and a little brother who now sleeps in his mother's room because the world is too dark and strange at night. They lie together in the same bed, mother and son, one of them awake and the other snoring tiny, six-year-old snores, while the strangeness of the midnight world wheels toward dawn.

She is a good mother, isn't she? She was a good wife, but now Charlie's dead. Questions haunt Beth like the puzzle of the dead M'busai and their strange rituals. Maybe her life needs ritual, maybe it's missing something. Maybe Nate ran away from home because he was missing something too.

Beth rises and goes to the window.

This time, lightning flashes. Thunder rumbles all around. She sees their faces, dozens of them drawn with dark ink, with impossibly big, white eyes. Charlie is in the middle, smiling. He's alone among the warriors. For a moment, she'd hoped to see Nate standing next to him. The nighttime yard flashes with light again. The lightning bolt strikes the shed and it burns, sending the sweet odor of marijuana—some of Charlie's hidden stash—into the sky. Maybe Nate is hiding in the shed, she thinks, and the thought catches her heart with a sudden squeeze. But no. In life, puzzles aren't solved so easily. Never so easily.

Then, only then, as the emergency sirens swell, does she sink to her knees and cry.

ABOUT THE AUTHOR
JAY CASELBERG

Jay Caselberg is an Australian author who now lives in Germany. His unique brand of dark fiction has appeared in many languages in venues worldwide and spans many genres. Caselberg's long history of work has received a number of honorable mentions on many Year's Best lists.

Caselberg's work crosses the boundaries of science fiction, fantasy, mystery, horror and the literary, with all of his pieces containing an especially dark edge. He is the author of several novels, including his *Jack Stein* series and *Empties*, a brutal tale of psychological dark fiction.

Caselberg's visceral tale of psychological horror, "Collage" is featured in the Bram Stoker Award®-nominated *Dark Visions: A Collection of Modern Horror - Volume One* and his disturbing "Compartmental" appears in *Equilibrium Overturned: The Heart of Darkness Awaits*, both published by Grey Matter Press.

PENUMBRA

JAY CASELBERG

You know, it's a funny thing walking through the valley. Thy rod and staff and all that stuff. None of it matters a jot. There is no tunnel. There is no white light. There is no comfort. All of that is there to mollify, to give the fearful something to hold on to. I, for one, am not one of the fearful.

There were no particular fireworks when I passed. It was something of an anti-climax, truth be told. The only things that really change are the priorities, and now that the priorities are set, I have a plan.

You've got to have something to hold on to. Do you believe in love at first sight? That place where you connect with someone and you know, without a trace of doubt that you two are meant to be together for ever. It was a rude awakening that it didn't quite work like that, was not necessarily meant to be that way. I'm not sure which was greater, the shock of my passing, or the magnitude of that realisation by itself.

Suddenly, without warning, I was gone; she was not.

* * *

ghost \ˈgōst\ (*noun*)

1. The spirit of a dead person, especially one believed to appear in bodily likeness to living persons or to haunt former habitats.
2. The centre of spiritual life; the soul.
3. A demon or spirit.
4. A returning or haunting memory or image.
5. a. A slight or faint trace <just a *ghost* of a smile>
   b. The tiniest bit <not a *ghost* of a chance>
6. A faint, false image, as:
   a. A secondary image on a television or radar screen caused by reflected waves.
   b. A displaced image in a photograph caused by the optical system of the camera.
   c. A false spectral line caused by imperfections in the diffraction grating.
   d. A displaced image in a mirror caused by reflection from the front of the glass.
7. *Informal* A ghostwriter.
8. a. A nonexistent publication listed in bibliographies.
   b. A fictitious employee or business.
9. *Physiology* A red blood cell having no haemoglobin.

* * *

When I read that definition, it makes me laugh. Apparently I am a ghost. But Jennifer, to all intents and purposes, is my ghost.

Can a ghost have a ghost? Apparently so. See numbers 2 and 4.

Well, having been convinced that was the case, I set about to exorcise the particular ghost that was haunting me. Is that recursive? Perhaps so, but it's real. Then again, I wonder whether 6c. provides an adequate description of the separation of realities between the corporeal and non-corporeal worlds, if we were to think of them that way.

I needed to pass that diffraction grating to deal with my non-corporeal nature. Only then could I set about doing what I desired, to step beyond that veil between. I was more than a false spectral line—so much more. And I planned to do something about it.

* * *

The very first time I saw Jennifer, it stopped me in my tracks. I knew right then and there—in that very instant—that we were meant to be together. We were at a coffee shop. I was waiting for my drink to be delivered—a nice, skinny cappuccino—and she was in line, waiting to be served. Shiny, auburn hair, pale complexion, perfect skin and blue eyes almost verging on indigo. She happened to glance across as I was watching, and in that brief moment of eye contact, she gave a little half smile before looking away to attend to her order. I knew with certainty that that look contained my destiny. It was only the first of many. In the weeks and months to follow, she would show me how much she loved me in so many different ways, all of them full of the meaning that only Jennifer could convey. She was so very special. And, of course, I loved her back.

Imagine my surprise when I made my unplanned rendezvous with the truck that smashed me against a wall. That hadn't been in any of my plans, and it was just too cruel. There was so much more I still had to do. Of course, above all, there was my life with Jennifer and everything that went with it. That was the most important thing.

I loved her with all my heart and soul. It's an interesting concept that last one—soul.

So, here I was, removed from the mundane, transported, aware, but still removed. It took me a while to adjust. In this place, the sunlight filters through like greenish, glimmering water. The moon is no different, though the touch of its light is more blue. It is as if we swim in the world, amongst you, in an out of the streets and buildings that we used to walk in body. Although I could sense that there were others here, I could not see them, could not touch them directly. I didn't even bother reaching out to them, trying to make contact, for there was only one sole thing that mattered.

For the first few weeks, I laboured over trying to get Jennifer to notice me. Perhaps I would have given up and simply drifted away were it not for the fact that our bond seemed so strong. I had to be with her and I knew she had to be with me. I concentrated all my will into manifestation, becoming solid, whatever it was, and that was part of the problem. I didn't know what it was. There is no primer, no instruction manual that tells you what to do. One moment you are there, and the next you are here, slowly spinning around, seeing but not understanding, trying to come to terms with what has happened. The whole thing with the truck took place so fast and then, here I was. Sometimes I wonder if it would have been different if my death—there, I've said it—would have been slow and lingering, giving me time to prepare.

It seemed that I would have the time to prepare now—all the time in the world.

That's not to say that there wasn't some sense of urgency about my plan. I was, now, just as I had been when the truck wrenched me from life, or at least that was my perception. I had not changed, except for the fact that I was whole again, instead of some gruesome smear on a wall. I presumed that would hold true for her.

I wanted us to be together as she was right now, maybe not as she might be in ten or twenty or thirty years. Sometimes we mark the passage of time by the frequency of those periods of boredom. Since I had been here, I have never been bored. But then, watching my Jennifer was never boring.

First, I tried to whisper in her ear. I thought if she could hear me, there was the chance she'd recognise my presence and we'd be partway there. I did that for a few days, but with limited success. The most it elicited was a brush with one hand at the side of her face, as if she'd been bothered by a persistent insect. It was something. I took hope.

Next, I tried touch. My fingers passed through her arm, drifted unregistered through her shoulder, passed uselessly through her hair and left me grasping nothing. I jumped up in front of her, but she walked right through me—not even a shiver. My frustration grew.

My next recourse was her dreams. I'd heard about people being haunted in their dreams, though I preferred not to think of what I was doing as *haunting*. But I couldn't help but think about it in those terms. You know the stories. Someone sees their long-lost love in their dreams. And then, one day, they meet somebody new and get the blessing from their dream lover, allowing them to move on with life and set up house with their latest love. Well, that wasn't going to happen here. I was sure of that. It was me and me alone that she was destined to be with. Our love was pure.

I returned to waiting, watching, desperate for that moment when she would close her eyes and drift to sleep, her form curled within her bed, shimmering vaguely through the water veil that separated us. I moved closer to watch her eyes, hungry for the tell-tale movement that would signal she was deep within the throes of a dream. At last it came, and I was there, at the perfect moment.

I was lost.

How was I supposed to get into her dreams?.

Several times I tried, and each time I failed. Awake or asleep, she was unaware I was there. If I didn't manage something soon, I feared she would move on with her life, despite her love for me, despite my love for her. Eventually, people do. It might take some of them longer than others, but eventually they moved on. I had to face up to that.

I was weak.

The next few days I took a different approach. I followed her. Over and over again, I summoned my will, tried to make myself known, tried to make her see me. Nothing. I felt myself fading. I started to question the purity of our love. If I couldn't make her see me, if she didn't recognise my presence, how strong could our bond really be?

Then came the moment I'd been waiting for. I saw her striking up a conversation with another man.

Something sparked inside me, something raw, something that blossomed like a flame and filled my senses. It was fear. Jennifer was talking to someone new. It was her first step to moving on. There was no way I could allow that to happen.

The fear—the desperation—filled me and I grasped it, held it and shaped it. I forced it through my resolve, my desperation and gave it a new form, willing myself to be there, to be there with her.

She gave a start.

"What was that? Did you…?" She shook her head.

The guy she was with looked around. "What?"

"I just thought that, for a moment… No, forget it. I guess I'm just seeing things. Just my imagination. I haven't been sleeping that well."

I haven't been sleeping that well. Had I managed, at least in part, to achieve what I had set out to do? I wasn't sure, but now it didn't really matter. I had my proof.

For the next two weeks, I practiced. I needed to get this right. I stayed away from Jennifer altogether. I tried it on other people, those that I had known before. I didn't want her to get used to me, not yet. Too much depended on it.

Gradually, I became more confident. Little by little I gained strength, bunching that will, that raw emotion, and shaping it into something I could use

Once I was secure enough with my new ability, I formed a plan. I started following her again, tracking her movements, re-familiarising myself with her daily routine and the moments that would serve my plan. And finally, at long last, the time was right.

It was the end of the work day, even though time was not really something that mattered to me. Jennifer left her office amongst the rest of her colleagues and headed down the street for her journey home. The evening was dark, chill, an oily sheen across the buildings and streets. There was something special about the look of the evening, even through the watery green of what I saw. It was auspicious. About ten minutes later she reached the station. As she passed through the barriers, I followed close behind. Already I was holding my will, starting to build it, forcing it into a tight, bunched shape deep within me. She reached her platform and passed along its length. Still I followed.

Jennifer stood there on the platform edge. All around her commuters stirred. I had to pick my moment. If I was the slightest bit off, my plan wouldn't work. Perhaps it would be today, perhaps tomorrow, but the conditions had to be right. Below, the rails started to thrum, rattling slightly in their stays. We were close. I summoned my will, driving my energy, all my power, all my desire into a hard knot, ready to release.

Further down the track, the square silver front emerged, pushing out of the tunnel, the broad glass windows, yellow and opaque, oily in the station lights. She and others turned to track the approach. Now. This was my moment. I released my hold on that balled up energy and thrust it into a single effort of will. There! She saw me. This time she couldn't ignore me.

She drew in a sharp breath. "What the—"

She took a step back, her heel twisting in the confined space, forcing her to stumble backwards. Her ankle turned.

And then she was falling back, back and down.

Her descent played out in slow motion, and I watched as the faces around her turned to open-mouthed stares A hand reached out to grab her too late, and still she was falling. The train swept down and impacted, consuming her tumbling shape.

And then she was gone.

Within me, the joy burst upwards, filling me with the love I had for her.

Finally, finally, she was there and I was there with her. At last, we could be together. We would be together, forever.

"Jennifer," I said. "Jennifer." Drawing her out of her initial confusion. I understood that disorientation. After all, I had been there too.

There was a little frown and she spun slowly to look at me. Her gaze travelled up and down and then fixed on my face.

"Who the fuck are you?" she asked.

Not quite the reaction I had expected.

"Now, come on Jennifer, don't be like that. It's me, Adrian. I know you're confused. It's a bit hard to come to terms with at first, but you're here now. Just take a few moments. Take your time. You need to get used to it. It will get easier soon."

She drifted back, away. "I don't know you," she said. Her voice was expressionless. The statement was flat. "I don't know you."

"Jennifer. Please. Come back to me. I worked so hard to make this happen, so we could be together."

"I repeat," she said, her features becoming severe. "Who the fuck are you? I don't know you. I've never seen you before in my…my… life." She turned around and around. "My life," she whispered.

Realisation of what I had said came to her then and she turned back.

"You prick, whoever you are. You did this? You did this to me? What gave you the right? What made you think this was something that—"

She ran out of words.

"Jennifer, please," I said, imploring now. "We were meant to be together. You must see that."

She lifted an incorporeal hand then, warding. "I don't know you. I have never known you. Stay the fuck away from me." A moment's pause. "It was you. It really was you. I remember now. I remember… what…happened."

Her face transformed—a grimace, teeth bared—and then a growing growl that issued deep from within her.

"You prick! You sick fuck. Stay the hell away from me."

Little by little, she backed away, bunching her fists. For a moment the light grew, cutting through the watery waves of greenness, and then she was gone.

What she said was true, I suppose. We never really met. We never had a conversation. That didn't mean I didn't love her with all my being. I thought she understood, that we had a connection. She sent me so many little signs. Those fleeting glances, those little half-smiles. All of them told me I was right. How could I have been so wrong? I couldn't have simply been mistaken for so long, could I? I knew she loved me.

Jennifer was gone. I didn't know how to find her, not in this place. Whatever dreams I had had dissipated with her.

I was alone again.

I couldn't be alone. Not here.

I turned my attention back to the world beyond the veil, back to where we had all come from.

I knew now that Jennifer had been a mistake. She misled me. She was crafty. But she taught me. My desire for her, no matter how misplaced it had been, schooled me in what I needed to do. Now I knew better.

Somewhere out there was my one true love. Her name might be Bronwyn, or Samantha, or Jane. I would find her and I would love her, and she would love me back, once she realised I was there.

And then, then I would make sure that we could be together, that we could be together for ever.

ABOUT THE AUTHOR
JG FAHERTY

JG Faherty is the Bram Stoker Award®-nominated and ITW Thriller Award-nominated author of four novels, seven novellas and more than fifty short stories. He is the author of *The Burning Time*, *Cemetery Club*, *Carnival of Fear*, *The Cold Spot*, *He Waits*, *Hellrider* and the Stoker-nominated *Ghosts of Coronado Bay*. In 2014, he released *Castle by the Sea*, *Fatal Consequences* and *Thief of Souls*.

Faherty writes both adult and young adult horror, science fiction and fantasy. His works range from quiet, dark suspense to over-the-top comic gruesomeness. His short story with a new take on the zombie apocalypse, "Martial Law," is featured in the Grey Matter Press anthology *Equilibrium Overturned: The Heart of Darkness Awaits*.

He enjoys urban exploring, photography, watching both good and bad horror and science fiction movies, hiking, playing the guitar, good wine, and Guinness–not necessarily in that order.

As a child, his favorite playground was a 17th-century cemetery, which many people feel explains a lot.

FOXHOLE

JG FAHERTY

Gaston pushed his body as far against the muddy wall of the fox-hole as he could. I'd already done the same. Even so, we couldn't keep ourselves from trying to force our way further into the soft earth. Another inch. Hell, another half inch. Anything to escape the shrapnel and bullets raining down on us from the South-Am Alliance troops a quarter mile away.

Tree roots poked our bruised, wet flesh, easily tearing through uniforms gone soft and mildewy from weeks of rain and humidity. I've never met anyone who fought in Vietnam—that was way before my time—but surviving those jungles couldn't have been any worse than trying to fight your way through the Amazon basin during the rainy season.

"Jesus, Pierre. What we gonna do?" Gaston's eyes were two white-and-black circles peering out from under the chocolate mud coating his face. He'd be seeing the same thing when he looked at me.

My parents and his came from Haiti to New Orleans on the same makeshift boat back in '88, and they still live on the same street to this day. Me and Gaston were raised more like brothers than friends. We even looked a lot alike, although he'd always been more the athlete and I'd always done better in school.

When the rumors of war started, we both figured it was better to sign up and get our hitch done before the real fighting broke out.

Things hadn't gone like we'd planned.

"I doan' know, brother," I said. "But we stay here, we gonna die, dat's for sure."

Our platoon had been making its way across the seemingly endless rain forest and swamps, moving through the southeast portion of South-Am occupied Venezuela until we reached the Allied headquarters in Guyana. Along the way, we was to lay down some new kind of sensors. When enemy troops crossed the sensors, sniper drones would target the area with high-intensity laser fire. The technology was getting its first battlefield test, courtesy of thirty-something Army grunts.

No one had counted on us stumbling into a damn guerrilla training center.

Now they had us surrounded, outnumbering us twenty to one. And that was *before* we'd started taking casualties. What was left of our unit had been hunkered down for six hours as the South-Am forces slowly closed the circle around us.

Incoming nano mortars screamed their fury, and I tried to make myself one with the earth while whistling, semi-living shrapnel buried itself all around us. With each heartbeat, I expected to feel the sudden punch of scavenger bots tearing open my belly and spilling my guts into the brown puddles at my feet.

Somebody screamed nearby, the throat-tearing, soul-stabbing kind of shout of another soldier meeting their maker.

Heavy volume sonic-cannon fire followed on the heels of the mortars like little brothers tagging along to see what the big boys were up to. A laser round hit the edge of the foxhole and came right through the wet soil, burning a line across my left shoulder.

"Goddamn!" I could barely hear myself over the death-peddling din filling the air.

Then it was over. That first silence after a barrage ain't really silent at all. Your ears ring like you spent the night at a rock concert with your head between two speakers. Underneath that is the *bang-bang-bang* of your heart as it battles the adrenaline shooting through your veins.

I looked at Gaston. His eyes were open and his mouth was going up and down, but I couldn't hear anything. I thought maybe I'd gone deaf and I panicked.

"Gaston!"

He put a finger to his lips. When he spoke again, I could just make out his words. "They think we all dead, maybe they go 'way."

Gaston wasn't no dummy. We both knew we'd be lucky to ever see Bourbon Street again. I started saying prayers in my head.

It didn't take long before things got hot again. More whistling overhead. Only this time it was deeper. Louder. And it seemed to go on forever.

I knew that sound. "Firecracker!"

"Shit!" Gaston dove into the mud at the bottom of the hole. I did the same.

Only thing to do when the firecrackers come is cover your ass and pray. I've seen one turn a double-armored tank into nothing but scrap metal and memories.

Sound waves tore through my ears, leaving a terrible buzzing in their wake. The earth moved underneath us like it was throwing a fit.

Something heavy hit my back and everything disappeared.

* * *

The first thing I noticed was the pain. Then a voice calling my name. I tried to get up, but my body didn't obey. Terrified I'd been paralyzed, I flexed my arms and kicked with my legs, but they wouldn't move. I screamed. Bitter, gritty mud filled my mouth. I froze.

I'd been buried.

Jesus only knew how much water-soaked earth covered me. I got my arms under me and pushed, not much, but enough to get my head up so I could draw a breath without sucking mud.

"Pierre! Pierre!"

That voice again. Gaston's. He was alive. He was *free*.

"Help!" Fear overtook me. I saw myself dying in the ground, slowly going crazy until my air ran out. I shouted the word over and over, my voice a little more hysterical each time.

"Hang on, I'm comin'!"

I pushed and kicked and hollered some more. I rolled in the mud until I faced upwards, then turned to the side as handfuls of dripping muck poured into my mouth.

Just when I thought I couldn't take it anymore, something burst through the earth and grabbed me.

I screamed. I knew it must be Gaston's hand, but I screamed anyway. For a moment, that hand looked like something evil, all gray and pale and dead, like the walking corpses the bocors in Haiti call from the ground to do their evil work.

Then it was Gaston's hand again and I grabbed at it. He pulled. I clawed and kicked. I came shooting from that wet grave quick and easy, not like the earth was giving birth to me, more like it was shitting me out.

"Damn, I'm sho' glad to see you." Gaston pulled me close. I couldn't even answer him. I just squeezed with all the strength I had left in me. No two brothers in the whole world could have been closer than we were right then.

"How long?" I asked.

He shook his head, sending brown water droplets all over. It'd started raining again, hard. We must have looked like two chocolate snowmen melting.

"Doan' know, Pierre. I woke up, dug myself out and den started lookin' for you. But I t'ink we be safe, least for a while."

"How you know that?" I didn't feel safe. We had no guns and we were deep inside enemy territory.

"Look." He pointed to the ground a few feet away. Slowly eroding away in the rain were dozens of boot prints.

"I t'ink dey already come and gone, while we be buried."

I took a deep breath. Their trail led in the opposite direction we had to go. Good news for us.

But we weren't safe, no way. There'd be plenty of other South-Am soldiers between us and Guyana.

I remembered something. "I heard screamin' just before the fire-crackers."

Gaston nodded. "Pretty sure it was Waters. Or maybe Freed." He hung his head. The warm rain ran off his bald dome like he'd just waxed it.

"We should check for survivors," I said.

He grabbed my arm. "Ain't no survivors." I started to pull away, but he held me tighter. "Look 'round, Pierre."

I did. What I saw stopped me cold.

Gaping holes made the area look like we were on the moon instead of in South America. Body parts grew from the mud like obscene alien plants. Acres of trees either knocked down or blown to bits. For the first time, I noticed something in the air, something other than jungle rot and burnt explosives.

Death. Blood and guts and shit and roasted flesh. There's no other smell like it.

"Pierre. We gots to leave this place, get back to the base." He put his arm around my shoulder and I winced. "You hurt?"

I shrugged him off. "It's nothin'. I got nicked. C'mon." I checked my belt compass. We needed to go southeast. A hundred klicks or so, and we'd hit the roads. From there, we'd just follow the signs.

One hundred klicks of jungle swamp. No weapons, no radio, no food. Alliance forces all around us.

How could it get any worse?

* * *

"*Be careful what you ask for, Pierre*," my Mamma always said.

The first three days we did okay. I still had my belt knife, so we were able to cut down fruit when we got hungry. There was plenty of rainwater to drink.

At night we'd huddle under the biggest trees we could find, use branches and leaves to keep the worst of the rain off us. We didn't sleep much. During the days we'd pick our way through the undergrowth, keeping an eye out for trip beams. It was hard going, but we were doing all right.

Until my shoulder started acting up.

The morning of day four I got up to gather some bananas for breakfast. The rain had eased up, and we were hoping to cover some extra ground. I reached up, and next thing I knew I was sitting on my ass.

"Pierre? *Tout bagay anfòm*?" Gaston came running over, still asking if I was all right.

"Doan' know," I told him. "Musta stood up too fast."

He took the knife and cut the fruit down. "Eat somethin'."

I reached out and that's when I felt it. Something achy and tight in my shoulder. I couldn't stop myself from swearing.

"Lemme take a look." As soon as Gaston touched the wound, I cried out again.

"I think it gettin' infected." There was a note of concern in his voice that told me he didn't think so, he *knew* so.

"Ain't nothin' we can do," I said. "'Cept keep movin'."

And that's what we did. Walk all day, rest at night. I was okay when we were walking, but soon as we'd stop, that's when my knees went weak and I felt lightheaded. By the fifth day, Gaston was building the shelter and cutting the fruit all by himself. In the mornings, he'd have to slap me a bit to wake me.

Things got a lot worse on day seven.

I was leaning against a tree, taking a whiz. Gaston was nearby, gathering some passion fruits. Something caught my eye.

A red dot, moving across the tree trunk towards me.

"Down!" I dropped to the ground. Gaston did the same. Sniper fire blew apart the quiet afternoon. As soon as it stopped, we were up and running, my weasel still hanging from my pants.

"*Prese!*" Gaston yelled. *Hurry*.

He didn't have to tell me twice. More gun fire. Sonic rounds turned leaves to confetti all around us. We hunched over as best we could. The trees protected us some but slowed us down, too.

I don't know how long we ran. At one point, Gaston went down, and I feared he'd been hit. But when I helped him up, he gave me a pained smile and shook his head.

"Tripped, dat's all. Keep goin."

We did. An hour. Maybe two. Until it grew too dark to see, and then some. I thought my heart would explode. My legs, they were two pieces of dead wood. My lungs hurt worse than the time I spent Christmas in Boston and caught myself a nasty flu.

Every time I thought I couldn't go any further, Gaston was right there, holding me up, pushing me on. His face was gray and there was a stink rising from him. I swear he must have shit himself, but he didn't let me stop. No, sir. Not until we were safe.

When he held up his hand, I fell to the ground right there. The whole goddamn South-Am army could have been right behind me, I wouldn't have moved.

"Stay here, I'll look around," he said. I couldn't even answer him. It was all I could do to keep from passing out.

Gaston took off his shirt and disappeared into the night. Not long after he left, distant screams roused me from my stupor. I pulled myself up against a tree, but I still couldn't stand.

More screams. Someone getting hurt real bad. More than one someone. Gun shots.

Silence.

I waited against that tree for death to appear.

Footsteps. I closed my eyes, thought about Marlee, my girl back home. I wanted her to be the last thing I saw.

"Easy, boy. It just me." Gaston appeared from the darkness as if it was a doorway. In the traces of moonlight weaving their way through the leaves, he looked gray and ghostly.

In one hand he held a sonic rifle. In the other a demo pistol.

"I dogged three of them," he told me as he put his shirt back on. "Good t'ing I so black. I stab one wit de knife, take his gun. I shoot his two friends. Now at least we got weapons."

He handed me the pistol. It was a Sanchez Model Ocho. Twenty-four in the clip, every round tipped with armor-piercing explosive. A heavy gun, but I could probably shoot it one-handed.

I'd have to. I could barely lift my injured arm. Worse, if I turned my head in that direction, I could actually smell pus and rotten flesh. Forget antibiotics and stitches. I was praying I'd keep the damn arm.

"Can you walk?" Gaston held his hand out to me. His grip was greasy and cold. I wasn't the only one pushing things to the limit.

I walked.

Five more days brought me to my knees. We hadn't seen any more soldiers, but we'd seen signs. Flattened ground where someone had made camp. Candy wrappers written in Spanish. Narcorette butts.

When I collapsed, Gaston got this worried look on his face. I couldn't tell if it was for me, or because we'd stopped.

"I gotta rest. *Mwen pa byen*." *I'm not well*. I was lapsing into Creole, not a good sign. I tried to stay awake, but I had no strength.

Darkness claimed me.

* * *

I only remember bits and pieces of the next few days. Gaston carrying me in his arms like a bride over the threshold. Feeding me. Forcing my cracked, peeling lips open and pouring water or fruit juice into my mouth.

Sometimes he disappeared into the jungle at night. Once I heard distant cries for help and guns going off. Or maybe I dreamed it. When he came back that night, I saw a double image of him, the Gaston I knew overlaid by a ghostly spectre riddled with bullet holes. My heart stuttered like the machine guns I'd dreamed—or heard?—and I rubbed at my eyes. When I looked again, only one Gaston stood before me. Still, it took me a long while to get back to sleep that night.

Gaston smelled of dirt and mold and rancid beer, but I smelled worse. Every time I moved my shoulder, hot fluids oozed down my back and arm, filling the air with the reek of spoiled meat. I was turning into one of those animals you see on the road in the summer, all putrid and gassy.

When we reached the first road, I was sure I was hallucinating again. I'd been doing it for the past two days. Weird visions of Gaston's mother kneeling before a black candle. Him sitting Indian style, watching me while I slept, a nasty, hungry look on his face. When I cried out in fear, he told me to hush.

"You always safe wit' me, brother."

Gaston made us wait until dark before we started down the highway. He seemed to know where he was going.

I don't know how many miles he carried me before we came to a road sign.

Gaston read it out loud. "Guyana, 5 kilometers."

He didn't sound happy. I wanted to shout for joy, but my mouth wouldn't work. I wanted him to shout for me. Instead, he sighed and kept walking.

Dawn was still hours away when the border came into view. We moved into the high grass of the savannah bordering the highway. Under cover of darkness, Gaston crawled the last hundred yards, me laying on his back and holding on with my good arm.

Once we crossed the border, he set me on the ground.

"Pierre, dis be all for me."

"Then rest, brother. We safe now. In the morning we'll make our way to camp."

He shook his head. "No, you doan' understand. I can't go to camp wit' you. I got a job to do."

I tried to make sense of his words, but it was hard to concentrate. "You can't leave me. *Mwen malad." I'm sick.* He knew that. How could he go?

"I gotta make them pay, brother. You take dis." He put something in my shirt pocket. "When the sun come up, walk down da road. Make sure you go in da right direction." In the darkness his teeth glowed white as he grinned.

"Fuck you." I tried to smile back. I don't know if I did. I hope so.

"Goodbye, *mwen fré,* my brother. I see you back home."

He got to his knees, held out his hand to me. I took it, gripped it as hard as I could. I refused to let go, even when he tried to pull away.

"Doan' go," I pleaded.

I passed out with his hand still cradled in mine.

* * *

Bright sunlight, the first in days, woke me. I still held Gaston's hand. I opened my eyes.

I was alone.

And *still* holding Gaston's hand.

The flesh was green and gray and falling off the bones. Greasy slime covered my palm, and I dropped the loathsome remains. Sickened, I wiped my hand across my shirt. Something rattled in my pocket.

I reached in and drew out a simple metal chain. On it were two dog tags and a Saint Christopher medal.

The one Gaston always wore.

I didn't have to look at the tags to know they were his. Just like I recognized the rotted hand in the grass. I knew it as well as my own.

Had he died when the firecrackers hit? Or maybe when the bullets took him in the jungle? Had he ever been there with me at all? If not, how could I have killed those South-Am soldiers when I could barely stand? I had a lot of questions, but I knew I wouldn't get answers, not until I got home and spoke to his mother.

I wondered what kind of trouble he'd be causing for the South-Ams. I remembered the hungry look I'd seen on his face in my dream and thought that maybe I was better off not knowing.

I hung the dog tags around my neck and wrapped his hand in my shirt. He hadn't left me behind.

I wasn't going home without him.

ABOUT THE AUTHOR
GREGORY L. NORRIS

Gregory L. Norris writes full time from his home at the outer limits of New Hampshire.

Norris grew up on a healthy dose of creature double-features, and his work can be found in numerous national magazines and fiction anthologies. He has written for television, including *Star Trek: Voyager*. He is presently working with the Canadian production company, Space Opera Society, on various TV and film projects.

Two of Norris' short stories are featured in volumes from Grey Matter Press. His grisly tale of life in the aftermath of the mortgage crisis, "Violence for Fun and Profit," is included in *Splatterlands: Reawakening the Splatterpunk Revolution*, and his dark and prescient take on a future where advertising has run amok, "Third Offense," appears in *Ominous Realities: The Anthology of Dark Speculative Horrors*.

DROWNING

GREGORY L. NORRIS

Invisible fingers tightened around Palmveist's throat. He was in the water again, drowning a hundred million miles from shore beneath a black velvet sky filled with diamond flecks. Intense cold embraced his body, invaded his marrow. The flicker of sanity in his consciousness that told him to breathe, told him he was only dreaming, also tried to reason that the deadly chill had been there all along. It hadn't left, really. When he went into the drink the first time, ice had formed somewhere deep beneath his bones. In his soul, perhaps? That vein of permafrost would always exist under the surface, a reminder he'd cheated death. Barely.

The last bottled sip of breath burned in his lungs.

Breathe, an inner voice bellowed. *For the love of God, now!*

He woke enough to expel the stale air from his chest and to drink in a gulp of new. The ice jumped out of his soul and onto his skin, and the illusion of freezing to death, of drowning, continued for another tense second. Then Palmveist shot up in his bed, a scream lodged in his throat. He expected to taste the foul brine of the Atlantic and even believed he saw another man lolling in the waves beside him. It was the face of one of the many doomed on that night, the living dead—not to be alive much longer, the man clearly knew that, judging by the wideness of his eyes.

Palmveist blinked, and he saw that the dead man floating nearby wore his own face. He had returned fully from the dream to his rented room above the hardware store and woke staring at his reflection in the mirror above the sink.

Gooseflesh prickled on his arms and legs despite his dressing gown and the warmth from the iron radiator ticking in the corner. The sensation of freezing in the water, of sinking and choking, persisted. So, too, the certainty he wasn't alone. There was someone else in the room with him.

Edgard Palmveist pinched his eyes and willed his galloping heart to calm. Someone? Not exactly. It was a ghost that had haunted him for thirteen years, from the moment he jumped into the ocean with two life jackets tied around his waist.

* * *

Palmveist dressed in his work clothes, went through the motions of buttoning buttons, combing his hair and adjusting his spectacles.

He plodded along the sidewalk. *Ghosts?* "No," he huffed aloud.

The cold March day pressed down from a sky the color of slate. His breaths came with difficulty. For a terrible instant—

He wasn't standing on Main Street in Little Dodd, Connecticut; he was once again falling, falling, given no other option but to jump. The behemoth had split in half, forcing Palmveist to dive into the black water to save himself from going down with the ship.

He struck the Atlantic, like so many others, so many bodies already frozen to death ahead of him. He didn't want to die, no, and so he started moving, swimming. Screams filled his head. Most were his own, contained internally by ears that went numb before hitting the water, partially deafened by the death throes of *Titanic* as she surrendered to the Atlantic.

Screaming, he paddled. For how long, he couldn't be sure, because the rules of time had lost all meaning. His arms stiffened but still worked, according to the splashes as his body cut the ocean's surface. As a boy growing up in Sweden, he'd swum in cold water on plenty of occasions. Maybe that helped save him.

A shadow loomed ahead, lolling on the waves. His first thought was that he'd come across a coffin. The oblong length of wood materialized—a stateroom door, torn loose in the night's violence. He scrambled for the door's edge. Somehow, his fingers grabbed hold. It wasn't the safety of a lifeboat, and the Atlantic feasted on his body's heat without mercy. Still, he was alive.

The foul, fishy stink of the ocean poisoned his desperate sips for air. Sobs reached beyond the ice in his ears. The cacophony echoed into the distance. A ghostly wind's howl replaced it, and Palmveist blinked. The dark panorama of black sky, and blacker ocean, sank. He rose up from the waves to find himself in the present, holding onto a different door—the worker's entrance to Bridgeport Tool and Die. The image of the stateroom door hovered before him, growing less distinct between the shutter-clicks of his eyes. The wind howled.

Right before the memory evaporated, he again saw the dark shape and heard the scrape of nails digging into the wood. Someone else had been holding onto the stateroom door.

* * *

He'd landed a decent job as a machinist, thanks to the man who owned the hardware store and rented him the upstairs room.

The smell of the gear grease and the heat from the metal drill nauseated him. Everything, in some way, reeked of that night, now nearly thirteen years gone. Sweat flowed as it normally did, and his flesh crawled. It was the Atlantic, soaked deep into his soul and now leaching out of his pores.

During work breaks he sipped water. His stomach knotted, and his gorge threatened to rise. How much of the murderous ocean had he swallowed that night? Enough to gag on, so many seasons later. Enough to drown.

Only he hadn't drowned, Palmveist's inner voice reminded.

Water was no substitute for ale, and the memory of a stout, cold drink worsened the ache in his gut. Industrial ethyl alcohol lurked somewhere under the same roof, but the federal government of his adopted land had poisoned all of it to prevent bootleggers from defying the Eighteenth Amendment, curse those pure Protestants and the Anti-Saloon League. The temptation to drink even a finger of the stuff was great. Plenty—thousands, in fact—in nearby New York City had and they'd paid with their lives. Legalized murder, according to the growing throng of voices calling for repeal.

A drink. A night on the town with a fine lady. Anything to feel whole again.

He worked, sweated and did his best to ignore the sensation of being watched.

* * *

Other hands, clawing for purchase on the stateroom door.

Palmveist sat on the edge of the mattress. His dressing gown hugged his skin with an awkward, damp fit, like the clothes he'd worn on his leap into the ocean. Bare feet absorbed the chill radiating up from the wooden floor. The lone candle on the nightstand launched flickers off the mirror and the porcelain sink. He fell into the whirls and concentric ripples of his imagination. Holding onto the door, drowning—*dying*. The screams, the jagged wind tearing above the water and his heart pounding in counterpoint. It was difficult to see clearly given the dark and bitter cold, the latter attempting to freeze his eyes shut.

"Hold on," he said to the owner of those other hands holding the stateroom door, first in Swedish and then in English, his second tongue.

Only when Palmveist blinked away enough ice to see clearly, that other soul was gone, lost to the ocean's hunger.

The cold worked its way up from the floor and into his soles, radiated into his blood, deeper. He forgot how to breathe because he was there again, alone and clinging to the stateroom door. The other man had let go and surrendered. But he wouldn't—he didn't want to die. A new and prosperous life waited somewhere ahead in the distance, but it was still so far away as to be completely out of sight, almost beyond his ability to believe. On this deadly, dark night, the unfeeling stars over his head seemed closer.

Let go, too, a voice whispered. *Less pain this way.*

Palmveist turned to his left. No one was there. The voice originated in his head, he reasoned. Or from the dark brine of the Atlantic, whose appetite for human suffering wasn't yet satisfied. Then to the right, where movement formed in the terrifying seascape, one degree darker than the surrounding night.

A splash of water. Frantic words followed, though at first Palmveist wasn't sure if they were real or in his imagination.

"Hurry—or we risk being dragged down with it!"

It—the *Titanic*—had already sunk. A lifeboat passed close by, maybe one of the last, and as such, Palmveist's last chance. The same voice that had told him to let go of the door and drown now attempted to coax him to hold on. He willed his fingers to detach. The ocean lapped him up, but instead of sinking, he was buoyed by the two life jackets still tied to his waist. He paddled, cut water, kicked. The door, which he'd mistaken for a coffin, drifted away. He was back in the drink.

In the present, a shudder teased the nape of Palmveist's neck. He fought it, failed. The chill spilled down his spine, blurring the details of the rented room above the hardware store in Connecticut. It struck him that he was only half there, aware of the lamb stew from dinner sitting lumpy in his stomach and the wan glow from the streetlamps, which gilded the window frame. The other half had reached the lifeboat.

Alive—he so desperately wanted to live. To begin the new life that had led him from Sweden, and all he knew as familiar, to a place called Yonkers, where his older brother and his wife waited. *Yonkers.* What a strange and mystical-sounding place, promising new opportunities and adventures. First, he had to survive the night.

The lifeboat towered above him, as big as *Titanic* in his growing panic.

"Help me," he cried out in English.

"No!" a woman answered.

He reached up for a hold. The lifeboat renounced its gargantuan mass.

"No, we'll capsize!" she shrieked.

A sharp pain raced up his arm, delivered by the nearest oar. Palmveist slid back into the water. He tried again. The next strike nailed him across his right collarbone.

"Please," he pleaded to the dark figures huddled above him. "I don't want to drown!"

A small, scared face peered over the edge of the lifeboat. A young girl, he realized. She was wrapped in a shawl. The waif opened the shawl and lowered it toward him.

"Here," she said, and nothing more.

He wound the cloth under his injured shoulder. He was aware of movement—the lifeboat's or the ocean's, he couldn't tell. A numbing fog engulfed him.

The rescue ship drew near, and the hands of strangers hauled him from the water. He later learned the young girl who'd offered the life-line to which he'd clung had died from exposure.

* * *

His time in Yonkers hadn't been long or particularly pleasant. Palmveist and his brother's wife, Hannah, were incompatible beneath the same roof. And there was the matter of the violent night-mares that plagued him, the proximity of Yonkers to the water.

He moved to Connecticut, first to New London, but the ocean drove him steadily inland, to Little Dodd and the rented room above the hardware store.

Palmveist blew out the candle and curled his body beneath the covers. He craved a drink, something that would ignite on its way down the throat and warm the insides. But of course, such a luxury here was almost impossible. He often dreamed about returning home to his true home, Sweden. That land, however, was far away, reachable only by crossing the Atlantic. He was stuck with the choices he'd made. Cursed by them.

The permanent chill in his marrow—his soul—made getting warm impossible. His breaths came with increasing difficulty as the weight of memory pressed down on his chest. The room drifted on imaginary waves of darkness and icy ocean water. He thought that at any moment death would pull him under. He was drowning again; maybe he had been for thirteen years. The stink of the Atlantic ignited on his next shallow sip of air.

And then he was sure that another presence had invaded the room. His eyes shot open. He sat up, gasping for breath.

"Who's there?" he sputtered. "Tell me, who goes there?"

Nobody answered.

* * *

Palmveist was not an unattractive man, but the events of his adult life had heaped decades onto the lines around his eyes and mouth. Without regular contact from the little family he had in America, and no true friends outside his connections at work, he was for the most part alone. He convinced himself the loneliness was to blame. The ghost haunting his life wasn't born of the supernatural but instead the natural world, in which circumstance had isolated him, an apparition taking form from an absence of human company and comfort.

Little Dodd was hardly New York City, where a man could easily find companionship with a woman, even of the temporary sort. On occasion, Palmveist had—another of the reasons that had so offended his brother's wife. A rented room was no place for a bride, let alone suitable for starting a family, but it allowed him to save his earnings. Sweden was far away and effectively lost to him. Still, he could begin anew if he, too, found a wife. He was certain that then all the ghosts of his past would vanish.

Not far from Bridgeport Tool and Die was a tailor renowned for his exceptional cut and execution. Before work, Palmveist hurried to the storefront whose windows displayed men's suits on mannequins without heads, showcased by drawn black velvet drapes. He tried the door but found it locked. He was too early. The exquisite clothes mocked him. Twice he spun in the direction of the factory, only to turn back. After checking his watch, he entered the alley between Choice Tailoring and Haberdashery and the brick building that contained, according to an understated tile, the shop of Madame Cataldo, palmist.

Palmveist dug in his heels and faced the simple blue door, which lacked windows. The tile, also blue, creaked on its hinges. His intention had been to cut through the alley, see if the tailor lived at the back of his shop as he assumed many tailors did. But thoughts of a new suit and vest, and a button-down with a stiff white collar, vanished.

The March wind whistled down the alley and rocked the sign. Such an out of the way place—likely set in a remote corner of the downtown to keep it removed from Protestant eyes, the same puritans behind Prohibition's dry America—was also surely closed at so early an hour. But Palmveist knew that if he reached for the door, the knob would turn, and he would find himself speaking with the mystic, Madame Cataldo, in her sanctum.

He extended his fingers and then recoiled, as though the tips had been flash-frozen. Shaking his head, he turned, hurried back to the sidewalk and marched to Bridgeport Tool and Die with his hands shoved in his pockets for warmth.

* * *

Palmveist studied his reflection. "Are you certain?"

Rudolpho Choice, the tailor, smoothed out the shoulders of his new jacket. "The wider trouser leg? Absolutely. Oxford bags are in fashion."

The jacket was higher waisted, the lapels thinner. Choice called the color *midnight-blue*.

"The look suits you."

Palmveist agreed. He exhaled and indulged in the rare flicker of happiness.

"Besides," Choice continued, "new clothes are an expression of a man's prosperity."

The narrow neckband of the shirt collar was softer than he expected. New trends. New beginnings. Palmveist almost believed in the possibilities.

He studied the jacket and vest, and a chill gossiped over his skin. He willed his eyes higher, up to his face, but they refused to cooperate, as though knowing he wouldn't be there. The only reflection would be that of his new suit, not his old flesh, the image like one of the headless mannequins in the display windows.

"Is something wrong?" the tailor asked.

Palmveist realized he'd stopped breathing and exhaled a lungful of air. His eyes darted north and recorded the expression that had given Rudolpho Choice such concern. "No, no, I was only thinking."

"Thinking?"

"Yes, regarding your nearest neighbor, Madame Cataldo."

"What of her?"

"Is she...?" Palmveist's voice trailed to silence.

Choice completed the sentence. "Is she legitimate? Some would say no, others yes. Are you in need of a glimpse into the mysteries of the future?"

"Perhaps. Or maybe the past."

"*Caveat emptor*." Choice sighed and again brushed his bony fingers across Palmveist's shoulders, smoothing the already smooth material. He then presented him with the bill.

A restless wind gusted down Main Street. The long walk to his rented room loomed, and whatever lightness of spirit he'd gained from his new clothes scattered with it. His new Oxford wingtip shoes felt like cement hardening around his feet. Palmveist reached the mouth of the alley. He turned right. The tile rocked on its hinges. The doorknob turned. He entered Madame Cataldo's shop.

A scent of citrus infused the air. Delightful, but hardly the exotic spice he expected. Missing from the mental décor he'd laid out in his imagination was the crystal ball; the gnarled gypsy with the wart on her nose, a dark yarn shawl around her hunched shoulders; the stuffed black cat frozen in taxidermy, its spine arched, its eyes bugged out and its mouth open in a permanent silent scream. No mummy's sarcophagus. No jars of dead things floating in solutions, or potions, or smoking cauldron.

He entered a sitting room, quite charming and ordinary, with a camelback sofa, upholstered in a claret-colored velvet, and two Queen Anne chairs, those in the same summer blue as the outer door. A candle flickered on a table set between the sofa and chairs, more for effect, he thought, given the electric wall sconces. A mirror with a gold frame sent back the room's reflection, creating an illusion that it was twice as large.

Another door connected the room to wherever. Palmveist wondered if this were an anteroom of sorts, a parlor. The gypsy with the crystal ball surely saw her clients beyond the other door. He opened his mouth, intending to call out, only he couldn't conjure his voice.

The mirror drew him over to the wall. The same room. Of course it was. He hadn't noticed the simple landscape on the opposite wall— a painting of the ocean of all things, with white-capped waves crashing beyond a spare anchor of beach.

Palmveist turned around, and no such painting hung on the wall. He again faced the mirror. The painting was gone, a hallucination that had jumped out of his mind for a second and had returned to the territory of the imagination.

A woman now stood in the mirror's reflection. He spun around, stirring the scent of citrus, and found that she was real. Blonde, not unattractive, she wore the kinds of clothes women of the decade had embraced with brashness—shorter, tighter, showing off what the catalogues scandalously referred to as 'boys' bodies.

Hers was trim and boyish. Where the woman showed her age was in the eyes.

"May I help you?" she asked in a voice that lacked accent, so far as Palmveist could tell.

He cleared his throat. "Yes, thank you. I seek Madame Cataldo."

"I am she."

"You?" he asked, and then felt foolish for the question.

"How may I help you, Mister...?"

"Palmveist. Edgard. I seek the truth."

She waved the slender fingers of one hand toward the Queen Anne chairs. "Have a seat."

Palmveist shuffled to the nearest of the chairs. As he passed the section of wall where the imaginary seascape had hung, the temperature in the room plummeted. Madame Cataldo shivered.

"Did you feel that?" he asked.

Though it was clear in the language of her body that she had, she took the other seat without formalizing her answer. Madame Cataldo extended both hands. "This is my left hand, in which you'll place a coin for my services."

He reached into his pocket. "How much?"

"That's for you to decide."

He fished out a Walking Liberty half-dollar and placed it in her hand.

"Generous," she said, though the statement lacked enthusiasm. She closed the left, opened the right. "And this is my right hand, upon which you'll lay yours, palm side up."

The connection unleashed a numbing rush of cold up Palmveist's wrist. His instinct was to pull away, like the time in Yonkers at his brother's home when, reaching to turn on an electric torchiere, he'd received a shock. But Madame Cataldo's open palm, far smaller than the back of his hand, held him frozen.

"*The water*," she said in a voice that sounded half-submerged. "Stay away."

Palmveist gasped an expletive in his native tongue. "Tell me...the *Spöke*—?"

She coughed.

"The *ghost*," he said. "Is it real? Following me?"

Madame Cataldo attempted to mouth an answer. Instead, a gout of brackish water flew from between her quivering lips. Palmveist jumped out of his seat, breaking their connection. The vomited liquid splashed across the floor. He no longer smelled citrus; the brine of the ocean poisoned his next breath.

"Yes," she spat. Thick tears clotted her eyes. "The *Spöke*—for an instant, I almost saw his face!"

"Him? Not a young girl with a shawl?"

She shook her head. The clotted tears spilled down her cheeks. "He's angry, so angry—"

Movement at the periphery drew Palmveist's gaze away from the mystic, to the wall. No painting of waves crashing beyond a thin strip of shore materialized. It was, a rational man would see, merely the light of the candle, distorted by their sudden movements and projected onto that stretch of horsehair plaster. Still, the way the reflection flickered, rolling in waves, painted the same study in strokes of fire instead of oil pigment. Palmveist shook.

"I must go," he said, and turned toward the door to the alley, praying it would still be there. It was.

Madame Cataldo called after him. "Stay away from the water! The next time you go in the water, you will drown."

* * *

The midnight-blue suit haunted him in the growing shadows. Palmveist studied the cut of the vest and the Oxford bag trousers, dangling from the bottom center of the clothes hanger. New clothes for old skin. He again remembered the mannequins without heads. Here he was, a suit on a hanger suspended from the hook on the back of the door to his rented room, a being without form. There were times when he no longer felt solid, a man made of memories.

Any second, he expected the clothes on the hanger to come alive, the shoes to scuttle across the floor independent of feet.

Dusk deepened and night rolled in, casting dark waves over everything in the room, including the suit. Palmveist resisted the urge to light the candle. He struggled to breathe; he felt like drowning.

* * *

On March the twenty-seventh, he donned his new suit and headed out of his rented room, down Main Street. He stopped at the barber's for a shave. Johansson was a Swede and what conversation they shared was made in the language of their mother tongue.

"Moving?" Johansson asked.

"Yes. I'm seriously considering a change of place," Palmveist said. "Somewhere new. The mountains, perhaps."

"It would be a shame to lose a friend from home, and you have everything a man needs here in Little Dodd."

Palmveist chuckled. "Everything? I have no family, no wife."

Johansson's eyes glinted with mischief. "I have a solution to that. My wife's sister Annika, a Swedish beauty who is in need of a husband…"

* * *

He planned to dine at the best restaurant in Little Dodd, with or without Annika Christoffer as his guest. The leisurely stroll to the Johansson house in the remote countryside dragged out before him. His feet complained, and the new wingtips absorbed as much spring mud on the outside as sweat inside. He considered turning back, which would label him a cad and destroy any chance at courting the woman described to him as "a fine beauty, sadly alone and far from home."

The road wound through a dense stand of fir trees growing so close together that their linked branches formed a living wall. The afternoon sun floated behind the clouds, a platinum disk offering little warmth. Patches of the last of winter's snow prevailed at roadside and beneath the hemlocks.

Handsome, Johansson had said, and the image of his potential new bride was one of hard expressions and wide hips, not of the flapper girls dressed in short, flowing frocks that sang and clanged from hems of beads and bangles.

The company would more than compensate for actual passion. Another body to heat the bed, to keep away ghosts. A fresh start, with him walking toward it dressed in his sharp, new clothes. At the Johansson place, out past the stone quarry. Maybe.

A scuffle of footsteps sounded behind him. Palmveist spun. No one was there. They came again, this time from the direction ahead. He turned back around in time to catch a darting ripple of color, midnight-blue, as it dipped into the nearby trees. His next breath clotted in his throat. He looked down to make sure his new clothes were still on his body, that they hadn't jumped off him in search of the hanger.

Someone in a similar suit moved at the tree line, just out of sight behind the branches.

"Who are you?" Palmveist demanded. His voice rose to a shout. "What game is this?"

The only response was a man's laughter.

Turn around, his consciousness urged. *Run back to your room, fall deep beneath the covers where it's warm and dry.*

Palmveist shook his head. *Spöke.*

He pursued.

The figure zigzagged, staying always ahead, always barely there, a flicker behind the gray-green branches.

"Who—"

Hemlocks pawed at his face. His new suit wouldn't be so crisp once he emerged from the woods, and he was past caring.

"I demand to know, who are you?"

Palmveist broke through the trees and found himself standing on the precipice of a hollowed-out hillside. The stone quarry. A damp, stale smell assaulted his nostrils as he gazed down the scored, exposed walls to the pond that had formed in the vast bowl far beneath. The water was as black as the ocean on that night. He froze.

Footfalls scurried behind him. Palmveist turned. A moan escaped his lips. The face of the ghost haunting him was his own. His reflection pushed.

And then he was falling again from the deck of the sinking *Titanic*, spiraling toward the ocean.

Before reaching the water in the quarry pond, he remembered the stateroom door and that other set of hands. In the rapid flash of the memory window inching open for a brief view, less than a second's worth of time, he saw the hands were his own, the image recorded out-of-body. The ghost was his. He hadn't fully survived that night. Part of him had died, drowned.

Palmveist struck the water.

* * *

On April the fifteenth, 1925, Edgard Palmveist's body was discovered floating face down in the Little Dodd granite quarry. The undertaker who examined the remains concluded the cause of death was drowning.

ABOUT THE AUTHOR
JANE BROOKS

A native of the southern United States, author Jane Brooks ultimately escaped from her birthplace below the Mason-Dixon line to the general safety of the West Coast, where she now makes a living turning numbers into stories for a large software company.

Co-written with author Peter Whitley, her short story "Release" offers a fresh new take on the zombie genre and is featured in the Grey Matter Press anthology *Dark Visions: A Collection of Modern Horror - Volume Two.*

THE WEIGHT

JANE BROOKS

There was no precipitating event, no fall or car accident or lifting of too much weight. It started a few days ago, this dangerous feeling in my back, like my spine was being tugged very slowly apart. It quickly became alarming enough to bring me here to endure a series of what are supposed to be quick, routine X-rays. The orthopedist wants to blame it on age, but I'm not that old.

The tiles are cool on my feet. This is all I can take in of the room, cool tiles and everything brightly white around me. Standing still, I'm flushed with adrenaline, like smoldering coals in my gut pushing heat outwards where it's trapped and sizzles on my skin. My feet on the cold floor assure me that I won't dissolve into steam.

The X-rays, of course, require several unnatural positions, and with each comes a new pain. I've learned to expect it. Moving in unusual ways invites a new intensity and flavor. But expecting the pain doesn't make it any better.

The cool on my feet isn't enough anymore. I'm unstable and unsupported, and I ache and burn along the length of me.

"Just pull on this bar. Hold...and relax." Jeff, the X-ray tech, is professionally amiable. It doesn't help, but to his credit he doesn't make anything worse.

Another shot, another position, another knife slicing from shoulder to hip. Tears chase each other down my cheeks and I concentrate on not sobbing.

And then the last, with me facing a detached metal wall, its arms extended over my head like a Halloween ghost. Stupid wall, you don't scare me. I'm counting breaths until I can sit down again. I may soon not remember how to count. Or how to breathe.

"Okay, stretch your neck back a little, Leigh. Last one. Deeeeeep breath. Hold… Hold… Hold it… And…"

Click-hum-click.

I feel a sudden sharp crack and clutch the metal in front of me for support. It feels like something is swinging from my spine, stretching it out of shape left and right. My gorge rises, then blackness surrounds my vision.

I hold my breath, waiting for him to say, "Relax," but he doesn't say it.

Looking across my shoulder I see his pale face, eerily lit by the monitor. His brows are knitted in confusion, as if trying to untangle something monstrous with his mind. He's looking, I know, at the image of my spine.

"That can't be right," he mumbles to no one in particular. Then to me, "Leigh, we're going to repeat this one." He steps out to reposition me again, then jogs back behind the partition. "Just take a deep breath and *don't move.*"

I grit my teeth.

Click-hum—

All at once the weight of my body is too much to carry. I hear what sounds like a truckload of candy canes being crushed by a wrecking ball. This is followed by screaming that I think might be me, and I feel—

Pain is just not enough word. It can't possibly cover this. This is more than pain. It's different. It's transformative, identity-shaking, disorienting—an absolute, permanent loss so profound that I may no longer be me. It doubles me over, as if gravity has tripled, and when I fall to the tile floor the stages of grief pass by in a single, tragic, nauseating millisecond. This is a tectonic shift in everything I understand to be true about my body, physics, the universe.

Fundamental things about me no longer work.

From outside my body I listen with mounting alarm to the soprano wreck of noises coming from my throat. Then, turning to the booth, I see Jeff's wild eyes riveted to the screen in front of him and I realize I'm not the only one screaming.

* * *

I am floating into a pool of light on wobbly clouds, moving toward faint sounds of machines. Everything seems very far away—my hands, my feet, the room, people. I try to speak and my voice is far away. It may not even exist.

I don't remember anything that isn't crazy. I know that something's wrong, something's happened, something awful, but that's all I know. All I have is a muscle memory of cold hands grabbing my spine from the inside and pulling me down.

My awareness gutters like a candle, and through the uncombed cotton of my mind I hear voices—confident and educated voices—and words I struggle to recognize. *Catastrophic. Surgery. Paralysis.* The words are musical syllables choreographed like Ziegfeld girls, harmonized and trilling and sparkling around my head. I have no anchor in time. I have even less anchor in meaning, they're just sounds cascading down staircases wearing feathers as I drift in and out among them.

Sometimes the voices are accompanied by the noise of machines—staccato ticks, rhythmic beeps. Cold things skip across the skin of my face or my hand, and I feel a great squeeze on what might be my arm. Mumbled numbers repeat themselves in my dreams.

Occasionally I hear voices I know. My husband Rob's calm bari-
tone. Dear friends I want to reach up to but can't, whispering lightly
and sometimes cooing very near my ear. The nurse who's stopped by
to check on me. My neighbor. These are the voices I listen for. They
are the sounds that remind me I'm not lost.

* * *

I am awakened from sleep by cold pressure on my back, then a
sharpness that climbs through the center of me to a terrible, icy peak.
The pain is yellow behind my eyes, chaotic and loud, like screaming
children beating the skins of snare drums.

There are hands on my face. Familiar, cool hands.

And then her voice.

"Leigh Ann, baby."

A sweet, tidewater drawl, heavy and long, like satin ribbons dipped
in wet plaster. She whispers, but her words echo in my head, melodic
and jarring and harmonizing with the cacophony of my pain.

"Leigh Ann, baby doll, can you hear me? Do you know who this
is?"

Of course I know her. How could I not? Hers was the first voice I'd
ever heard. It has been with me all my life.

"Mama," I croak, a broken rasp of a whisper.

I open my eyes to her wet, puffy, desperate face.

"I'm here to take care of you, Leigh Ann. I know it hurts, but
when you're better I'm gonna take you home with me. Fanny Helm's
daughter will get the best care possible, I swear. You won't want for
anything."

I'm not comforted.

I know that something is wrong but I can't remember what. It's
more than just the fact that I'm in a hospital bed aching and unable

to move. Something about her is wrong. I know it's important, and I almost have it, but then I feel a sharp stab in my back that violently disrupts everything and I lose the thought. Something is pressing my bones through the mattress and towards the floor. I lose track of her, of the room. There is only pressure and pain and breath and then darkness and the memory of Mama's voice.

* * *

I see toes at the end of the bed, covered with a blue hospital blanket. I see tubes and wires connecting me to bags of fluid and illuminated monitors.

There is also this…this *thing*. This figure. A shape. Not like a person or an animal. Like a symbol. It's faint and translucent. A curve sweeps out to the right at the top and bows down and to the left before turning back to the center at the bottom. It's like a question mark scrawled by a child. Though it moves around, it persists. It's always somewhere in the room.

I see it everywhere and not everywhere all at once. It appears in the folds of the blanket. It floats in front of the curtains and walls.

Often I see it on the back of my eyelids in the darkness, like a sigil marking a terrible, invisible doorway.

* * *

I hear my husband's voice, my Rob, the cadence of his questions to the doctors, intelligent and patient, cataloguing everything. I can't follow what they say for very long—the drugs are too thick. But I know when he's nearby, so I have the space to relax and let it all happen around me. With him I'm always safe.

His warm, thick hands hold mine for a long time. I listen to him breathe and I breathe with him. I'm accustomed to this, no words between us, just comforting warmth, safe and solid. The weight on me is lifted, and I can float within that cloud and sleep.

* * *

Here is Mama's voice now, a familiar sandpaper whisper accompanied by her cool hand on my arm. She talks close to my ear about me getting better and coming home with her. I want to believe her. I want her to save me.

When she's with me my body feels different, especially weighted down, pulled and stretched into the bed. Her presence makes me nauseous. I brace for something awful to happen, and the pain blooms and throbs throughout my body.

I'm not so far gone that I don't know why, of course. This is Mama. She has always been problematic.

She has always been my burden. I took care of her even when I was a child. We all did, but for reasons I never understood, out of all the family I was the indispensable one. I was her "special baby," and it was my job to keep her calm. Entertained. Distracted from whatever it was that made her sad or angry or sent her searching for weakness in those around her. It was my job, when everything and everyone else failed, to stay next to her and hold her hand and *take it*.

Her voice summons all my memories of her.

Mama on the farm at Easter, when I was three, my navy blue dress matching hers like I'm a silent echo, a little Fanny doll made to match everything laudable about her, and on the way home her long list of my transgressions.

Mama smoking in the den, drinking a glass of sherry in the headache of late afternoon, the rest of the house braced for a storm that may or may not come.

Mama screaming at everything that was wrong in the world,

scattering the cats to far corners of the property and leaving me paralyzed just inside her blast radius waiting for her hand to come down on my face.

Mama in her bedroom, in the dark, a cool cloth on her head, crushed by the weight of her sadness, reciting all the ways I let her down. Sometimes she would gesture for me to lie down with her, and she would squeeze me like a rag doll, my teenage body grinding against itself as she desperately pressed her weight and strength onto me.

Mama in the hospital, surrounded by pinging machines, her cool fingers squeezing mine until they felt like they would pop out of my knuckles.

And again the feeling that seeing her here is wrong.

Her hand squeezes mine constantly. Her fingers, I know, communicate our lifetime covenant: never leave, never leave me alone. It's how she designed us, what she wanted, and Mama always got what she wanted, one way or another.

I think we all want our parents to be good parents. Despite everything, despite decades of proof to the contrary, I've spent my life hoping somehow she could learn to be the Mama I needed or, failing that, that I could teach her how. If I was just wise and calm enough, then she would understand and become my good Mama, a Mama I'd never really known but missed every day of my life.

Hearing her voice now, I remember that hope and also the disappointment into which it always dissolves.

When I struggle to understand it all—her presence, our life together—the pain moans like whale song, like a failing suspension bridge, and my architecture bows as the weight of her pulls itself hand over hand up my spine.

It's all so heavy.

I welcome, again, the blankness of sleep.

* * *

"I'm here, Leigh. Don't worry. I got you. I'm in charge now."

Rob.

I'm not sure I'm actually smiling—I don't know if I can—but I imagine all the warmth and relief I feel beaming out the top of my head. That phrase, "I'm in charge now," that's what he's always said to me when I can't sleep. He knows I'm the vigilant one who can never sleep when there's something for which I need to be responsible. He learned early to take the burden and hold onto it himself. We both know it's just a metaphor, but it's our signal, the way we make it okay for me to rest.

He's whispering to me, a litany of the day's events spoken to my eyelids, a steady patter of all the dumb things. Lunch. Nurses. Coffee. Home. The cats. His business. Our friends. The plot of a terrible movie he's seen. His best friend's love life. The things he has to accomplish tomorrow. I can stay here and listen to him, feel him, for a very long time. With him, the pain subsides. I can feel the drugs pushing the ache away. It's still there, but it doesn't grip me so tightly.

As he talks I drift in and out. His voice makes my fog pleasant and allows me to let go and float among the listing clouds. When I return, there he is with his soothing voice. I let it hold me, make me warm, for as long as I can remain aware.

* * *

In my dream it's summer and we're hot, even with the breeze. She's singing a corny love song and dancing with me in the living room of our old house in Virginia. I'm a toddler at most, diapered and vulnerable, tucked on her hip as we sway around the room. I recognize the tune, but the words are muffled. Something about love and bushels and wrecks. I try to ask what it means but I can't talk. The tune is a swing I can sit in and rock, though, so I relax into the back and forth of it as she dances more and more vigorously through the house.

After a while the swing goes too high.

Suddenly, my location shifts back to the hospital room. I feel a grinding sensation and the sound of gravel underfoot. With each crunch of rock upon rock I feel a new spark of pain up the center of my spine.

Now there are many noises. A loud, urgent beeping, Rob's worried bellow for help, then concerned, professional voices speaking about heart rate and blood sat and blood pressure. Numbers, more numbers clearly spoken, but they mean nothing to me.

Then next to me, Rob and a woman with great authority in her voice.

"...deteriorating quickly...act soon..."

"...you said she isn't strong..."

"...too much for her heart if we wait..."

"...but the risks..."

"...you've seen the lateral distortion..."

"...I know, like a question mark..."

"...so you must understand..."

And then the crack of fear in Rob's voice as he says, "Look, *you* don't understand. This condition, this surgery, is the reason her mother is dead. I can't lose her like that."

I'm awake now, from the pain and the activity around me, adrenaline and alarm inflating me until I can speak.

"Rob. ROB!"

He turns to me and kneels by the bed. "Leigh, you're awake. I was so scared—"

"No, Rob, listen. Tell me... Mama... She's dead?" My head is exploding with hot ache.

"Yes, of course. Are you feeling okay? Do you know where you are?"

My words slide around in my mouth like oysters. "Not dead, Rob. Not dead. Mama…"

I hear a hot, red alarm next to the bed, accompanied by agony slicing through me. Everyone in the room leaps into action, and darkness closes in. The last thing I hear is Rob whispering in my ear, "Stay with me, Leigh. You're going to be all right, just stay with me. Okay?"

I feel movement. The bed is rolling quickly, surrounded by running feet. My vision narrows to a pinpoint and then pops out of existence like an old TV picture.

* * *

I'm standing in a large, black space. A fragile old woman is facing away from me in a powder-blue hospital gown that leaves her back and thighs exposed. Her shoulders stoop forward and her frame leans unnaturally to the right. She's holding tight to one of those four-footed nursing-home canes.

Her figure is awful but familiar. A twisted spine threads in and out of her muscles below the skin, surrounded by flesh squeezed into unnatural shapes as it conforms to her back's meandering line. It's difficult to imagine that her back can carry her weight, the muscles and curves and knots of vertebrae squeezing right and then left bend her into a question mark.

On her papery skin there is a faint image, as if projected by the dusty and unfocused lens of an X-ray machine. A fuzzy, wide line starting at her neck follows her spine out to the right just below her shoulder before sloping down and slashing diagonally across her back. Above her left hip it curves back to center.

Of course. This is where I've seen that shape before.

"Mama."

She turns her head, using her cane to keep steady, and shuffles around to face me. "Leigh."

Memories crowd my mind like panicked horses—the last five years of her life spent in crippling pain, her back slowly collapsing under the weight of her flesh, getting from doctor to doctor, the increasingly strong narcotics that left her depressed and frightened and more angry than normal. She lost six inches in height, my tall and powerful Mama shrinking into desperate frailty.

Near the end she found a surgeon who said he could rebuild her spine using a titanium mesh cage. She begged me to come stay with her through the many surgeries required, emailed me her terrifying X-ray—that horrifying, distorted question mark that inhabited her body—and I flew back east to her. I knew that it wouldn't be— couldn't be—pleasant, but it was my job. Taking care of her had always been my job.

Mama had never been emotionally resilient. She was always ready to tumble into panic or fury at the least provocation, a condition I was all too aware of as I was usually the target of her rage. She had always been weak and dependent and very, very mean. However, before each surgery, she became more terrifying and predatory than ever—teeth bared, claws unsheathed, sniffing out vulnerability and biting viciously at everyone around her. The closer you were to her, the meaner she got.

Rob had tried to shield me from her, but he couldn't. He didn't understand that I'd been raised for this. I was the one she had created to bear her weight. I was the one who had to take the punishment.

When Mama wasn't in surgery, I sat and held her hand, taking the terrible blows of her anger and fear. She dragged out my every failure for everyone to see, blaming me for everything wrong in her life and in mine, inventing elaborate wrongs from the everyday facts of our lives.

I couldn't leave without sending her into a fierce rage, so Rob brought me coffee and juice and covered me with blankets when I fell asleep at her side.

Just before the last procedure we fought. The topic, as usual, was my profound inadequacy as a daughter—how I had continually abandoned her, tortured her and disappointed her. She accused me of leaving her for Rob, whom she lambasted as no-account, stupid, pussy-whipped, weak. It was as if she knew this would be her last chance to hurt me.

She died on the operating table a few hours later.

I was ashamed at how much relief I felt.

Seeing her now, that relief shrivels and blows away, replaced by an old, familiar dread.

Mama had always haunted me. I laugh now at how nothing changed with her death. She has found a new way in. Once again, my life is no longer mine. Literally, in fact. My spine, the structural center of my being, now belongs to her.

"Mama. Why are you here?"

"Because you're hurting, Leigh." Her voice is that perfect Southern combination of kindness and condescension. She leans in to touch my cheek.

"But Mama, you're—"

"Shhhhhhh." Her finger crosses my lips. "Don't talk. You need your strength to get better so we can go home."

"But, Mama—"

"No, baby. Don't be confused. They have to keep you see-daaaaaay-ted." Her accent stretches the word out like taffy.

I take her hand from my face and hold it in mine, searching for the right things to say to loosen her grip on me. Grief and resentment battle behind my reddening cheeks, and I fight the temptation to crush her cool, brittle fingers. Perversely, I have missed her but I know she is lying, trying to convince me to hold onto her distorted version of a world where she is never wrong. I follow her without question. This is the world in which she feels safe.

"You're dead, Mama."

Slow, fat tears spill over her bottom lids. "No, baby doll. I'm here to take care of you. Don't be mean."

My breath audibly leaves my lungs as my chest compresses with the emotional weight of her. "Do you not know, Mama? You died. Four years ago. Can't you remember?"

"Sweetheart, no. It's all those drugs they have you on. Once you're home, we can take care of that and get you strong the old-fashioned way."

I step back, releasing her hand. "Mama, stop this. You died. We buried you. What are you now? A memory? A ghost?"

My gorge rises as I say the word, its wrongness lingering on my palate. I begin to cry just like her, silent and wet like a heartbroken young girl.

I'm terrified and full of rage, though I'm doing my best not to show it. This feeling is old, very old. It's the panic of a child whose responsibilities exceed her power. I'd had this panic at seventeen, at fourteen, at twelve, seven, four. This is the constant condition of being her daughter, knowing that I would be asked to answer for something I had no control over, made responsible for something I couldn't affect. I know her state of mind is still my job, and this time, especially, I won't be able to please her.

Her voice is more firm. "Don't be mean, Leigh. I know you're mad. I can't help that. I'm here to take care of you.

"Dammit, Mama, no."

"But Leigh! Don't you understand?" Her voice is pleading now, pitiful and squeezed. "You're so awful to me when you don't get what you want, Leigh. How did you grow up so selfish? You lie and you say terrible things. Why are you doing this to me now, when all I want is to be with you?"

"Mama, no! Stop twisting everything around. I'm not being mean. I'm telling you the truth. I can't help that it hurts." She stares at me with wet, injured eyes. "Mama, you can't be with me. You can't take care of me. Don't you remember? Four years ago in the hospital you told me to go away and never come back, and now, now you've come back and—" The truth is so ugly that I don't want to say it out loud. "Mama, I don't know anything about what happens when you die, but *you shouldn't be here.*"

"But Leigh, I need you."

A chunk of truth lands hard in my throat. Its weight pulls me farther down, squeezes my lungs and neck and shoulders down into my chest. I don't want to believe it, but I know her. I know how she has always worked. She always knew how to keep me weak so that she could get what she wanted.

"Mama, are you…are you doing this to me?" Of course it was true. I knew it like I knew the sound of her voice.

"No! Of course not. What is wrong with you? What kind of a girl could believe that about her own mother?"

"Mama, you *are* doing this. I just don't know why. Are you punishing me? Because I wasn't good enough?"

"No, sweetheart, I would never punish you for that."

"Are you trying to take me with you? Is that it?"

"Leigh Ann, no, it's not like you think. I need to take you home with me so you'll get well. You need me to take care of you. That's why I'm here. Don't you understand?"

Of course. "I understand. You're the one who doesn't get it. I don't know how you're doing this but it's not okay. I always took it from you, whatever you gave me, because I thought it was my job. But it's not my job to let you hurt me anymore. Especially not this way. This isn't right."

She stands a little taller next to her cane and sighs. "Leigh Ann,

I'm not like you. I'm not strong. I need you, sweetheart. Am I such a terrible mom that I can't even raise one daughter to take care of me?" Her plaintive voice wedges itself into the upper octaves of her range before it turns to an impossibly high croak. "Don't you love me?"

"Mama, stop. I'm not being mean. I'm sorry, I swear." It feels like I'm peeling her sticky hands from around my neck. "I'm just telling the truth. I love you, Mama, but you died. You're gone. I don't know why I can see you and talk to you, but you shouldn't be here anymore. Can't you see this is hurting me?"

"You listen to me, Leigh Ann." Her voice is suddenly firm, drained of its pleading tone. "That's enough of that. You're just being stupid. Now let it go. We have to focus on getting you home."

Inside me there has always been a little girl who couldn't help but comply with that voice. Maybe as a child I had no choice. Mama always had so much more will than I did. As an adult I never had enough time to teach myself any other way to react to her.

I take a deep breath, then reach out to touch her free hand, ready to support her as she takes me wherever she wants to take me. *I can fight her later*, I think. *This is a long game. Right now, she's not reasonable.* Of course, part of me knows there's a chance I might never fight her again. She was always so much stronger in her weakness than I was.

Mama stands a little straighter as I bend under her weight. Her hospital gown has changed into a perfectly pressed, powder-blue pantsuit. She absently brushes invisible lint from her jacket, releases my hand, and looks down at me with hard, dry eyes.

Her smile is perfect and chilling and oh so sweet. "You just remember that I know what's best for you, sweetheart. Everything I do, I do for you."

Capturing my eyes with hers, with one bent finger she touches my collarbone and traces beneath my shoulder the meandering line of her old spinal X-ray. As she traces, I feel my own spine collapse further, the pain making me hot and nauseous. When I look down, the shape that had been drawn on her back is now on me, glowing faintly through my hospital gown.

"Mama, no. Please."

She walks away from her cane and comes around beside me to help support my weight. "Let's just get you home, baby doll, and then all this won't matter."

In the distance I see our old house in Virginia, its wide porch and gables, the gravel driveway and the path around to the semi-detached kitchen. I lean against her and am honestly grateful for the support. Of course, the more I give her my weight, the more my strength drains out through my flimsy hospital slippers.

Hot tears roll down my cheeks.

She looks over at me sweetly. "I know, honey. This is how it always should have been. You and me against the world. Just us. Forever."

I know this isn't right. I know that isn't really our home she's leading me towards. But between us she has all the power. The weight of my childhood is so much heavier than the few years I've spent learning to be independent.

We approach the kitchen door through a thickening fog. I can barely see, and I feel as if I'm growing fainter with every step. Meanwhile, the pain in my back has wrapped itself around me like a cold, wet blanket, numbing me until I don't know where it ends and I begin.

Maybe this is right. Maybe this *is* my destiny. Maybe caring for her is what I'm supposed to do with my life, no matter how hard it is or how much it hurts. I lose my footing on the gravel path and she loosens her grip, letting me fall. When I look up, she's smiling, holding out her hand for me. I take it.

"Don't you see how much easier this is if you let me help?"

I cringe. "Yes, Mama. Thank you, Mama."

"We're gonna get you your own pillows and blankets, your own bed, and all our cats to set up around you. It'll be nice. You'll see."

"I know, Mama." I pause for a breath. "Thank you, Mama." My voice is soft like cotton candy, almost not there at all.

I shuffle up the two shallow steps to the kitchen door, and she turns the knob, looking back over her shoulder at me. She turns her back to the door once it's open, so she can help me with both hands.

My vision is fuzzy and dark and my mind is hopelessly clouded, but over her shoulder I see what she doesn't. Through the doorway is not our warm kitchen but a howling black vortex. It pulls gently at her clothes and hair as she backs closer to it.

Whatever this place is, it is not home. But if I don't follow her, I will have failed her one last time. I will be the terrible daughter she has always known me to be. Whether or not she believes in this charade of our house and our porch and our kitchen door, her end game is clear to me. She wants to be taken care of, to be cared for, in all the needful, desperate ways she always demanded. That will be my duty, just like she always planned. A few more steps will seal my fate and her gnawing hunger will be satisfied forever. I know if I go inside I will be gone forever.

I stop at the top step and take both her hands. "Mama, I love you so much. You know that, right?"

"Well, of course you do, honey. I'm your Mama."

"I took good care of you, didn't I, Mama?"

"Don't worry about that now." She smiles, tugging me towards the threshold.

"I did, Mama. I took good care of you. We both have to understand that." I pause and square my feet. "Because now it's time to say goodbye."

Her eyes flash with anger. "Leigh Ann, don't be so stubborn. You always thought you could live without me, but don't you see you can't? Without me, you're a failure. You need me to show you what's right. Now come with me. You know it's the right thing to do."

With that she yanks hard on my hands. I stumble and the pain in my back screams at me to stop resisting, to let her take me, to finally allow myself to rest. I muster all my strength to remain on the top step. I cannot let her win.

"Mama, no. I'm not going, not with you. Your time is over. It's my life now." My voice shakes as I say this, my body breaking with grief and anger and exhaustion.

"No, Leigh. Don't you see how much I love you? I want us to be together. We can start fresh, build a new life together."

With all the strength I can find, I push. As she falls back across the threshold, a great, hot wind suspends her in the air in front of me, pulling her back into the nothing that is supposed to be our kitchen. She clutches at my wrists, pulling me dangerously close to the vortex. Her scream lashes out at me like thorny vines.

"Leigh! No! Stay with me. Please, I want to be with you. We were always supposed to be together."

My voice is calm, almost sympathetic. "No, Mama. Now it's time for you to go without me."

Her face grows hard and cold and proud. No longer is she the pleading, syrup-sweet mother she's always wanted the world to see. She holds her head high, hair whipping behind her into the void. Her voice is like a sponge, wet with contempt.

"You stupid, useless girl. I always knew that you would fail me."

I have to tuck my hips beneath me and lean back to avoid being pulled in with her. She is tugging hard with desperate hands to dislodge my stance.

"No, Mama. I won't go."

I feel all her weight and strength yanking me towards her. "You're too weak to do this yourself. I have to make this decision for you."

And she does, but not the way she would have wanted.

"You're right, Mama. You were always right." I shake her hands loose and watch her fly back into the yawning gulf.

As blackness closes around her, the house disappears as does the path and the driveway and everything else. I fall backwards into my hospital bed, surrounded by beeping and wires and tubes and nurses. The sheets are cool around me. The bed is firm and reassuring.

And there is Rob, smiling. He leans down and kisses my hot forehead.

I can't feel my body. I don't know what has happened in the real world while I was lost outside Mama's terrifying Hell. I do know that inside I feel tall, taller than I've ever felt before.

And very, very light.

ABOUT THE AUTHOR
BRIAN FATAH STEELE

During the last ten years, Brian Fatah Steele has written a number of both short- and long-format horror fiction pieces, much of which is being published by an independent co-op.

Steele is the author of the novel *In Bleed Country* and the single-author collection *Further Than Fate*. His work has appeared in several magazines and journals. Steele's short story, "Wet Heavens," appeared in *Blood Type: The Anthology of Vampire Sci-Fi*, a charity volume that benefits The Cystic Fibrosis Trust.

His dark tale of the supernatural, "Delicate Spaces," was published in the Bram Stoker Award®-nominated *Dark Visions: A Collection of Modern Horror - Volume One* from Grey Matter Press.

HARDER YOU FALL

BRIAN FATAH STEELE

Rain. It felt like it had been raining every single day for the past month. Maybe it had. Madeline slouched her shoulders uncomfortably beneath her jacket, careful not to dip the umbrella. Not that it mattered; the damp weather was slowly soaking its way into her regardless.

She stared off at the gravestones, her eyes unfocused. Little gray fingertips pushing through the dirt. Rows and rows of tiny, rotting teeth. No, the handful of scattered trees ruined that illusion. The trees, and the workmen currently lowering the casket into the ground. Into the ground. Down, down, down. This cemetery might actually be pretty if it wasn't for all the damn rain.

That made her pause.

Madeline glanced around, examining the landscape. Why was it raining so much? They weren't in Portland.

"Where are we again?" she asked, turning to Cavallaro.

He grimaced, his eyes never leaving the casket. "We're in Ohio."

Madeline nodded. "I didn't think it rained this much here."

"I don't believe it usually does."

Perhaps it didn't. The cemetery workers certainly seemed

unaccustomed to it. Not only were they having a difficult time keeping the integrity of the grave walls in place, their machinery kept slipping in the mud. The entire complicated affair had almost spilled over once. Both Madeline and Cavallaro stood by on the hill and passively watched the whole comedy of errors play out.

She had been surprised her first few times at gravesites like this, watching caskets being lowered. She expected dozens of mourners surrounding the grave, a wailing mother, and a child or two standing there solemnly as they watched a loved one lowered into the earth. Cavallaro had laughed at her. Turns out that was mostly Hollywood fakery. The graveside funeral was a thing to add drama to a tale. Oh, they happened, most definitely, but only in regions that could accommodate them, not in Ohio.

Before things started happening, before Cavallaro, the only person she knew that died had been her grandmother. It was a small, private affair for her family. She had been seven.

Ruminating on that, she was broken from her thoughts once again as one of the workman came trudging up the hill towards them. She felt herself stiffen, preparing for the worst, but she heard Cavallaro snort his little chuckle beside her. She said nothing and followed his lead.

"I'm guessing you're the family?" the man asked, wiping rivulets of brown water from his face with the back of his ball cap.

Cavallaro said nothing for a moment, then, "Is there a problem?"

"Well," the man began, staring up into the sky as if answers might be found there, "I guess that's up to you. You have a choice, I mean. The ground is saturated and we can't keep fighting it. We can try to finish lowering him now but it won't be regulation. Or we can wait, and I can understand that. But sir, I don't know when—"

"Bury him now," said Cavallaro. "Three feet or two. It doesn't matter."

The man's eyebrow rose, obviously surprised. Six feet under was another little myth.

Cavallaro reached into his pocket and pulled out five twenty dollar bills. "You and your crew go out, have fun tonight. But get it done now."

Taking the money and nodding, he said. "It'll be done within the hour."

Madeline watched the man slide and stumble back down the hill. Everything about what just happened was probably illegal. Illegal she could deal with. It was what would come later that put a sour taste in her mouth.

Another glance at Cavallaro. Immaculate Brooks Brothers suit, Burberry trench coat, handmade Italian shoes, Rolex watch. He was attractive, no doubt about it, but alluring in the way of a predator. Dark hair cropped short, sharp features, pale eyes that showed no emotion. There were no emotions there to show, as far as Madeline had deduced. Greed, rage, contempt. Did those count?

"Are you actually going to stay for another hour?" she asked.

"Yes," he replied, not even looking at her.

Madeline sighed. "I'm sitting in the car."

Cavallaro said nothing as she walked away.

The wind hadn't been bad where she stood next to Cavallaro on the hill, but as she made her way back to the car, she found herself gripping the umbrella tighter to keep it from blowing away. It was doing little to stop the rain from drenching her at this point, but Madeline stubbornly refused to give up and close it. The fence along the perimeter of the cemetery was a short, wrought iron design that had probably never done much in the way of keeping out trespassers. Her Gucci heels were already ruined, so she decided not to tempt fate on her jacket. Instead of trying to climb over it, she kept on walking all the way to the exit.

A part of her laughed at the part about the heels. Had she become so corrupted by Cavallaro that she cared that much now about a pair of shoes? Maybe that was proof. Or maybe it was proof that she realized the change in herself.

Madeline reached the black Escalade, hit the button and pulled open the door as she lowered the umbrella. Just as she moved to sit, she saw the teenage girl in the backseat. Blood poured from two jagged wounds right above where her heart should be.

The girl's eyes went wide with fear, looking past Madeline. "Are you alone?"

"Yeah," she said to the ghost. "He's still waiting on his next score."

* * *

She could remember a time before the nightmares walked out of her dreams, walked into the day. That's when things were easy, silly and bright. She rode the school bus every morning, sat with Taryn and pretended not to notice the boys goofing around in the back. Different classes, different kids in eighth grade, but lunch was always the best. Everyone crowded together, some with lunch boxes and some with cafeteria trays, everything seasoned with petty arguments, awkward flirting and crude jokes. It's where she felt safest, felt the farthest away from the nightmares.

It's where the nightmares first walked into the light.

So much screaming. More screaming than blood, really. The dead man with blood on his hands, staring at her, begging her to help him. But there was no dead man, no blood, not that anyone else could see.

Madeline didn't see Taryn very much after that.

* * *

Dropping the passenger side visor to fix her hair in the vanity mirror, Madeline tilted it to look at the ghost in the back seat. The girl couldn't have been any more than sixteen when she died. Sad.

Looks like she had been shot, too. The part of Madeline that always ached for the dead wanted to ask how it happened. Instead, she silently continued to fiddle with her long black hair. No good would come of asking the question. No good ever did.

"We have enough," said the ghost. "More than enough."

"All right," said Madeline, leaving it open for the ghost to report more on her own.

"We—I mean some—don't think you'll go through with it."

"I see," replied Madeline.

Silence.

The ghost shifted in her seat. "You are, right? Going to go through with this?"

"What's your name?"

"My name? Um, Gabby. It was Gabby."

"Gabby," said Madeline. "I'm most definitely going to go through with this."

* * *

No more doctors, no more tests. No more nightmares, being pests. Look, a rhyme! Too bad that last part wasn't true. A sixteen-year-old runaway, what a wonderful cliché. But you can't outrun the dead.

Madeline had no idea what this place had once been. Some kind of factory, maybe a warehouse. It was a whole lot of nothing now. Run down, half caved in, filled with mold, rats and cockroaches. Her new pets. Fortunately, her petite frame fit perfectly on this broken desk. Broken, just like her.

She had so many new friends now; they just refused to keep coming. They clung, and pleaded, and sobbed, and babbled. Most wore their wounds like badges of honor. Gunshots, car accidents, slit wrists, seven story falls. No cancer or heart attacks for her. The bloodier the better.

And it gushed, dripped and ran everywhere.

Madeline hadn't eaten in three days. Eating was difficult when you were a sixteen-year-old runaway lunatic. She lay on top of the desk, staring at the ceiling, and waited to join the dead shuffling around her.

She spent so much time ignoring them, it took her a moment to realize they had been worked up into a frenzy. Most were trying to flee, but some were cowering around her, begging her for protection. Madeline just stared at this new turn in her madness. Then a man in an expensive suit stormed into the room.

He ripped through them, literally, the motion of his hands tearing the essence of the ghosts to shreds. Two he gripped and drew to his face, their substance growing denser as he sucked them down. Like inhaling smoke, he devoured them, then a third, and a fourth. In under a minute, he had obliterated over a dozen of the dead that had failed to flee.

Madeline just gaped at him, terrified. He returned her gaze, a look somewhere between disgust and amusement. Almost as if he was trying to make a decision.

Finally, he sighed. "Get up. If I'm going to be bothered teaching you anything, it won't be in this shithole."

Madeline didn't move as he made his way back to the door.

"Are you coming or not?" he asked.

"Who are you?"

He snorted, something akin to a laugh. "My name's Jacob Cavallaro and I'm a necromancer. Just like you, Madeline."

* * *

"So he's buried?"

"He's buried," replied Cavallaro. "And tonight, when there's finally no one around, I can get what I need at my leisure."

Cavallaro spun the Escalade out into traffic and headed back towards the hotel. The rain had let up some, but the day was still wet and dreary. Everything seemed muted a slight gray. A series of strip malls, fast food joints and big box stores rolled past them outside the window. A group of young people, undaunted by the weather, skate-boarded in the parking lot of an abandoned furniture emporium.

"What are you smiling about?" Cavallaro asked.

"I don't know. This place, I guess."

"Dear god, why?"

Madeline shrugged. "It reminds me of home."

"Home is an executive suite in a five star hotel," he replied with a sneer.

She didn't bother responding. Cavallaro hadn't had anything re-sembling a home or family in a very long time. Once she had come to understand her powers and had them under control, she thought about trying to reconnect with her parents. Cavallaro had strongly advised against it, but she decided she had to at least see them. It had been years, and while she knew she had aged into her early twenties, she hadn't been prepared to see how old her mother and father had become. How old they looked. After spying on them for an entire day, she left without saying a word. What answers could she possibly give them?

Not just her parents, but anyone. How could she tell anyone what she and Cavallaro were? How could she ever explain what they did? How they did it?

"How do you know he didn't have a partner? Someone to move the money for him?' Madeline asked, speaking of the recently de-ceased.

"A man like that? No, he died trying to hide his misdeeds. On Wall Street, ten million is nothing, but here in Podunk? He had it stashed, waiting for the IRS mess to blow over. And the anxiety gave him a stroke. Bad for the IRS, good for me."

Me. Not us. Never us. Cavallaro had read about the situation in a trade journal while they were in Chicago. He found it, so that made it his. Sometimes Madeline wondered exactly what he thought of her. Definitely not as a partner. Still a protégé? Could he even muster up enough human feelings to call her a friend?

It didn't matter.

* * *

Controlling them came easy, once she realized she could do it. It was nothing to banish them, to send them away. No more nightmares hovering over her. That was the best part. She felt bad about making them do things, especially menial tasks she could easily accomplish herself. She refused to "kill" them and continued to balk at eating them. That's where Cavallaro put his foot down.

Turned out Jacob Cavallaro was born in 1932. Now, so many years later, he still appeared to be in his late thirties. This he directly attributed to the eating of ghosts. Not only had it allowed him to age at an incredibly slow pace, but he had survived being shot on seven different occasions, stabbed four times and nearly hanged once.

With his personality, Madeline wasn't surprised.

Cavallaro teased her about her reluctance to eat. He also taunted her about other things lurking out there in the night other than necromancers. In those early days, he loved to frighten her by spinning tales of vampires, wendigo and werewolves. He tried to convince her that while these creatures were wary of their kind, a kind that casually shattered the wall between the living and the dead, those creatures wouldn't hesitate to prey upon one as weak as her. Still, Madeline wouldn't feed.

Finally, one morning in Tampa, as Madeline was doing her hair in the mirror, she heard him enter her hotel room with bagels and coffee. She turned to find a knife plunged into her stomach. Now it was feed or die.

So she did, three of them, as she lay there in a bloody mess on the bathroom tile. She tried to apologize to them, but she could barely speak. And when it was done, not even a scratch remained on her.

She still had not met any vampires, wendigo or werewolves.

* * *

A hot shower helped.

They had hours before they were to go back out again, and Madeline wanted some semblance of comfort. The heat from the water, instead of reinvigorating her, relaxed her. She wondered why she wasn't more nervous.

Drying off, she used the towel to wipe the mirror. A pale face with large dark eyes and long black locks peered back. At twenty-four and only five-foot-two, a quick change of clothes and makeup could allow her to pass for older or younger. Cavallaro had made her utilize this on numerous occasions. Obtaining keys and passcodes, learning building layouts and personnel counts, she mastered this skill to gain a variety of information and bypass security. And then they waited.

Waited for a celebutante heiress to overdose. For a renowned surgeon to lose his battle with cancer. For a scandal-ridden senator to hang himself. For a CEO to have an "accidental" wreck in her limo. They waited, and then Cavallaro swooped in and tortured secrets out of them. Money, money, money. Those Brooks Brothers suits weren't cheap.

He had amassed millions in his decades doing this. He had spent just as much. A lavish lifestyle built on fortunes stolen from the dead.

Madeline stared at her muddy Gucci heels and knew she was just as guilty.

* * *

It was her nineteenth birthday, but she hadn't said anything to him. He wouldn't have cared. Still, the noise in the adjoining suite was getting to be too much. She was trying to concentrate. She had almost focused enough will into Brock to allow him to pick up the plastic cup.

Brock was terrified, even though she promised she wouldn't eat him. She had eaten before, yes, numerous times, but only when necessary. This didn't seem to reassure the sad-eyed young man who drooled blood from the corners of his mouth. Ignoring his terror, she asked him to try the cup again.

Unless a ghost gathered up enough energy on its own, usually through malevolent intent, they were incorporeal and couldn't affect the material world. A necromancer, however, could focus his or her own energy and lend it to a ghost, allow it to do minor tasks. Madeline was still having some difficulty mastering this.

Get the cup, get the cup, get the cup, getthecup.

Another loud moan from the adjoining suite broke her concentration.

"Damn it!" Madeline screamed.

A bang, a swear, and Cavallaro came through the door with a sheet wrapped around his waist.

"What's your problem?" he asked.

"I'm trying to practice and you're shaking the walls with a hooker."

He looked back and forth between her and Brock.

"Well, practice harder then," he said. "I don't care."

Madeline just stared at him.

"What?"

"I'm just surprised that you never..."

"Never what?"

"I'm surprised you never tried to get me in bed," she finished.

Cavallaro walked over to her and looked her up and down. Appraisingly, obviously undressing her with his eyes, making it apparent that he liked what he saw. Then he raised her chin, locking their stares.

"Have you ever heard the expression, 'don't shit where you eat,'
Madeline?"
Madeline nodded.
Cavallaro walked back to his suite, slamming the door behind him.

* * *

Any comfort from the shower had been short lived.

At least this time she dressed more sensibly for the weather—a heavier, waterproof coat, thick black jeans and boots. Sensibility did not apply to Cavallaro, still decked out in similar attire as before. The rain had slowed to a drizzle but it was still cold, wet and irritating.

Cavallaro gestured dismissively at the ghost who had once been a middle-aged mom. It walked over to the gate and plunged its hands into the lock mechanism. Her hands shook—almost vibrating—as they were diffused through the lock, a look of sheer anguish on the ghost's face. It tried to pull its hands out but Cavallaro kept them fixed in place. Suddenly, the lock gave way and the ghost fell back. Everything below its wrists, *her* wrists, was in wispy tatters. Streams of shattered ethereal smoke, her spiritual cohesion breaking down. She looked at Cavallaro with eyes that would have produced tears if possible, eyes that questioned the need for her suffering.

In three steps, Cavallaro condensed her with a motion of his hand, drew her in and drank her down. Without hesitation or doubt. Without regard to whom she may have once been.

They had been in many graveyards before. This one really wasn't any different from the rest, although Madeline didn't recall ever being in one quite so muddy. The excessive rain had started to drain a brown sludge down from the slopping hills onto the wide brick pathways. It was a mess, and she found herself grateful for her choice of boots. Cavallaro swore the whole time he made his way through, almost falling twice.

The gravesite of the recently deceased Thomas J. Newmare was a giant puddle. Most of the dirt had been washed away, leaving a depression in the ground of at least a foot. Only so many inches of wet earth lay between them and his casket. Not that such a distance mattered to Cavallaro. It could have been miles, but the first resurrection was more easily accomplished with closer proximity.

"What a monumental pain in my ass," he said as he removed his leather gloves, preferring bare hands for this ritual.

Madeline watched as he stood before the grave, arms out in front of him. Palms up with his fingers clenched as though he was gripping large swathes of cloth, he started to raise them. The tension in his fingers grew visibly as his arms rose higher, and she could see him grinding his teeth. Fighting against the natural order, he raised his arms yet higher, his grip stronger. With a roar, his hands flew up into the air.

And Thomas J. Newmare stood upon his grave, looking both dead and bewildered.

"What... Where am I?" he asked.

"You're dead, Thomas," Cavallaro replied. "But I have questions for you."

"I don't…I don't understand."

The necromancer sighed, reached out and twisted his hand. The dead man doubled over in pain. With a flick of the wrist the pain subsided.

"Thomas, you're going to answer my questions, or I'm going to cause you agonies more excruciating than you ever knew existed in life. Do you understand?"

The ghost stared at Cavallaro, a look in his eyes that was almost impossible to define. Then Thomas turned to look at Madeline. She returned his gaze for only a moment and then looked away.

"What the hell do you want to know?" Thomas asked.

* * *

The picnic table sat back from the others, discreetly hidden among the tall pine trees, far enough away from the jogging path. Madeline wondered how many couples had found their way here. How many couples had quietly made love on this bench only fifty feet away from people walking their dogs or going on a morning run? Madeline wondered if she'd ever get a chance to experience something like that.

"Most of what you've said is true," the Confederate soldier said.

"Wonderful," Madeline said.

"No, I don't think you understand. The dead haven't experienced a plague among our kind of this magnitude in a millennium. His name is known among us all as a bane, as a curse. Beyond the fact he's just a bastard, his utter disregard for the dead marks him as our greatest threat."

Madeline glanced at the soldier sitting beside her. "You have other threats?"

"Don't worry about that for the moment. If you can't destroy Cavallaro, you need to get away from him. Now."

"And do what? Go where?" Madeline asked as she watched a young mother push a stroller through the Georgia State Park. "He saved me. I've been with him since I was sixteen. I don't know anything else."

The ghost sighed and took off his hat. "Have you ever asked yourself why he saved you?"

Madeline just blinked at him. The reasons hadn't ever really crossed her mind.

"Someone like that doesn't care about a protégé or an heir. He was a protégé once. One of two. He was found just like you were. The older necromancer already had an apprentice, but he took on a second. Then twenty years later, Cavallaro killed them both."

"Why?"

"*Same reason he killed another necromancer in Europe about ten years ago. The ghost of a necromancer is the most powerful. Tastes the best. Why do you think he's so adamant about you feeding? He's trying to 'fatten you up.' It's all he cares about.*"

Madeline sat back on the bench, stunned. She didn't want to believe it, but a part of her knew it was true. Cavallaro never cared about her, never saw her as anything but a means to an end. But to be killed and eaten?

"*I'm not powerful enough to take him on,*" *she whispered.*

"*I know.*"

Madeline chuckled. "*I wish I had some of those vampires or were-wolves—or whatever—to call on.*"

The ghost didn't respond, silently pulling on his beard as he peered out through the pine trees.

"*What?*" *she asked.*

"*Remember those 'other threats' I told you not to worry about?*"

* * *

While the rock quarry wasn't large—only a few miles wide—it was old and desolate. At one time roughly shaped like a rectangle, the layered cuts had eroded away along with their angles, and the pit now resembled something more like an uneven oval. Miles from the outskirts of town, forest lined three sides of the pit, the trees rising high above the jagged rock walls of the excavated quarry. One could have easily dropped a four-story building into the quarry itself, walked out upon its roof, and seen straight across to the tufts of grass shooting out from the rim. Instead of buildings, however, there were mounds of discarded dirt and rock. Mostly aggregates with some chunks of slate mixed in, the quarry had been mined down to these last four mounds and left abandoned.

According to Thomas J. Newmare, he knew of this place because it had belonged to his uncle. It was the last thing he screamed before Cavallaro devoured him.

There was a small, one-room shack made of rotting wood that had once served as an office. After driving through the quarry to ensure they were alone, Cavallaro parked up front by the shack. Newmare confessed that he had buried the money in a briefcase behind it, a location Cavallaro had not been pleased about. Stepping from the vehicle into the rain, he summoned a half-dozen ghosts and commanded them to start digging.

Madeline watched the dead work, against their will, slaves for the necromancer. Suffer unto death, suffer thereafter. You could die twice at the hands of someone like him. Someone like them.

"So this is it, huh?" she asked.

"What?" he barked back.

"We run around the world, scamming cash off the recently dead, using ghosts as our flunkies until we decided to snack on them? This is our life?"

"Yes, and it's a damn good life. What else do you want? What else do you expect?"

Madeline said nothing, only watched the ghosts struggle with the hard packed earth. Cavallaro had lent them enough energy to dig with their bare hands in the ground, mud caking between their fingers. None of them had enough strength to flee, let alone fight back, never to fight back.

"So when were you going to do it?" she asked, watching the hole grow deeper.

"What are you talking about?" he snapped,

"Kill me. Kill me and eat my ghost. When would I have been strong enough?"

Cavallaro went very quiet and very still.

"Tomorrow? Next year? Ten years?"

"I haven't decided," he said. "I wanted you powerful, but not too powerful, of course. But you've been taking your sweet time with feeding, so probably sooner than later just so I won't have to deal with you anymore."

The rain kept coming. The ghosts kept digging. The hole got deeper.

Madeline sighed. "I see."

"I've stayed on top for over eighty years, Madeline," he said. "Killing anything that got in my way. Anything that might have been a threat. I am rich and powerful, and of course, unstoppable. So I'm going to get that money out of that miserable hole and then you're going to get back in the car, and we're going to go back to the hotel for a nice little chat."

She chuckled. "Harder you fall, Cavallaro."

"What did you say?"

"I said you might want to check that miserable hole you just mentioned."

He stomped over to the space behind the shack where the ghosts were working. They had excavated a relatively large area. There was nothing. He had been so busy in his exchange with Madeline he hadn't noticed it was empty. No briefcase. No money.

Cavallaro spun, ripping through two ghosts in a rage before his sights turned back to Madeline. Ignoring the remaining dead, he started back towards her. Before he made it half way, she held up her hand, her face passive.

"Yes, I knew there was no money. I knew Newmare was going to lie to you. I helped set this all up."

"Why?" he spat. "What could you hope to accomplish? And when the hell did you—"

"I never spoke to him. The dead did. They told him. They told him who you were, what you were going to do to him regardless of what he said, and they told him to lie. To get you here."

For once, he looked honestly confused. "Why?"

"Because they hate you!" she screamed, losing her composure. "They hate us for what we do. And they should. I hate us too."

The downpour continued, drenching both of them. Mud splashed up from the droplets around their feet, the effects of the rain the only sound, nothing else for miles around them. Shaking with tears, Madeline stared at Cavallaro, willing him to say something of merit. To give a reason, or at least an excuse. Anything.

Instead, he gave her a sneer and said, "So what?"

Her face collapsed for a moment. Then she pulled herself together, pushed her dripping black hair back, tried her best to stand straight, and looked directly at her mentor. There would be no wisdom or purpose gleaned from him.

"Do you know why it was here? Here of all places?"

"I assume you're going to tell me," he replied.

"Vampires, wendigo and werewolves," she said.

"What are you babbling about?"

"You used to taunt me about those monsters. But there are no monsters in the walking world, except us of course. But there *are* monsters. Horrible ones."

"Are there now?" he asked, taking two steps towards her.

"Yes. And they're all dead."

Now Cavallaro paused, looking concerned. "Dead monsters? I've never heard of any such nonsense."

He didn't notice the darkness between the trees behind him start to thicken, to coalesce. Shadows elongated, grew more dense, becoming something more tangible. They rolled down over the edge of the quarry like liquid smoke. Throughout the mass were pockets of deeper black. A substance that hurt to look at, a material never meant to rise this far into the material world. The mass of it shuddered and moved forward.

Madeline smiled. "The dead knew. They always knew. Why would they tell you? They only told me so that we could destroy you."

Cavallaro finally noticed her line of sight and spun to see the living darkness building behind him. Bellowing, he tried to use his powers to stop it. Nothing. He forced the few remaining ghosts upon it, but his effort was like throwing pebbles at a hurricane. Stumbling back, he fell in the mud, gaping up at the monstrosity that formed above him. The sections of deeper black merged into a central core, while lesser parts branched off into what appeared to be rudimentary appendages. These whipped around, smashing into the mounds with incredible strength.

"It lives here somewhere, I guess. I don't really know," Madeline said. "I was just supposed to make sure you got here."

He screamed her name, sliding back in the mud.

"Why haven't you ever seen one? Because it took one thousand ghosts sacrificing themselves to this thing to raise it. A thousand ghosts willingly feeding themselves to this to stop you from feeding on a million more. That's how much they hate you."

Something within the deeper black shifted. It more than moved in space, it tilted on a level beyond comprehension. An orifice opened, revealing a light that had no color. It didn't shine, or emit warmth, or in any way illuminate. Perhaps it was all things to the dead leviathan—eye, mouth, ear, other unknown sensory organs. The giant limbs unraveled and grabbed Cavallaro to draw him into that light.

He screamed and scrambled in the mud as the lengths of blackness whipped around his legs, pulling him down, begging and pleading with Madeline as the dead nightmare dragged him closer. She didn't move and neither did the ghosts he had brought as slaves. They all stared in horrified fascination. They stared as Cavallaro tried to bargain and threaten and then finally wail like an animal as he was lifted into the light.

"That's how much I hate us both," Madeline whispered as she watched him be devoured.

She stood there, the echoes of Cavallaro's screams fading from the quarry. And she waited. She didn't expect to leave this encounter alive. Never had. While her sins were nowhere as great, she had enough. Resigned to her fate, she closed her eyes and accepted the inevitable.

It didn't come. Looking up, she saw the darkness diffusing and slipping back up into the tree line. Part of her wanted to run after it. After everything, why?

Then a single thought came to her. A single word roared into her mind by the disappearing abomination in the chorus of a thousand voices. One that sent her running for the Escalade.

* * *

"Are you sure that's what you want?"

The ghost nodded. "Absolutely. Even if she ends up marrying someone else. I mean, I want her to be happy. But I want her to know I loved her. And that I wanted to marry her."

"I'll make sure the ring gets to her," Madeline said. "You said it was in a shoebox in your closet?"

"Yeah, it's the only one. Box my hiking boots came in. It won't be hard to find. Like I said, it was my grandmother's."

She wrote it all down. The ghost fiddled with the laces on his jogging shoes. She could tell something was bothering him, and it wasn't the memory of getting hit by a car while out for his morning run. She was pretty sure what it was.

"Go ahead and ask," she said.

"What?"

"Go ahead. You want to know why I'm helping you."

"Um, yeah. I heard necromancers weren't exactly the friendly type."

"That's usually true. But I got some advice once."

"What was that?" the ghost asked.

She smiled at him. "One word. I was once like other necromancers. Maybe not as bad as some, but I'd still eaten ghosts. And profited off their misery. But I was willing to make a sacrifice and, well, I was given a second chance."

"So, don't leave me hanging! What was the word?"

Madeline picked up her notebook and gazed out over the sunny cemetery.

"Change," she said as she walked away.

ABOUT THE AUTHOR
MARTIN ROSE

Martin Rose writes in a wide range of fiction genres covering the fantastic to the macabre. Rose's work has been published in a number of anthologies and highly respected literary magazines. His story, "Dark Rose," received an honorable mention from editor Ellen Datlow. He is also a contributing reviewer for *Shroud* magazine.

His tale of dark religion, "How to Make a Human," is featured in the Grey Matter Press volume *Ominous Realities: The Anthology of Dark Speculative Fiction*. His zombie novel, *Bring Me Flesh, I'll Bring Hell*, was published in 2014.

When not hunting the Jersey Devil in the wooded areas near his home, Rose focuses on his dark, literary writing while sometimes also moonlighting as a graphic designer.

MIRRORWORLD

MARTIN ROSE

Jude falls back against the wall with a smoking hole in his expensive business suit. Divorce papers fall to the floor.

Salazar holds the gun. The end of the barrel forms a toothless mouth ringed with lips of iron.

"But I'm not dead," Jude whispers.

He presses his hand against the hole in his suit. The bullet has penetrated deep through the fibers of cloth, through the shirt beneath and ventilates his interior pocket. A single, high-pitched twitter of bird song prevails through the smoke, and then all is silent.

"Why?" Blood bubbles up over his lips.

He regrets not taking the time to think of something better. The last moment of his life and all he has to show for it are lines purloined from melodramas and low budget films.

Salazar's face divides in half with a lean smile. "I traffic in black magic mirrors."

"Mirrors?"

"I need dead men to make them."

Jude opens his mouth to ask another question, and that is how he dies; frozen expression of eternal surprise and one hand clasped at his wound. A bullet in his heart, a canary stowed in his breast pocket.

* * *

Jude awakens.

His memories of waking in his life before are nothing like this. His coming to is automated and without transition from one consciousness to the next. He arrives from blackness to find himself reduced to a doll whose wind-up key is touched off once and then set loose, eyes opening.

He stands in a new room. Blood snakes down his suit and stains his clothes from his chest to his belly.

His breast pocket pulses like a heart and he reaches into it.

"There you are, Jenny."

The canary hops into his palm, talons pricking at his skin. Pale yellow. He brings her to eye level. Her wing feathers are singed around the edges where the bullet clipped her and punched straight through to the other side of him.

"Does that hurt?"

Jenny hops onto his finger and gives him a reptilian glare. He deposits her back into his pocket where she flicks her head over the top and watches their new world from the warm nest of his body.

The time before remains faded and dizzied in his memory and difficult to recall. A man named Salazar. A drawn weapon. Dying. Did that happen? Did he die, just like that, so easily? At the hands of a man who marketed in black magic mirrors. Some two-bit Satanist with a reputation for posing like a punk rock singer but was just a greasy con artist telling futures to old ladies for blow. Jude quietly tacks on murderer to the list.

Would anyone even know he was gone? Jude analyzes his quiet, solitary life and draws a mental portrait of himself, sad and disappointing in its smallness: a man who enjoys chess, classic novels and birds. Never married, never loved. With dismay, he finds the mark he made upon the world is insignificant—so mediocre, no one will notice his absence.

Is this death, then? Heaven?

Jenny tweets from his pocket and then falls silent.

The room remains unchanged, yet like no room he ever inhabited. He moves toward the couch, and it shimmers and pixelates like an image from the LCD screen in his office—flat and two-dimensional.

He touches it. Fingers press into a gossamer resistance, invisible and unyielding, an object with no height or width or depth. The couch is like a cardboard cut-out.

He rubs his fingers together and they feel greasy and coated in oil. He wipes them on his pants leg in disgust.

Beside the couch stands a crib. A dangling mobile above it. All these things, the bookshelf beside it, even the window through which summer light pours, gives an impression of life—but life without substance. He draws closer to each. Jenny whistles and punctuates his rising panic with ululating song. The furniture are as pages torn from a magazine, fluttering, insubstantial. Artificial.

"Jude."

The voice drifts in like a foul wind. He spins and comes face to face with a window, an oval pane of glass set in the wall.

Like a mirror.

A man stands on the other side of the portal, and Jude recognizes the dark brown hair, the cruel slant of his features, the steady hands behind the trigger that authored his death: Salazar.

Memories detonate. Firecrackers in his head. A dark-tinged recollection of the divorce papers he was sent to deliver to the residence, office rumors of Salazar sacrificing goats. Men and women claiming to be witches engaging in unholy congress with him by the light of the moon. How bad could it be? Gossip, tabloid nonsense, Jude had said.

Jude remembers—his fingers moist with the humid summer—bending the pages as he waited for Salazar to answer the door, impatient, tapping his foot against the floor. All they had to do was just sign the damn divorce papers, but they always gave him trouble. They always stalled and hemmed and hawed. He had planned on stopping at the vet's office in the next hour. The bird cage broke in transit, so he had his canary huddled in his pocket. The entire day had been nothing but a series of small travesties.

Then Salazar answered the door with gun in hand and shot him through the heart.

"Do you like your new home, Jude?"

"What is this?"

"You're in the mirror, of course. You're dense for an attorney, you know that?"

I'm in the mirror?

It did not seem possible.

Jude recalls his father, who passed away from a heart attack when he was a child. His mother tore through the house, drifting from room to room like a sad ghost, covering all the mirrors with scarves. He considered it an old superstition as tired and banal as stories passed in the high school hallways about Bloody Mary and conjurations in narrow bathrooms between the toothpaste and the soap. Games played by bored teenagers.

The difference is this is real.

Fury spikes through him. A lifetime's worth of pent-up frustration propels him forward to reach out and break the glass, shatter Salazar's face.

Nothing happens.

Jude's hand hangs on the air like a stalled puppet and will not obey his will. Salazar pulls out a comb and brushes back his hair with a vain gesture. Jude follows and matches the movement with his own hand in uneasy pantomime.

"Oh, I wouldn't start becoming violent now, Jude. I'm afraid that won't help you very much. You might want to make yourself at home. You could be in there a very long time."

Jenny flutters against his breast. Presses hollow bones against his heart. She burrows deeper into the pocket lint as though the sound of Salazar's voice sends her into a panic.

"There's no such thing," Jude protests.

"No such thing? You're in it now. All it takes is your blood, your signature—which you handily provided with the divorce papers from your firm—a few symbols and spoken words over your dead body. You didn't think witches were the only ones who could work spells, did you?"

"I'm just a lawyer. I've done nothing to you. This is criminal!"

"Haven't you? What, did you think criminals need a reason?" Salazar snorts laughter. "I'm no more evil than you are. How many shady clients have you ever saved from prison and set loose on the street? Well, making mirrors like this, that's my job, and it pays well. It's business—just like getting chumps like me to sign unfair divorce papers is your job. Nothing personal."

Jude considers the nature of evil, reflects on the subpoenas, indictments and divorces he'd delivered in the past, before dismissing it in a burst of rage.

"There's a world of difference between delivering an indictment to a criminal and imprisoning a man for no better reason than you can't keep better terms with your ex," he snaps.

A baby cries in the distance.

Salazar arches his head toward the crib nestled in the corner. Jude struggles for autonomy to move in the other direction but mimics Salazar's motion against his will, his body not his own.

In the crib, a child turns uncomfortably in her blankets and cries again.

"Shut it, Amanda!"

Salazar continues to yell, walking away from the mirror.

Your father's a bastard, little girl, Jude thinks bitterly.

"You shouldn't treat your child that way," he says.

Salazar makes a sound between a growl and a hiss. Jude pulls closer against his will when all he desires is to shrink back from the man who bares his teeth, as though he might come through the mirror itself and deliver a worse altered reality than the one he already occupies.

"Oh, you think so? Well, you should pray this cough syrup never runs out. You got a fancy education, lawyer man, you know your Shakespeare. What is it? '*The devil hath the power to assume a pleasing shape*?'"

Salazar moves out of sight.

When the man passes the limits of the mirror's frame, Jude experiences a tremor like a line snipped in two. A cord snaking up through his spine and from the top of his head severs and sets him loose. His joints, his limbs and legs are his own again, to move as he pleases.

I'm a mime, he realizes. "Good Lord, this must be Hell."

Jenny tweets her despair. She recognizes cages when she sees them, after all.

* * *

Time takes on new meaning in the Mirrorworld, as Jude comes to think of it.

He remembers and catalogues all the mirrors he had seen in his life—bathroom mirrors, hand-held mirrors to shave with, pocket mirrors for grooming, rear and side view mirrors, mirrors in a woman's make-up case. He wonders now if lost souls like his were not imprisoned in them all, forced to carry out the actions of their owners.

Salazar visits the mirror every morning, and again in the evening, to arrange his hair or to examine the fit of his clothes. In each instance, Jude finds himself trapped in dreadful pantomime, aping Salazar on the opposite side of the glass.

When Salazar leaves, shadows follow him by bending in weird knots when he passes and then springing back into place as though nothing ever happened. It calls into question just how many items in the man's apartment are filled with unearthly vitality, their substance stolen from other lives. Who is trapped in the antique end table, and what poor soul might inhabit the arm chair?

Jude presses his face against the glass and peers into the Otherland. He tries breaking the surface again, but the glass remains as stone and the force of his assault knocks him back with proportionate energy. He succeeds only in exhausting himself. He tires of this and at last sits on the floor of his two-dimensional cartoon world, watching the toddler in the far corner, imprisoned in the crib while he remains imprisoned in the mirror. The child is far too young to be without supervision, he thinks. What was her name? Amanda?

She peers at the mirror from above the bars of her crib, a thatch of wild, brown hair and huge eyes.

Salazar doses her with cough syrup in the afternoon. She sleeps through the hours of his absence. Jude envies her drugged existence, as he has nothing but brutal sobriety with which to feel every throb of pain, experience every agony of a death and an afterlife without conclusion.

* * *

"I want you to let me go."

Salazar plucks a hair from the center of his forehead as Jude presents his case. He laughs. Tattoos of mysterious sigils and signs of planets and spirits mark his arms. His gaunt cheeks puff with the force of his derision. Jude mimes it, and through him climbs an insidious, rising hatred. His physicality may be commandeered by Salazar, but on the interior nothing remains of himself to regulate his jangling nerve endings and his seething animosity. A drive-train of agony running with the engine of his heart.

"Why would I do that? Look, you're what, forty years old? Think of it like this—you probably weren't going to last much longer. What did you have to live for anyway?"

Jude tries to protest and instead lapses into sullen silence. That he cannot think of a reason to defend himself only multiplies his rage.

Because I don't have a wife, or a meaningful job, or a particular pursuit, renders my life worthless? That's not fair.

Regardless of the utility of life and its meaning, overwhelming despair claims him. Escape from the mirror will not return his life. His condition is permanent.

So too, is his imprisonment in the mirror.

Defeat comes on the heels of despair, and a series of images shuffle through his mind's eye—the detritus of his consciousness left over from the days prior. The sound of the gun in the cold air. The hiss of the radiator in another apartment. The residents had surely heard his agony and chose to remain in their matchbox rooms and let him die. Jude thinks of the divorce papers he delivered to Salazar. His signature and the empty space where Salazar was meant to sign his name.

And then comes an insight, breathless in its power, that surely all of life is a series of contracts requiring signatures and agreements, and his imprisonment in the mirror is no more permanent than Salazar's marriage. While his death was irreversible, his place in the mirror was not.

It could be broken, just like any agreement. He did it all the time.

Jude holds a breath, his eyes expanding as he conceives the idea and wrestles it down and deep within him.

Salazar leaves down the hall with the spider legs of shadows snapping at him before returning to their sensible positions and linear places beneath the flow of sunlight. Jude feels the same as they do, warped into Salazar's wake and then allowed to return to normal in his absence.

It occurs to him that Salazar is the only thing he has left in the world, whether he likes it or not. A final last friend, a friend who killed him and imprisoned him in silver and glass.

Jenny tweets.

"Except for you," Jude whispers.

He takes Jenny from his pocket. Plump and yellow, she preens and puffs herself to twice her size and satisfies herself with his finger for a perch.

At home in his apartment, he collected canaries and other exotic birds had a crow who learned to speak his name. Some he rescued and others he bought. There would be no one to care for them or feed them now.

"I'm sorry," Jude apologizes to the bird. He strokes it with trembling fingers. "No friends, no one else to sing with you, or flock to you, eh? How lonely you must be."

Her beak opens and she breathes, yellow belly contracting and expanding. Rapid flaps of wing until she takes flight. She careens for the portal, the mirror.

"Don't!"

She fails to perceive the barrier dividing the worlds, and Jude appreciates the sad irony of birds who can't distinguish one glass from the next. He attempts to intercept her but can't pluck her out of the air fast enough as she sails past. He hopes the impact will only stun her and flinches against the sight and the sound.

Silence.

Jude opens his eyes and releases a breath.

Jenny's gone.

On the other side of the mirror, in Salazar's apartment, she tweets triumphantly as she alights atop the crib and cocks her head, examining the baby as she might a bit of enticing bird seed.

"Oh," Jude whispers.

The bird casts no reflection. Free of the mirror.

And suddenly, the child awakens from her cough-syrup stupor.

Amanda, with the tousled hair, jerks upright from her slumber. Her eyeballs jitter and then fly open. She turns her head with an automated snap, joints cracking in her vertebrae until she stares through the rungs of her crib at Jude on the other side of the mirror.

"You can see me?" he asks.

The child grins, her mouth stained purple with cough syrup.

"He left it out," the child says. Her voice plunges low and deep. Jenny flaps her wings but holds her place on the perch, wavering between fear and flight.

Jude hears a sound like crinkling paper, and when he looks down at the edges of the portal he sees ice form along the frame, frost crystallizing from the air.

He steps away from the mirror.

He thinks to ask *What*? but decides that he wants no more of this. Wants no more of what lies beyond in Salazar's collected curiosities. The unnatural child speaking with the voice of something much older.

"He left the bird out," she whispers in answer and rises up.

A movement of uncoordinated limbs and then her hand whips out and seizes the bird. Jenny squawks and falls to silence as she succumbs to the child's grip.

"These spells are very exact. One thing off and they mutate or unravel, like a string of Christmas lights," the infant says.

"You don't sound like a child, Amanda."

"I'll hear your case now."

Jude licks his lips and stares at her. Her eyes roll and they now appear to him jaundiced and yellowed at their corners, with her veins creeping in green and her neck arching to stare at him from the side of her eyes.

"Present your case," the child husks in a voice too old to be a child's. Pitched as a trembling soprano, it makes for a weird and laughable tone whose very humor invites the gooseflesh to rise and his skin to crawl.

He thinks of bird song and wonders what such a voice is designed to impart with its malignant sound. It calls invisible things to it the same way Salazar's shadows trip over themselves to slither and grip at him.

"My case?"

"Salazar asked you what you had to live for. What is it, Jude? What is it that you have that's worth leaving the mirror? Present your case. Convince this old and tired judge."

What did you have to live for anyway?

Jude cannot shake the feeling that a man with only birds for companionship did not have a right to live. He'd made no difference in the world by being in it, had saved no lives, had never even donated to a charity.

"I was in love once. That must mean something," Jude says.

"Love does not have to mean anything at all."

She turns the bird back and forth in her palm. The canary opens its mouth as though trying to take in air and smothers in the child's grip. The thing called Amanda opens her mouth in tandem with the creature, and Jude thinks she might stuff Jenny into her mouth and bite into feathers and cartilage.

"Just don't hurt her!" he begs.

"Then tell me what you have to live for. Are you not a lawyer?

There are many laws both written and invisible. Approach the bench. Tell me what you live for. Tell me what you die for, and why you should be granted clemency."

"I've done nothing wrong!"

Amanda doesn't answer. Her implacable eyes shimmer, and Jude sees that she has two pairs of eyelids. A thin film passes over her eyes like a lizard's and then disappears beneath her human, fleshy lid until he thinks perhaps it had never been there at all.

Jenny tweets.

"Love! Yes, love. I fell in love with a woman I met at a library, did you know that? She was taking out books on ornithology. She owned canaries and finches and cockatiels. She invited me over to see them, and I was looking through her cages, watching the birds. She kissed me when I turned around. Everything happened by accident. Maybe she didn't love me at all, but I know what I felt. A time later, she told me she was pregnant and I promised I'd marry her. I bought a ring and everything. And then, one day, I came home, and…"

"And then what happened? Did love not see the day through? What happens when at long last it doesn't conquer all, hmmm?"

"Just give her back. Give her back to me. I don't care. I don't care about living." His throat closes up and the tears burn hot as paper cuts at the corners of his eyes. "Hardly matters now, does it? What do I have to live for anyway? Give her back."

The child laughs and hiccups from her belly, and the sound fills him with nausea as her grasp on the bird tightens.

"You can keep your bird for now. But think on it, boy. Give me the bird and I can grant you a chance for release. You'll have to convince Salazar that he's the one in the mirror, you know. No easy task. And at the end of it, you'll still be dead, but at least you'll be free of the mirror and no longer a plaything for rich occultists with nothing better to do with their money."

"Is that what you are?"

She hisses and opens her hands. Jenny explodes into flight, her song puncturing the air. She arrows for Jude who catches her and holds her close as Amanda turns her back on him, collapsing into the crib as though she had never been awake.

* * *

"Good morning, Salazar," Jude says.

Jenny flutters in his pocket, yellow feathers against his heart.

Salazar smooths his hair back from his forehead, and Jude follows suit with fingers pulled by invisible strings. He does not fight but allows the magic to command him. The sensation of rain drops running along his joints, tidal and oceanic currents.

"You sound pleasant today," Salazar says, eyes narrow in his gaunt face. "I don't like it."

"Did you ever wonder, Salazar?"

"What's that?"

"If maybe you're the one in the mirror? And I'm in the real world."

Salazar is expressionless. His heartless eyes flicker, and Jude detects the moment when the idea registers and catches hold on the edge of his consciousness.

Jude holds the posture, unable to move until Salazar chooses to do so. He returns the occultist's blank stare, measure for measure, caught in his supernatural cage.

Jenny, in his breast pocket, moves against his dead heart.

Salazar makes a face of disgust. A twisted leer of his lips. With an angry snap of his wrist, he plucks the bottle of cough syrup from the cabinet as he leaves. Jude follows him until the invisible cord that pulls and stretches him into action is released, freeing Jude to wander his two-dimensional Mirrorworld once more.

* * *

"Amanda. Little girl! Wake up, little girl!"

Shadows undulate through window light and Jude makes out her face through the rungs of the crib. She drools with violet-tinted saliva, then her mouth snaps closed and her eyes fly open.

"Amanda?"

The girl sits up and stares at him. He looks for signs and traces of the thing she'd been before. She looks vacant and groggy, no trace of her otherworldly self until her face bisects with a grin longer than the circumference of her head, extending endlessly to the other side.

"*Yesssss?*"

"Take her," Jude chokes out the words. "Take her and give her back her life."

The child climbs to her feet and grins, opening her hands.

"What happens when you have her?" Jude asks, pulling Jenny from his pocket. She peeps from her hiding place and hops upon his finger.

With her fingers, the child makes the gesture of a person running.

"Your bird pops my cage open," the child growls, "and then you use your wits to make the most of my absence, eh?"

"Fine." He kisses Jenny on the top of her head and lets her go.

She ascends the air in a yellow puff.

The mirror glass parts for her like a wizard's curtain, a shaft of light passing through her feathers.

"Go, Jenny," he whispers and presses against the glass. The tip of his nose brushes the hard surface of the mirror portal.

The bird bobs and weaves through the apartment. She dives down and alights on the edge of the crib. The little girl coos and blurts a string of excited nonsense words, as though the glittering lizard intelligence lying dormant beneath her child's flesh never existed. Her thatch of corn-silk hair stands out in all directions as the blue blanket falls away. The child offers a chubby fist, fingers grasping for the yellow bird above her. She opens her mouth hungrily, and Jenny stares at her before hopping along the rung and poising above the crib lock.

Amanda blinks and the monster inside her is back. Or does it only pretend, Jude wonders, when it wants to seem a normal girl?

"There, little friend," she hisses. "Right there."

The shadows around them bend and beckon in their direction, as though all the sleeping, energetic lines of earth and electricity pull along a tide, conspiring to lull the bird and make it see things it could not recognize before. Then Jenny cocks her head and, in a flash of light, spots the bright crib lock for the first time.

C'mon, Jenny.

Tap tap. Jenny sets her beak against it. The little girl swipes at her and the bird dances out of reach, fluttering wildly and then diving in to *tap tap* again at the lock.

With all the appearance of a normal child, she laughs with her open mouth in a pink curl, the beast evaporated from her eyes.

The devil hath the power to assume a pleasing shape.

Jude wonders what kind of devil she is. Any minute the thing residing deep inside her will rise to the surface with its yellowed eyes and green veins of rot.

The thing inside her swells. She slams a fist against the crib door. Her fingers hit the mechanism in her desperate grab for the prize. The canary flutters, the lock snicks open and the door casts wide.

Amanda spills out onto the floor, trailing blankets behind her. A monster pretending to be a toddler.

"Yes," Jude whispers.

Jenny describes a drunken figure eight in the air as though she were no more than a child's mobile. She dances in and out of Amanda's reach, and the little girl stretches her arms in a desperate bid to defy gravity and pluck her out of the air. Jenny dives and tumbles, teasing and tempting the toddler. Shadows cast from furniture and window blinds contract like fingers, becoming shaded tentacles that swat the bird to the ground. She lies flat over wood flooring with wings outstretched, dazed.

Amanda giggles, scoops her up and disappears into the closet beyond. The door snicks shut. Laughter, giggles, the bird singing from behind the closed door.

You use your wits to make the most of my absence, eh?

Jude passes a hand across his forehead, his lips moving in silent prayer.

He sits down on the floor of the Mirrorworld and waits while the little girl with something big inside her hides in the closet with the only thing that made his life worth living.

* * *

Jude does not quite doze but senses himself suspended in a netherworld. He thinks of his birds. Had anyone found them in their cages yet? Would they beat their wings against the bars until their hearts gave out, losing feather after feather to the cruel isolation?

He snaps awake to the sound of Salazar whistling.

Jude races to the mirror, hoping to peer through before Salazar enters, but he's too late—suddenly slapped back from the surface. Jude feels himself posed erect and placed into pantomime, unfurling like a cardboard cutout.

He seals his lips shut against a cry and greets Salazar because he can do no other. He advances upon the looking glass as though they are dance partners engaged in a complicated waltz until Salazar himself appears.

Jude musters all his enthusiasm.

"Salazar! Why, did you have a good day?"

The smirk disintegrates and dissolves into Salazar's face. His eyes ossify into stones.

"Why on earth do you keep doing that?"

"Doing what? I do everything you do, Salazar."

"Why aren't you miserable, like the rest?"

Jude follows Salazar's motions with cool dedication and loosens the collar around his throat. He pretends he is acting a part to a movie or a play, and this comes naturally to him. All of his future will depend on his talent for litigation and persuasion. His private play, his personal courtroom. Setting the stage and parading before the footlights for the benefit of an unseen audience. An invisible jury.

For Jenny. For liberation from this hell.

"What reason would I have to be miserable?"

"You're in a mirror."

"Am I? Still so sure that you're the one in the real world? Not the other way around?"

Salazar's face turns a shade of red beyond blood, his lips settling in an anemic line. What he shrugged off as a joke before no longer strikes the Satanist as funny.

"Stop it. *This* is the real world."

"Well, anyone would think so, eh? Where's Amanda? That little girl you're always screaming at?"

Salazar pauses, frozen, before slowly regaining his composure, staring at Jude measure for measure.

"Don't go anywhere, boogeyman," Salazar sneers and turns on his heel to dart through the room and lean over the crib.

Jude watches a slice of the man, silhouetted against a window, fists on the bars, looking down at the empty sheets before snapping back toward the mirror. Salazar's steps echo, impatient staccato against old wood.

"What have you done with her?"

"With the apple of your eye?"

"I can unmake you, you know. I've got a hundred ways to send you to Hell."

"I've been trying to tell you, but you won't listen."

"Where is she!?"

"*You're* the one on the other side of the mirror, Salazar. That's why your precious girl isn't with you. I'm on the right side. The life side. You're the one dead and trapped in the mirror."

"*Mirrorworld*," Salazar mouths. "You're lying."

"Really, Salazar? Can you afford to be so hasty? You're all alone."

"I was just outside. I can go outside again. I can leave anytime I want."

"Suit yourself." Jude makes his voice casual. *Tread lightly. Be convincing, dammit! Make the closing argument too strong to be denied.* "Where do you think I go when you're not here? Turns out, I go anywhere I want as well."

From beyond Salazar's erect figure, a streak of yellow bolts from the closet, fluttering and flapping wildly into the room.

Jenny tweets furiously, and Salazar starts at it and his mouth parts in confusion. Jude stares wide-eyed at the bird and leaps upon the opportunity afforded him.

"If yours is the real world, why is there no reflection of that bird in mine?" he asks.

Salazar snaps his gaze from the bird to the glass. His eyes widen and his lips part, mouthing a single word: *No.*

"I wouldn't be too hard on yourself. I mean, what do you have to live for anyway?"

Jenny tweets. She hovers at the window and then streaks to the ceiling fan and remains there, preening.

Salazar stumbles against the end table. He jerks open the drawer. Inside, a gun rattles along the bottom, a box of loose bullets clinking together like change. He picks it up and Jude remembers the firearm. The mouth with no teeth.

"This gun proves I'm real," Salazar insists. His finger lines the barrel.

"I have one too, Salazar."

Jude holds the fluctuating, flat-imaged pistol in his own fingers, waving it before him to demonstrate his power.

"It's not yours. I shot you with *this* gun. This is the real gun!" Salazar's voice becomes ragged, the rhythm of his breath uneven. "I can't be in the mirror."

As though to prove it to himself, he places the cold muzzle against his cheek.

Unable to do otherwise, Jude follows the motion.

"See," Jude pitches his voice to soothe. "See how you lift the gun as I lift it? The magic compels you to follow *my* motions."

Salazar gasps. His arm trembles and strains. Reality tumbles and swaps places and disorients his reason.

Jude grinds his teeth to hold every small emotion within, to keep for himself the secret. He holds his breath and touches the pistol to his head along with Salazar.

An explosion.

The blue flame licks from the muzzle.

Jude is suddenly everywhere at once as molecules of his own self struggle to follow the progress of Salazar's broken skull and splattered brains across the wall and carpet, a thousand shards of mirror reflecting every tiny portion of himself.

He fractures and splits and divides, helpless but to share the same fate as Salazar.

A death rattle from each of the men plays in two-part harmony, filling the empty apartment with a woeful sound.

The little girl with the growling voice and the jaundiced eyes slumbers in the closet, her lips stained with cough syrup.

She dreams of yellow birds and other pleasing shapes.

ABOUT THE AUTHOR
MATTHEW PEGG

Matthew Pegg lives in Leicestershire in the United Kingdom where he writes fiction, stage plays and shopping lists. Since his first job as a painter of canal boats, he has moved on to become an actor, teacher, graphic designer, bureaucrat and director of a community arts company.

Pegg is working on his first novel, *Black Annis*, a black comedic horror about a shape-shifting witch who eats children and wears their skins as a skirt. His most recent theatre work is entitled *Escaping Alice*, a love story that combines chains and handcuffs, produced for the York Theatre Royal.

MARCH HAYS

MATTHEW PEGG

At first I was blind, swimming in and out of morphine-fired dreams. Again and again I saw the aeroplane bank, its engines howling as it came in to attack. I heard the explosions and the screams, saw the earth thrown up, the Jeep in front of me tracing a lazy pirouette in the air as its passengers came apart like toys hurled at a wall, felt the impact like a slap in the face and awoke trapped under a smouldering vehicle. Friendly fire. Over and over again.

For a long time, all I knew were the hands of those caring for me. Brisk and business-like they changed my dressings, washed me, checked my temperature and injected me, before letting me slip into unconsciousness once more. I was rolled over, prodded and maintained like a temperamental piece of machinery to be discarded if all else failed.

I began to recognise one particular pair of hands amongst all the others, the fingers long and delicate as they lingered tenderly on my brow and gently teased dressings away from wounds.

Later I could see. The bandages were removed from my eyes, and I could identify the face that went with those hands. Her name was Lily. Lily's eyes were dark and perceptive, her hair mousy blonde; not pretty but interesting, which was better. She treated me as a person, looked me in the eyes, spoke to me even though I couldn't answer, told me about my case as if we were colleagues.

Later, when the worst was over and I was on my feet again, I learned where I was and remembered I had met Lily before.

* * *

It was when I was ten. There was a garden party. Everyone from the villages that surrounded March Hays, the big hall, had been invited. I remember the day because after a week of dismal cloud the sun broke through and turned the grounds into a blinding vision of white and green and blue and ochre. Tables had been set up on the lush lawn, covered with crisp snowy cloths and piled with food and big jugs of cider and lemonade. Adults clustered in groups, the men stiff in Sunday suits, the women in the patched and carefully preserved dresses of yesterday the colours of crocus, daffodil, pinks and clover, befitting a day straddling spring and summer. Around the adults eddied tides of children, uninhibited by their parent's social awkwardness.

I left my mother's side to get a drink. A harassed maid thrust a glass into my hand, and I discovered she had given me cider rather than lemonade. My first instinct was to exchange it, but I realised I had been offered a chance to experience a forbidden pleasure. So I wandered off, sipping the unfamiliar, sour-sweet liquid that formed cloudy whorls in the glass.

For a while I stood in the arch of a coach house watching grooms saddle a recalcitrant stallion. With the cider and the sunshine making my head swim, I drifted to the other side of the hall where younger children were chasing up and down on the lawns. I decided to explore the graveyard of the nearby chapel. It was overgrown with grass, nettles and foxgloves. Slate gravestones poked up like fingers from a fur cuff.

"Who are you?" A small girl with long, fair hair tied with a plaid ribbon was perched on top of an ornate granite tomb. A little rough-haired dog sat below her in the shade, tongue lolling.

"Sam Meachum," I said. "You?"

"Lily Siddons."

"You live here?"

"Yes."

"Don't you go to school?"

"I have a tutor. Next year I'll go to school."

"In the village?"

"Boarding school. Devon." She pulled a face.

"They're sending you away?"

"It's where Mummy went to school. Supposed to be the happiest days of my life." Lily spat into the nettles. That impressed me. The dog scratched himself, wheezing like an old man.

All the girls at school were as familiar to me as my family. They giggled and played skipping games and had inexplicable rules and secrets. Sometimes we all ran riot together, and at other times they were a species apart. They were part of the unquestioned landscape of my childhood, flowers planted in the same soil. Lily was new and different.

I can't remember everything we talked about, no doubt the inconsequential things that seem important when you're ten. We threw sticks for Monty the dog and tossed pebbles at the chapel, trying to get them through the corner of a window where the glass was missing. We wandered round the little graveyard, and Lily showed me an ancient tomb with a hole at its base where the stone had broken away.

"It's a murderer's grave," she said.

"No it isn't."

"Yes it is. Hundreds of years ago Lord Radcliffe Siddons murdered his gamekeeper. And they hanged him."

"Why did he murder the gamekeeper?"

"He just did. Have a look inside. You can see the bones!"

I knelt down and peered into the hole.

"Get closer. But be very quiet or he might wake up and grab you."

I got closer.

"Don't make a sound."

I peered into the murk, the gap was full of dead leaves and dirt, but beyond that I thought I could see something. I pressed my eye firmly to the hole.

"See anything?" Lily whispered, very close to my ear.

"No."

"RAAARGHHH!" she screamed, grabbing me under my ribs at the same time. I leaped away from the tomb and sprawled on my back. Lily convulsed with laughter. My heart pounded and I gasped for breath. I glared at her, which sent her into more convulsions of mirth. Her hilarity was so infectious that I couldn't help smiling and then guffawing myself. We rolled on the ground. Monty danced round us, tail wagging, not sure what the game was but wanting to join in.

We clambered back to our perch on the grave. Lily tasted the cider but pronounced it, "Foul stuff." I agreed, but thought I should pretend to like it so as to appear grown up. So it was that my mother found us lounging on top of the tomb with a quarter-full glass of the demon drink between us.

"Sam, I've been looking for you everywhere. Wherever have you been? Who's this?" She gave Lily a thin smile.

"Lily Siddons," I said.

"Oh. You're the daughter." Mother rearranged her face into a more polite mask.

"Pleased to meet you," Lily said, hopping down to extend a hand, playing the polite little girl.

Then Mother saw the glass of cider.

"Sam, have you been drinking alcohol?"

Drink had played some unexplained part in my father's demise, and so my mother had always been dead against it.

"That's mine. My father lets me," Lily said.

"Does he?" Mother paused. I could tell that she doubted it was true, but she couldn't pursue it without calling the daughter of her host a liar. "How nice. We must be going. Come along, Sam."

Lily gave me a wink. I grinned at her and followed my mother. I looked back to see Lily in the gateway, sun striking her fair hair, Monty at her feet. She had rescued me.

That was the moment when I fell for the girl perched on top of a tombstone in the everlasting sunshine of the 1930s. Did she realise the wounded soldier she tended was the friend she'd made so many years before? I didn't know. But I remembered her.

* * *

At the outbreak of the war, Lily and her mother gave over March Hays as a hospital for injured troops, especially those from the surrounding areas who could be looked after near their friends and families. The larger spaces—the ballroom, the upper gallery—were stripped of their fine furniture and period paintings and filled with rows of functional, iron-framed beds. The family migrated to the upper floors, to rooms formerly only fit for servants. Nursing staff and doctors were installed. Lily went to London to train as an auxiliary nurse and then returned to her home to repair shattered bodies and minds.

When I could move around, I spent my days drifting through the grounds, marking the changes that war had made to the fine red brick and stone house. There were few able-bodied men left to tend the gardens, so the lawns grew wild and tall and grass seed drifted in the breeze. Inside, a business-like clatter overlaid the dignity of the house like a mackintosh worn over a ball gown. I wandered the corridors, trying to avoid the doctors. Sometimes I found myself in the wards and looked in on old colleagues or friends from my boyhood.

On one of these occasions I found myself looking down on a poor, broken thing, swathed in bandages like an Egyptian mummy. The patient lacked an arm and a leg, a carving abandoned incomplete. As I stared, he thrashed for a moment, shuddered and then was still. A doctor hurried over, gave him a cursory examination and declared him dead. Curtains were drawn around the body, masking it from sight. Later, I saw Lily crying in the nurse's room. For a few seconds her calm, professional manner crumbled away and beneath it I saw the grief and strain her job caused her. I wished I could say something that would help. A moment later she wiped away her tears and went back into the fray.

* * *

My favourite room in the hall was the library. It was still much as it had been before the war, lined with bookshelves and boasting several comfortable armchairs and a large desk in front of windows that looked out onto a terrace. It became my habit to sit in the library every evening to watch the sun set and twilight flow up the lawn to flood the big windows in darkness. Few patients or staff used it and, mostly, I had the room to myself.

This changed one day when I was walking along the corridor that led to the library. I was talking to Ted Allenby who had been in the class under me at the village school. He joined the RAF and had been shot down over the Channel, crashing into the sea near Hastings. Suddenly Ted cocked his head.

"What was that?" he asked.

I had heard nothing and told him so.

"Sounded like someone calling me."

With that he opened the library door and stepped inside.

I waited for a few moments. "Ted?"

There was no answer, so I stuck my head through the doorway. He wasn't there. A glazed door next to the windows gave out onto the terrace. The only other exit was an anonymous panelled door on the opposite wall, between the high shelves. I stepped into the room.

The terrace door was closed so I turned to examine the other. As I gazed at it, I began to experience a peculiar feeling. It's hard to describe, but I felt as if the panelled door was somehow *wrong*. I hadn't paid it any attention in the past, in fact I couldn't remember noticing it at all. But now it set my teeth on edge. Perhaps there was something subtly awry in its proportions or placement in the room.

I realised I was now standing right in front of the door with no memory of stepping across the room to get there. Close to, it appeared perfectly nondescript. I reached out a hand and touched it. The polished timber felt cool, its surface smoothed and burnished over centuries.

With an effort I shook myself out of this odd reverie and walked back across the room. I was still in a delicate state, prey to unhealthy fancies and night terrors. This could have been just another instance of that. I looked through the window to see if Ted was on the terrace. At that moment, from behind me, I heard a furtive chuckle. I whipped round. I was still alone in the room yet I had distinctly heard someone try to stifle a gloating laugh.

I don't mind admitting that I left the library with undignified haste. Later, I berated myself for having been spooked. But still I found reasons to not visit the library. In the deep of night, when my more rational self slumbered, I imagined that the voice had not come from behind the door at all, but had been made by the door itself.

* * *

The war ended. There were celebrations and rejoicing with an edge of hysteria, an attempt to forget the deep scars of the last six years. The hospital at March Hays was gradually disassembled. Patients departed to return home or enter institutions offering long-term care. Medical equipment was removed. Stored furniture was dusted down and reinstated. The house returned to some semblance of its pre-war state.

With the wounded gone, I stayed on at March Hays to help elderly Jem with the horses, something for which I had demonstrated unexpected talent. My mother had remarried, sold the cottage and moved away, so with no other home to go to I established myself in a room above the stable block.

Though I didn't go back into the library for some time, I did try to work out where the door might lead. Pacing out the corridors beyond the library walls, passages turned away before they reached the right spot and featureless walls confounded me. In the end I gave up the search and decided to confront my fear, go back into the room and simply open the damn thing.

This time, the door was no longer there. In the space where it had been was a panelled alcove with an upholstered seat. For a moment I thought I had walked into the wrong room. I glanced around in confusion but everything else was as it had always been. The seat showed years of wear, and the surrounding panels perfectly matched the rest of the room. Clearly, the alcove had always been there. I slowly backed out of the library.

Trauma and injury affect the mind as well as the body. I had seen ample evidence of that among the injured here. While I felt perfectly sane and clear headed, it was becoming clear to me that I was not yet my old myself.

* * *

A year later, Lily married Edward Radcliffe, a big, barrel-chested man with curling black hair. Edward claimed to work in what he called 'acquisitions and supplies' but he was vague about what that involved. He made himself at home at March Hays, playing the local squire, occupying the family pew in the chapel and joining the hunt.

Once again, the library became my occasional, illicit refuge. If the phantom door was the product of my fevered imagination, there was no reason not to steal in and partake of the calm offered by the room. One evening as I sat in my favourite armchair looking at the sunset I noticed a slim leather volume that had been left on a small table: *Etchings*, by someone called Emily Nast, published by the Suffolk Press in 1878. I opened it at a random page and read:

Old Tod.

When they first came through the door many a traveller did not notice Old Tod in his overgrown alcove. If they did, they often mistook him for a statue, for he was the colour of ancient iron.

When he was sure all was right, Old Tod would creep up and strike the traveller down with his big hammer. Often this killed them outright, sometimes it only rendered them insensible. At other times he would employ a long metal spike or a stone club. Then Old Tod would take the traveller apart with the tools he stored under his bench. The tools were old, rusted and stained, but Tod kept them sharp.

He fed bits of the travellers to Dog, who liked the tenderest parts best of all. The bones Tod threw in the river. He made candles of the fat. Blood he kept to paint the floor of his alcove and teeth he sorted in jars to make mosaics on his walls. This was his only pastime and pleasure.

A skinny, pale, toothless traveller he would let pass, even
if they deserved his attention. They had nothing to interest
Old Tod, and further along the road The Fisherman or The
Crone would be sure to find them.

The book carried on in this vein—terrible, meaningless car-
nage, horror piled upon horror, described in almost childishly simple prose. Was it some kind of allegory? I didn't understand, and
I couldn't imagine anyone reading it for pleasure. I shuddered and
returned the book to the table, but I could not shake off the morbid
mood created by the tale of Old Tod.

The sun had vanished behind the trees and the library was now
swathed in shadows. As I stood up to return to my room above
the stables, I glanced at the alcove and there, once again, was the
mysterious panelled door.

For a long moment I simply stared, then I forced myself to approach the door. I dared not open it, but below the knob there was a
keyhole. Cautiously, I knelt down.

"Have a look inside. You can see the bones." I remembered Lily's
words from so long ago.

I leant forward.

"Be very quiet or he might wake up and grab you."

I applied my eye to the keyhole. I could see nothing. Then the
darkness seemed to shift as if a huge form was pressed up against
the other side of the door. I thought I could hear breathing. As the
shadows moved again, I drew back allowing a little light to enter the
hole. I could see my eye reflected in the depths of the keyhole. It had
a peculiar yellow tint as if seen through stagnant water. I wondered
at how bloodshot it was, the pupil slightly oval. Then the eye blinked
and I realised I wasn't looking at a reflection of my own eye at all.

I scrambled away on hands and knees, expecting that at any
moment the door would burst open and Old Tod would emerge,

hammer raised. But the door stayed closed, and I hurried out of the library and back to the horses and sanity.

* * *

It snowed that September. Lily was heavily pregnant. There was an old motorcycle in the stables and she had taken to using it, roaring fearlessly along narrow country lanes. One evening I was in my room when I heard raised voices in the stable yard below. I peered through the window to see Lily and Edward.

Lily was pushing her bike out into the yard. Edward was following her and he grasped the handlebars, arresting her progress. His face was scarlet. They argued furiously but I couldn't hear what was said. After a few moments, she wrenched the motorbike out of his grasp, mounted it and tore out of the yard. He stared after her, swore under his breath, paced back and forth for a moment, then went into the garage. A moment later Edward's car drove out of the yard and headed off after Lily.

I waited for them to return. I didn't think Lily should have been riding the motorbike at all in her condition.

As night fell it became colder. I eventually slipped into a fitful sleep. I dreamt Lily and I were in the library. She had her back to the dreadful door, which was slightly ajar. She was describing a book to me and waving it in my face. I tried to warn her, but she wouldn't listen, and she batted my hands away when I attempted to draw her further from the gaping portal that was slowly opening behind her. I was awoken from the dream by the sound of Edward's car returning.

Through the window I saw that Lily was not with him, and her motorbike was nowhere to be seen. Edward stomped off towards the house. I walked downstairs and out into the stable courtyard. Snow had begun to fall again and it sparkled in the light.

Sergeant, the big, black stallion stood in the centre of the yard, his breath clouding in the cold air. I didn't question how he came to be there, saddled, ready. I swung myself up into the saddle, and Sergeant walked under the arch and onto the lane leading away from the house. I could see the motorcycle tracks, now beginning to be obscured by falling snow. Sergeant and I followed them.

It was a strange journey, the horse's hooves muffled, crunching through the snow. There was little traffic, and like a dream we passed cottages lit up inside and sheep huddled together in fields. The tracks led us around the edge of the estate, eventually vanishing completely at a crossroads, erased by falling snow. I slid from Sergeant's back and looked round. All was white and midnight blue. Ahead of me in the ditch I saw a twisted, black shape, the handlebars of the motorbike. Lily was pinned beneath it. Her eyes were shut, but as I bent down they flickered and opened. She tried to say something. There was a fleck of blood on her mouth, her lips were blue. Her eyes closed again.

I looked round frantically. There were no vehicles in sight. The bike pinned her like a butterfly on a board. I grasped the handlebars and they slipped through my fingers. I gathered all my strength, put my hands under the bike and heaved. It shifted slightly. I heaved again and slowly, miraculously, lifted it off Lily's legs. She gave a moan but didn't open her eyes.

"Lily!" I said.

She muttered something under her breath.

"Wake up!"

Her eyes opened and she gasped for breath. She looked down, saw her situation, and began to slowly drag herself backwards, pulling her legs out from under the bike. It started to slip through my fingers, but I held on. Only when she was clear did I let it fall.

* * *

Lily returned to March Hays after a week in hospital, having recovered from her ordeal and given birth to a healthy baby girl, Amy.

Over the months I watched Lily's relationship with Edward unravel. He began to drink late into the night, spent more time in London and showed little interest in his new daughter.

A year after Lily's motorcycle accident it all boiled over. It was a grey November day, laden with iron-coloured clouds. I heard Lily and Edward argue throughout the afternoon, a portable row like a pocket thunderstorm that moved from the stables, through the gardens to the house and back again. I avoided encountering them but it was difficult not to overhear fragments of the argument.

"How can all the money have gone?" Lily cried.

And later: "I hardly see you! What's so fantastic in London?

Then: "Amy's your daughter. Make time!"

And finally: "I'm not stupid, Edward. Who is she?"

In the evening Edward locked himself in his study with two bottles of brandy. Lily went upstairs. I slipped inside and followed her.

I found her putting Amy to bed and stood in the doorway feeling awkward.

"Lily, are you alright?"

She gazed down at Amy in her cot. "You don't have to worry. Everything will be fine."

"I'm scared for you."

She didn't turn round.

"Edward is Amy's Daddy. He'd never hurt us." Her voice cracked.

I hovered in the doorway for a moment, unable to offer proper comfort, frustrated with myself. Then I turned away and went back to the stables.

* * *

I awoke in my room, coming from sleep to full awareness in an instant. I had the impression that someone had just been calling my name. A minute later I was running towards the hall without knowing why, except for having a powerful, urgent sense that it was where I needed to be.

I arrived to find Edward staggering to the bottom of the main stairs. Lily stood at the top gazing down at him. Amy was clasped in her arms.

"Edward go to bed. You're frightening Amy."

He pulled an old sabre from its mounting on the wall and marched unsteadily up the stairs. Lily drew back. He staggered towards her and lashed out with the sword. She fell and sprawled to the floor. The blow missed, cutting a chunk out of the banister. Edward raised the sword over his head. He looked quite insane, scarlet with fury.

I ran up the stairs and tackled him from behind. He shrugged me off, but I grabbed him and spun him away from Lily as he sliced the air between us with the sword. I could see the murder in his eyes. I rushed at him, pushing him back until he hit the banister rail. Edward twisted away, and this sent him tumbling down the stairs to sprawl heavily on the stone floor below.

I descended the stairs and he rose up to meet me, roaring his anger. His eyes were red and his hands smoked. He tried to make his way up to Lily, but I seized him again and spun him away. We wrestled, Edward struggling to reach Lily, I grappling with him, never letting him get free. Then he turned on me and spat his fury in my face.

We fought all the way down the corridor to the library, but now I had the measure of him and I was the stronger. I shoved him inside the room. I wasn't surprised to see that the door waited for us. I propelled him towards it, and now terror fought with his anger. I held him against the wall, raging and frothing. With my other hand I pulled the door open. Edward divined my intention and struggled harder, beating his fists against my face but they were as the touch of moths wings. With the remainder of my strength I lifted him up and thrust him through the doorway. He grabbed the frame with one hand, preventing me pushing him through. His other hand grabbed the front of my shirt. I shoved him, but I couldn't make him loose his grip.

Behind him I saw what lay beyond the door. It was a benighted landscape. A narrow path led between high, dank stone walls covered with creeper. In the distance I glimpsed jagged mountains rising from a barren plain. The sky was dark grey, and the whole was lit by a dull red glow like the light from a dying volcano. The air smelled of metal and burnt flesh.

Edward snarled in my face. He couldn't break my grip, but neither could I break his. Slowly he began to drag me with him over the threshold. In a moment we would both be lost. Then something emerged from an archway in the stone wall behind him, unfolding itself until it towered above us. It was hairless and thin like a praying mantis, with skin the colour of flint. Dull yellow eyes stared at us above a lipless grinning mouth.

Edward saw my gaze shift and he turned to look behind him. Then his body jerked. A rusting blade emerged from the centre of his chest. His eyes widened in shock and he gave a strangled cry. Gore spattered the ground. He was torn from my grip as Old Tod lifted him up with the blade like a speared morsel at a banquet. I turned my face away and slammed the door shut. From beyond, I heard a familiar chuckle, then silence.

* * *

Lily grieved for Edward but, to me, her grief was tinged with relief. I moved back into the house. One night Lily opened her bedroom door. I walked in. She pulled back the sheet and got into bed
and I got in with her. I held her in my arms and that is how we stayed.

* * *

Time passed as it does, drip by drip. Many decades later Lily died.
It was peaceful. She floated away in her own morphine clouds. She
was very old, and I suppose so was I. The funeral was held in the little
chapel and she was buried in the family graveyard.

I saw Lily standing with her daughter and grandchildren as they
lowered the coffin into the ground. She turned, recognised me and
smiled. She ran to me. I took her hand and we wandered away from
the place where we had first met so many years ago. All at once she
was Lily the little girl, the young woman and the old lady, images in a
flick book. I was the boy, the youth, the wounded soldier.

I remembered how we had rolled on the grass and laughed as
children, how I had looked down at my own shattered body and how
Lily had cried when the doctor declared me dead. I remembered the
other spirits like Ted and how they had all departed until only I remained. I remembered lifting the motorbike from Lily's body, dis-
covering I could still touch the world and how I had grappled with
Edward's murderous ghost after his fatal fall down the stairs.

I had shared Lily's life, though she had never known I was there.
She had saved me and I had saved her.

We all have a door, but where it leads us is not fixed. For some
there waits a blighted landscape and the attentions of Old Tod. But
that is not the only possibility.

Lily and I walked to the house and into the library. Hand in hand
we opened the door. The light that spilled out was not the red glow

of Old Tod's domain, it was spring sunshine. This time there was nothing to fear as together we passed through and the door closed behind us.

ABOUT THE AUTHOR
KAREN RUNGE and SIMON DEWAR

Karen Runge lives in South Africa and is a horror author, artist, and a teacher of English as a Second Language. Her work has appeared in *Pseudopod*, *Something Wicked*, *Pantheon Magazine* and *Structo*.

Her story "Hope is Here" was featured in the anthology *Suspended in Dusk*, and "Good Help" was published in *Shock Totem*. Horror icon Jack Ketchum once told her, "Karen, you scare me."

Simon Dewar lives in Canberra, Australia, with his wife and three daughters. By day, he is an Infrastructure Systems Engineer, specializing in building complex environments, application deployments and implementation of virtualization technologies. By night, he writes terrifying and gruesome tales that his wife refuses to read.

Dewar is the editor of the anthology *Suspended in Dusk*. His short story, "The Kettle," appears in *Bloody Parchment: The Root Cellar and Other Stories*, and his "The Wire Bird" was published in *The Sea*.

He is currently working on a novella titled *The House of Waite*.

HIGH ART

KAREN RUNGE and SIMON DEWAR

Her breath came in ragged pants, her mouth muffled against the pillow. Her firm, round ass rolled against him in waves as it slapped back against his thighs.

That's it—any second now, bitch.

She let out an inarticulate cry and began to tremble. He grabbed her hip in one hand and a fistful of her dark hair in the other as the last shuddering convulsions of his orgasm rocked him, and he exploded inside her. She shivered as she slumped forward on the bed, moaning in contentment.

As far as Raymond White was concerned, *this* was the life, and one of the great virtues of having money and power was that he actually got to live this life. While losers out there ground through the boring nine-to-five to go home to their plain Jane wives and brood of squealing, snotty children, he had Stacey Bishop, the face of *Channel 4 News*, face down and ass up.

Just the way life should be.

He rolled onto the bed beside her and took a moment to catch his breath. When he could breathe a little, he took a cigarette and lighter from the bedside table and sparked it. Stacey turned her head to face him, an indulgent grin on her face.

"Oh my god. That was fantastic," she said. With each pant of her breath she made a little mouse-like squeak of pleasure as the aftershocks rocked her.

"It was pretty good," he said, adding some warmth to his voice to take the sting out of the response.

It was more than good, but he knew how to play the game. To keep her eager to please and attentive, he couldn't let her know just how good she really was. He'd made that mistake before.

"Pretty good? Mmmn. Wanna go again? You can't come to the banquet and try only one dish." She smiled and gave her ass an inviting little shake.

"We'll see," he said, exhaling a cloud of smoke and ashed his cigarette into the half-empty beer bottle on the bedside table. He stretched his neck and rolled his shoulders.

"What's wrong, baby?"

He took a drag of the cigarette, but he didn't respond.

"Goddammit. Tell me you're not thinking about *her*?" Stacey said, her full lips—natural, by the way, no collagen necessary—pressed together into an unappealing thin line. A straight razor of red slashed across her face. Not nearly as appealing as when she held them plump and open for his finger, or his cock.

"I'm just tired. I need to get some rest," he said. He dropped the cigarette into the bottle and relaxed back into the pillows, shutting his eyes. Stacey pulled the sheet up from the end of the bed and rolled over.

One of the benefits of possessing both money and power was that it immunised one against such base emotions as regret. Apparently, however, this miraculous effect did not extend to the time when Raymond White had murdered his wife.

He shook his head. No, he didn't regret his actions, but occasionally he found himself being rocked by a strange feeling to which he was unaccustomed. That gut twisting feeling that strikes just before something goes drastically wrong. It couldn't be Stacey—she'd never tell anyone about the hit. She had just as much to lose as he did in her reputation alone. But what exactly it was that kept tugging at the edges of his consciousness, prickling his skin with a nauseating unease, he couldn't be sure.

He took several deep breaths. In through the nose, out through the mouth.

He'd made peace with the decision itself long ago. He was free from the endless nagging and the perpetual grind of domesticity; freed from the ball and chain and her relentlessly ticking biological clock. He knew he'd gotten away with it, and Ray was free to enjoy all the pleasures of life that their five-year marriage had denied him. But it was easier for Stacey, who hadn't had to get involved. Easier for her, who hadn't had to look at the postmortem shots.

The police investigation was ongoing, but their focus on him had been short-lived. They had arrived at the house and taken him in for questioning. Through his profession as a prosecutor, they knew him. A good guy, reputable.

They had been thorough, but his alibi stood up to scrutiny. Years of legal work in courtrooms, viewing and participating in cross-examinations, paid him due as he went through his story over and over again for their benefit. He did it flawlessly, faultlessly, displaying all the expected measurements of bewilderment and shock.

It was what happened next that really sealed the deal.

They opened the folder to show him the photographs they'd taken at the crime scene—a typical cop tactic to check reaction, match it against possibility of guilt. The second that smooth, yellow file slid open and he saw for the first time exactly what he'd brought on his wife of five years, revulsion blasted through his gut. The reaction was physical before it was mental. He felt his lunch of fresh, grilled salmon roll acid up his throat as his stomach clenched, his eyes stinging shut. He staggered to his feet with his hand clamped over his mouth, pink flesh laced with bile and olive oil bursting out between his fingers. Choking for air, he heard himself gasping, "Oh Jesus, oh Jesus, the fucker—"

The fucker hadn't told him he was going to do it like *that*.

For a wild, desperate moment he thought he'd given himself away, but when he looked up he saw the looks in the eyes of the detectives, cold professionalism suddenly stripped, now human and warm with sympathy.

They closed the file quickly, sat him back down, brought him tissues, water. They faced him from across the table with hands folded and promised him, in slow, sincere tones, that they would do everything in their power to bring the perpetrator to justice.

That's what they called the guy. The "perpetrator."

Raymond didn't know what to call him anymore.

As he left the interview room, tears still wet on his cheeks, the female detective had placed a comforting hand on his shoulder. By then he was over the initial shock, and he had a clear moment to appreciate what a piece of work she was. Tight white blouse, sleek black suit pants. Very tidy. He'd had to think unsexy thoughts very quickly.

Dead puppies. Dead puppies. Dead puppies.

Dead—

No.

Now, lying beside Stacey, he pressed his hands into his eyes to block out the memory of those photos. He was glad he'd only glimpsed them, glad he hadn't been made to flip through them, spend time poring over them, exploring in detail the peeled skin and mutilated flesh.

He needed to sleep. The cases he had coming up would be arduous and lengthy. Late nights reading briefs in the office fuelled only by coffee and blow. He didn't have the time or the energy to keep returning to the corner of his mind that kept flicking through those red-glare images in some kind of macabre, subconscious slideshow.

One by one, he tensed the major muscles of his body and allowed them to relax, feeling the dead weight of his body sink into the mattress and the tension slowly ebb from his muscles.

Beside him Stacey purred softly. Even her snores were sensual, somehow. Within minutes he slept and dreamed.

* * *

It's a cold night but Raymond doesn't hurry. It would not do to attract attention. Beyond that, one of the great benefits of having money and power is that you no longer need to hurry to do anything.

He turns into an alleyway dominated by the silhouettes of big dumpsters and piles of trash. Stray lamplight glints off the stagnant, filthy water pooling among the dips and cracks in the concrete. Steam rises from a sewer grate midway down the alleyway, the odourless smoke of treated excrement. A whole river of shit, just metres below his designer shoes.

Raymond reaches into the pocket of his thick woollen trench coat and removes his cell phone. It's an old model, pre-smartphone era, with a pre-paid SIM card registered under a fictitious name. There must be no trace of the night's event.

He sends a new text message, a single word to the only number held within the phone's memory: *Here.*

From the mouth of darkness, he hears a beep as the message is delivered.

There is a sudden rustle and a shadow emerges from behind the furthest dumpster. It shambles forward, feet splashing through the pooled water, uncaring of the sound.

Fucking idiot. If he is such a professional, didn't he know how to be quiet?

Raymond hisses softly and looks over his shoulder. The rest of the street is void of people, void of souls with eyes and ears to see and hear, mouths to speak. There is only him and the shadow, splashing to the mouth of the alley where it stops, leans against the wall.

He cannot see the face. Somehow he finds that he wants to, that maybe he feels like he needs to. But in this game, that would be stupid.

"I hear you're looking to take care of a friend." The man's voice is hushed, but there is a hint of dark humour in it. The tone is slow, but alert. The accent is sophisticated, a contrast to the foulness of the black, the dark, the alley and the dumpsters with their collected gore of rotting trash.

"Yes I am. A lady. I have all the details and the money for you."

"So what did she do?"

"Fuck off. It's none of your business."

"It is if you want me to kill her for you. Those are the rules—take it or leave it. You want me to snuff some bitch for you, then I want to know why you want her dead."

The humour in the man's voice thickens as he speaks, and Raymond realises that he's being mocked. Mocked for being a white-collar yuppie trying to call his first hit.

Raymond doesn't reply. The silence closes around them, finding rhythm in the sound of water dripping somewhere further down, in the low rumble of cars gliding down the nearby roads.

After weighing his immediate options, he sighs.

"She's my wife. Justine. Let's call the reason "marital dispute." Are you happy?"

"Justine. Terrible name. The Marquis de Sade wrote a book about a woman called Justine. Did you know?"

The man lifts his head and a trace of light escaping from a nearby streetlamp momentarily illuminates his eyes. Bloodshot, glaring. Sharp with focus and intelligence, dark with indecent knowledge. The man moves forward a single step and extends a gloved hand.

Raymond reaches into his pocket and pulls out the envelope containing money, photographs of Justine and a guide through her expected schedule. He slaps it into the man's gloved hand. "Half the money is there. You'll get the other half when I know she's dead."

"Any specs on how you want it done?"

"No. I don't want to know anything about it until after the fact."

"So she's open range?"

"Whatever. Just so long as I stay clean."

The man laughs, a soft chuckle stuttering out the back of his throat. "You won't stay clean, mister," he says. "Not in your own head. No way, no how."

"You know what I mean. How long will it take?"

"Not long. You'll see. Keep an eye on the news." The man grins at him. A lifeless smile full of teeth. "A pleasure doing business with you, sir."

"Yeah. Sure."

The man turns, splashing back through the puddles he'd crossed before with the same chaos of sound shattering the stillness, then disappears behind the dumpsters.

Like a fucking rat. Has Ray just handed his future, his money, his chances of a perfect life, all to a fucking quasi-cultured alley rat?

It is too late now. He was one of the best, Raymond knew that. He'd found the guy himself, after all, after weeks of painstakingly checking through all the tips and lists of names available to him as part of client-lawyer confidentiality. He hadn't made his choice lightly. He'd just have to put it out of his mind and trust that this guy really did know what he was doing.

Raymond thinks about going home to see if he can catch Stacey on the 11:00 p.m. edition on Channel Four. His cock stirs, just thinking about her.

Now he just has to wait.

* * *

"Hey, mister slick lawyer," the voice oozed into his ear. He turned from his highball to see Stacey wriggling herself up onto the barstool beside him. If she had one flaw, it was that she was a little on the short side. When they'd first met face-to-face at that cocktail club six months ago, he'd made a show and a joke of picking her up every time she wanted to sit down on one of the high bar stools. Everyone there had laughed and said how cute it was. Even Justine, smiling tight-lipped as she sipped her tonic water, too stupid, too damn trusting to let herself see how much Ray enjoyed putting his hands on Stacey's waist, her hips, sometimes grabbing her a little higher for the lift so that he could see her cleavage come together just inches from his nose.

"You're late," he said to her, signalling the barman.

"Vermouth, straight up," Stacey shouted across the bar.

The barman nodded, his eyes nipping to and away from her as he got to work. God, how Ray loved that. In his head he called it the "made you look" game. Wherever he took her, nobody could keep their eyes off.

"So glad you're not the jealous type," Stacey said, fluffing her hair, smiling. "I had a killer day at work. The last thing I could handle would be some sort of ego war between you and whoever looked at me."

"Nah," he said, picking up his glass. "What's the point?"

She giggled, slapping his shoulder. "Although a *little* jealousy wouldn't hurt."

"Jealousy is for dumb kids who don't have the balls to believe they can keep what they've got." He smiled at her, a cold smile, one he'd already got her well used to. "I'm not worried."

"So that means you wanna keep me?" She put her hand on his knee, sliding it up and around to his inner thigh, where she knew he was most sensitive.

He pushed her hand away. "For now, I guess."

Inside, he was roaring victory. Grinning at himself. Backslaps all round. He was a winner, all right. What had he ever lost?

Beside him, Stacey wasn't looking like such a winner. "Don't be a dick tonight," she said softly. "I wasn't kidding about my day."

This, of course, was the slippery slope. This was when emotional bullshit starts tying knots around perfectly functional physical bonds.

"Jesus, Stacey. Me too, okay?"

Stacey's drink arrived and she took a small sip, grimaced. "I need to talk to you about something," she said. "About Justine."

He felt a flare of irritation, a jolt of rabid emotion. He reached over and grabbed her knee, squeezing tight, digging his fingers into the soft of her flesh. "Not here, you dumb bitch," he snapped. "Are you out of your mind?"

Wincing, she crossed her leg away from him and took a large gulp of her drink. "It's professional, okay?" she said. "Pro-fes-sion-al. Christ."

He turned away from her, squaring up to his drink. "Out with it."

"We got a tip-off at the news room. Your wife's murder wasn't just a murder. There's a tape."

His blood pulsed from hot to cold.

"Apparently it was all filmed and sold as a snuff tape. Our guy got hold of a copy. I was wondering if the cops had got in touch with you about that. We've had to share the information with them, of course."

"No, they haven't said a word."

"Uh huh," she nodded, "I guess they're still verifying the information, hoping to confirm it before they tell you. Trying to spare you the added grief, I suppose. It explains a lot, really, about the way the murder went down. Abandoned garage, body in so many small pieces. All that blood, all those wounds inflicted before death. We're going to do a spot on it tomorrow night. I thought you'd like to know in case the cops don't get to you first."

Ray's highball wasn't kicking hard enough.

"The technique is an emulation of Chinese slow slicing," Stacey said, talking to herself now. "Or 'death by a thousand cuts.' It's an old method of execution, made illegal in 1905. It was almost always enacted for public display. Except the Chinese could keep it going for days."

Ray put his head in his hands. Behind his eyes, he saw Justine's eyeless face, black holes streaming bloody tears. Her mouth a meaty smile of blood-painted teeth, her lips snipped off in neat lines of finely sliced flesh.

Stacey wasn't talking to him anymore. She was reciting the facts for her performance the next night. She was running through the data given to her, probably thinking about her wardrobe options as she did it.

"They often took the eyes out first, so the victim wouldn't know where the next cut was going." Stacey took another sip. "Or so our researchers tell me."

Justine. Fucking Justine. She was supposed to be forgotten now. He'd already put her in the ground, hadn't he? He'd already sold off that ridiculous redbrick house—along with most of her possessions—hadn't he? He'd already torn up every photo and scrubbed every memory, and here she was, set to make a prime-time return to drag out all the gory details of her final hours on this earth.

Slow slicing. It made Ray think of carving beef.

"So," Stacey turned to him, snapping out of her reverie. "I think you owe me a thank you. Oh, and an apology for calling me a dumb bitch."

He glanced over at her, the elegant arc of her professionally plucked eyebrow raised accusingly.

He sighed and ordered another round.

* * *

Raymond White, nineteen, walks Justine Meyer out of the campus theatre and across the empty parking lot. It's autumn, early evening, and the light that surrounds them glows orange through the drifts of dying leaves, everything around them caught in the glow of the sinking sun. Her blonde hair catches it too, rolls in the breeze, turns a soft auburn. She shivers. Smiling, she wraps her arms around herself, hiding the sharpening points of her nipples as he puts his arm around her.

"You were really awesome in that play," he says.

She shrugs, her shoulders tense under the weight of his arm. "Yeah."

"Come on, you know you were. If you want to be a big actress someday, you've got to learn to push your profile. That starts by learning how to take a compliment."

"I never know," she says, "if compliments are real. Do you?"

"Sure they are," he says. "Even if people are only saying it because they want something from you, it doesn't make it any less true."

She relaxes a little, hesitates, and then allows herself to put her arm around his waist. Her fist bunches around a handful of his shirt.

This is a girl too uptight to even open her hands, let alone her legs. This one, Ray thinks to himself, is the biggest challenge I've had yet.

"I still can't believe you're talking to me," she says, giggling. She sounds younger when she giggles. It betrays how little experience she really has. "You know, all through high school, no one really paid attention to me. I was too bookish I guess. Then I get to university, I'm in one play and now the whole world wants to be my friend. It's kinda hard to know who's sincere."

He stops, and for a moment she's ahead of him; for a moment, he has to grab at her shoulder, pull her back. Facing her, he forces himself to relax, he bends to put his lips to her cheek. What this girl wants, he thinks, is Romeo. What this girl wants is sweet promises and sweeping gestures. She's too cautious for backseat groping. She's too artsy for bowling alleys and drinking games.

She smells amazing. Like cinnamon and vanilla-scented soap.

Speaking into her hair, he says, "Everyone is sincere, when they're in the presence of beauty."

In his head, crowds go wild. He can hear the cheers, can almost feel the backslaps. An older girl, one less country fresh, would've laughed him into his car by now. But not Justine. Not her. So far it's like he can do no wrong.

Careful now, he tells himself. Slowly now.

"You know what they say about you?" he says into her ear.

She shakes her head, a stiff little movement that rouses a drift of perfume, delicate and oversweet.

"They say you're the prettiest girl in town. And you know what they say about me?"

She nods.

"What do they say about me?"

"That you're the one who's really going places."

"What could be more perfect?" he whispers, closing his arms tight around her, amazed at the sensation of the muscles surrounding her spine twitching spasmodically under her shirt. A thousand uncontrollable nerve pulses working away like piano strings at his touch, his words, his proximity. "What could be more perfect than you and me together?" he asks.

She laughs now, a sudden explosion of sound that makes Ray jerk back, that rings in his ear. Oblivious, she says, "You and me in a big, redbrick house, with lots of babies, and..." She stops, thinking. "And..."

"And you famous in feature films!"

"Oh, I don't want that," she says, suddenly serious, shaking her head. "I don't want to be famous. I just want to make art."

"All right, beautiful Justine, whatever you want. I'll do everything I can to give it to you."

Giggling again, she takes the step forward, puts herself back in his arms.

Give it to her, Ray tells himself to internal laughter, high with a sense of victory.

Got it in the bag.

* * *

Stacey staggered over to the bed, snaking her dress up over her head before sitting down heavily on the edge. Tossing her hair over her shoulder, she fixed her eyes on Ray. "So, Mr. White, do you have any comment on the suggestion that your wife's murder was filmed and sold as art?"

Grinning, Ray leaned in the doorway, watching her. Even half-drunk and dressed only in her underwear, she was a born TV journalist. It wasn't only in the quickness of the words, or her style of matching callous quips with revealing information. Giving her audience the meat and the sauce all in one simple bite. She had it even in the sharp patterns her eyebrows made, conveying seriousness, sharpness, sincerity. Saying *Yes, I'm sexy, but I'm a professional, too*. She had that delicate balance that any journalist of her type needs, that ability to grab at her audience with her looks, and then trap them there with her skills. She was smart. He forgot, sometimes, how smart she was.

"No comment, ma'am," he said.

"Oh, call me ma'am again and I'll get my gaffer to ram his mic up your ass." She grinned, melting out of her pose and back into herself.

Ray tried to harden his features, found that he couldn't. But just as he was about to burst out laughing, the Stacey he knew and loved to fuck vanished, and the mask came up again.

Stacey Bishop, hardboiled news reporter. Purveyor of the nasty facts.

"Mr. White, what kind of justice would you like to see delivered to the perpetrator of this monstrous crime?"

His smile was stiff. "No comment."

"Mr. White, tell us how it feels."

Before he could respond, she collapsed in fits of laughter, rolling back onto the bed with her knees up, kicking her legs in the air, revealing the strip of black lace that covered her snatch and then narrowed, disappearing into the warm, smooth cleft of her buttocks.

"How does it feel!" she shouted up to the ceiling. "God I'm drunk. That's such a rookie question. Nobody with the experience I have asks questions like that. My producer would freak."

"I won't tell." He laughed, quickly working his way out of his clothes, eyes fixed to the view she offered him.

"What should I say? I should say that in ancient China, death by slow slicing was nothing short of artistry. Utilising their fine knowledge of human anatomy and acupuncture points, they were able to keep victims alive for days at a time whilst carefully removing pieces of flesh without disturbing any vital arteries."

Ray felt sick. He stepped toward the bed, hovering over her. She put her feet down, opened her knees.

"You think it's artistry?" she asked him, reaching between her breasts to unclasp her bra.

God bless the man who invented bras that open at the front.

It must have been a man.

"*This* is artistry," he said, bending to run a hand over her belly. She had the softest skin he'd ever touched.

"Home grown, thank you." She smiled lazily.

"God's artistry, then."

"Nope, there's no God." She rolled away from him suddenly, reaching for the cigarettes by the nightstand, wilfully oblivious to the sight of his erection, now painfully tense, already swelling.

"They gave me the videotape," she said, looking at him, then looking away. Drunkenness gone, playfulness gone. Her bare skin, her body, just moments before offered to him so enticingly, now tense and shivering. Something in that flash of her eyes, like a small child on the verge of crying. "I have to watch it tomorrow."

* * *

Ray sat at his desk, his head in his hands, breathing deeply, slowly, in and out. The police had asked him to come to the station, had offered to come to the office, had tried to insist on speaking with him face to face.

"To be honest," he'd said, keeping his voice low and bruised, in the pattern of the bereaved and the exhausted, "I don't think I could handle dragging any more of this out. Please, I'd much prefer to do this on the phone."

The officer, Walsh, had told him to brace himself.

Brace yourself.

What does that mean? Head to knees, hands to feet, the body curled into a shell, into a knot, a ball of tense muscles waiting for blows.

Ray had sat down on the armchair in the corner of his office. He'd put his feet up on the glass coffee table and closed his eyes.

"The murder of your wife was filmed."

He knew that, of course. Take the cue to fake a gasp of horror. Now stammer incoherently until the cop talks again.

"The footage is being sold as a snuff film. In the underground, it's become a…well, forgive me Mr. White, but it's making a lot of rounds."

"It's popular, you mean."

Silence on the line, then a sigh. "Yes, it is, Mr. White. I'm so sorry.

We're dealing with a very dark underworld here, where people think this kind of thing is art. They collect snuff films along with kiddie porn and torture footage. It's incredible even to me. Some of the guys who watched it, they're not going to be sleeping tonight. If I'm honest, I don't know if I will either. The good news is that the footage itself gives us more to work with. I hope that's some consolation."

Ray closed his eyes, trying to fight off the return of the macabre slideshow that suddenly projected itself over his mind's eye. What came into focus was a shot of her thigh, the skin a marble white, run red with a delicate lattice of blood. The wound itself a wide gape of red dried black. The muscle severed clean away from the bone. That bone, a slit shaped like a narrow eye pressed thin between its cushions of flesh, blinded by the light it was never meant to see.

Open range.

Meant opening her. Meant ranging knives into the soft of her breasts, her arms, her legs.

"There's more, Mr. White. A copy of the tape was sent to a newsroom. I'm afraid they're adamant about their right to cover it. Most likely, there'll be some kind of interest piece on it on the news tonight or tomorrow. It's a…well, it's a pretty sensational topic, and I'm afraid there's nothing we can do to stop them from going ahead."

He'd ended the call then, on high notes of outrage and indignation, cursing the media and the bastard who'd treated his wife's murder like an art project. He'd thrown in an admonition, too, threatening Walsh to do his goddamn job and take down those responsible.

When he'd put the phone down, he saw his hands were shaking.

* * *

Justine had been in one film, an artsy short she'd done as a favour for a director friend of hers. One of the friendships Ray had quickly put an end to; he didn't want men who wore eyeliner and junk jewellery swanning in and out of his house. It didn't suit the image he wanted to present of respected professional and his cultured, arm-candy wife.

In the film, Justine played Virtue. She wore a long white dress, Roman style, and her skin was painted gold. She recited knotty poetry and then stabbed herself in the heart.

The blood was too orange, too bright, and when Justine fell to the floor, she forgot to stop breathing. She lay in a spread of stained white and electric blood, and he'd watched as her chest gently rose and fell.

When Ray laughed at it, she'd cried.

* * *

In the air-conditioned calm of his office, Ray flicked through the manila folder on his desk with one hand while he picked up his phone with the other and answered a call.

"Raymond White, speaking."

"Ray." The woman's voice was tight, gripped hard over the single syllable of his name. "Ray, I watched it."

"Stacey?"

"Yes, you fucking monster, it's me. I saw the video. I saw what that fucker—"

"You shut your goddamn mouth—are you fucking crazy?" Ray hissed and tossed the folder into his open briefcase.

"Crazy? You haven't seen crazy. I just saw crazy. I just saw its fucking face."

Crying. She was close to hysterical—he could hear it now. The tremor in her voice taking hold, distorting the sounds of her words.

"Ray, you don't know…you don't know what you did…"

"Stace. Baby, please. Let's not do this on here." He had to take control of the situation. Fast. "I'll come to you and we can talk about it. It'll be okay, honey. I promise."

Her words broke down into sobs, and he waited patiently for them to slow before he spoke again. Keep her calm. Don't rile her up. Then get to her as fast as possible.

Then, through gusts of breath she said, "I think I'm going to puke again."

He shut his briefcase with a loud click. "You hear that baby?" he said. "I'm packing my shit right now. I'll come pick you up from work. Just fix yourself a drink and I'll be right there."

The sobbing stopped abruptly, but he could still hear her breathing down the line. The whisper of her voice, catching on suppressed tears. And then, suddenly, total silence.

"Stacey?"

No response. No sound at all.

He took the phone away from his ear, and just as he did, she spoke again. He almost didn't catch it, but the words reached him in a clear, smooth rasp, as cold as the sweat that slid down his back.

"You need to see it."

The screen flashed: CALL ENDED.

His heart slammed against his ribs in a tense staccato, outpaced only by the thoughts streaking through his head. God only knew if the police had his phone tapped as part of the ongoing investigation. Unlikely, but he couldn't really be sure. At least the call had cut off before she could go into detail.

He'd told her not to watch the goddamn video, but would she listen? She was a nice piece of ass, but she was also great at what she did. That inner truth-seeker of hers would never let that video go unwatched, no matter how disturbing.

Ray resisted the cold fingers of panic digging around his heart. The last thing he needed was Stacey freaking out on him. She'd ruin everything. There are few things more dangerous than a hysterical woman with questions, or a journalist with an axe to grind. Right now, Stacey was likely both.

He had to get to her quick.

In thirty seconds he was out the office door and into the elevator. He hammered the button for the basement car park.

From here on in, Ray was winging it. There was nothing to do but get her alone and try and calm her down. After a few drinks she'd relax into his arms, and, after that, he knew all the right buttons to push.

The elevator door opened, and a minute later he was leaning out the window of his Camaro, swiping his building pass and thumping his hands furiously on the wheel as he waited for the roller doors to open, granting access to street level.

* * *

Channel Four had been a wild goose chase. When he'd arrived and asked for Stacey, he was told, "Ms. Bishop is unwell and went home hours ago. Rosie Spicer will be filling in for her this evening."

Hours ago? He'd just spoken to her. He told her he'd pick her up. What the hell was she doing?

His hands tightened on the steering wheel, his nails digging into the leather wrap.

He ripped the Camaro up through its gears as he swerved in and out of traffic. Even as he fought back panic, he felt a sense of relief at the sound of the V8 engine's throaty roar. Four hundred and twenty-six horses assuring him that he was going as fast as he could go. He took a series of deep breaths, felt his heart rate slow a little and some of the tension ebbed out of his chest.

Justine never liked this car.

Well, fuck her.

He was driving on autopilot now, weaving through the traffic like he was doing slalom. Cars flew past him, a rush of sound and a blur of colour.

Justine had always complained that when he pulled up in the driveway the noise shook the windows in their panes. A few years into their marriage she'd tried her hand at painting, and had thrown out whole canvasses she'd declared ruined by his thunderous arrivals home from work.

Ray remembered how he'd pull up at the old redbrick house and leave his baby parked out on the smooth curve of the white gravel drive, the engine ticking goodbyes behind him as it cooled.

He never knew, really, what to expect when he opened that front door. Justine—a typical small-town girl who never could get used to having money—spewed her fads and latest ideas of taste out on every wall and every floor. Carpeting up, carpeting out. Hardwood floors, marble tops. Minimalist, then Baroque, then seventies throwback.

He let her have it. He didn't miss the money, and by then he was spending so little time at home anyway that it hardly mattered.

Usually, he'd find her in the upstairs room, which she'd converted into a studio for her projects. Pacing the hardwood floors barefoot, reciting lines. Or sitting at the easel in the corner, her clothes smeared with paint. With the sun shining through the windows and catching the red in her hair, she was beautiful. Always beautiful. That, at least, was one thing that never changed.

"Take a seat, honey. I want to show you what I've been working on."

She'd seat him on a ridiculously overpriced and equally uncomfortable Victorian chair for the big reveal.

"*This* is art," she'd say, and draw back the screen to reveal her latest piece. If he was lucky, it'd be some life drawing sketch and at least he'd get to see some skin. More often than not it was some ridiculously bright and floral landscape that made him nauseous just looking at it.

Ray would make various insincere platitudes of adoration and then lead her to their room where she'd lie back on the bed for him with all the grace of a wet dishrag. Fucking her was like fucking a sex doll, all open mouth and blank eyes staring up at him. Nothing but a body of holes, everything else unresponsive. Such a shame, to have those hips and not know how to move them.

The way he saw it—the bitch had practically driven him between Stacey's thighs.

Stacey.

He was only minutes away from her apartment block. He floored it as he rounded the final corner, turning heads as the rear wheels kicked out and he fought to get the car back under control.

When he arrived at her building, he locked the brakes and came to a screeching halt. Smoke and the smell of burnt rubber filled the car.

Two floors up he could see Stacey's balcony door open, her shadow moving back and forth against the light. Backlit. Backlight. It reminded him, for a moment, of Justine, of the way she paced the studio when she was memorising lines for one of her plays.

He killed the association and headed to the doors.

* * *

Ray remembered coming home to Justine, the day he found her sitting on the floor of her studio, her head against her knees, arms wrapped around her legs. She was sobbing so hard he could hear her from downstairs. When he stepped inside the room and saw her, she turned her face to look at him, her eyes red and swollen, her lashes wet, black mascara running.

"What now, Justine?"

"I can't do anything. I can't do anything right."

He'd sat on the floor beside her, put his hand to the back of her neck. Her skin was hot and wet with sweat. She trembled under his touch, trembled with all the things churning inside of her.

"I can't even make you happy."

"I'm happy," he'd said. And realised, just as he said it, that he wasn't. Or if he was, it wasn't because of her, with her shitty art and immovable hips. Did he want to keep doing this? Every night? Returning to a woman he kept solely out of complacency? A woman who was once the best of the best in a smaller town, in a different time? A woman who was nothing here. A woman who meant nothing to anybody anymore.

Worse, a woman who cried to him about it, too dumb to see that he didn't give a fuck.

"I'm going to get old and you're going to get sick of me. You're already sick of me, I know. That's why you're always out, isn't it?"

He was out because he was seeing Stacey, of course.

Was that when he first thought about killing his wife? With his hand pressed to the nape of her neck, feeling the heat of her skin, the damp of her sweat, listening to her cry?

It was her own fault for making him realise that he wanted something else.

It was her own fault for opening his eyes.

* * *

The door was ajar. Ray hadn't spent much time in Stacey's apartment, preferring his bed to hers, but he knew his way around. It was a cavernous apartment, three bedrooms—each with an en suite bathroom all their own—and a large, sparsely decorated living room.

He found her sitting on the floor in one of the spare rooms with nothing but a white robe on, her hair loose around her shoulders. It was still damp from the shower and, without makeup, her face looked raw, sickly, like a slab of scrubbed pork.

"Should have just got a fucking divorce," she said.

"It wasn't that simple, baby, you know that," Ray said, sitting down cautiously beside her.

"What was it? You didn't want to share your money?"

"That," he nodded, "and I didn't want a divorce to reflect on my reputation. We discussed this, honey. We agreed. Remember?"

She stared at him blankly, her eyes glazed over, struggling to focus. Drugged. She must have taken something. What was it? Xanax? Oxy?

Good. Better drugged out of her mind than hysterical and unleashing shit storms.

He reached a hand out to tenderly wipe the line of drool that was sliding from the corner of her lax mouth. Before he had the time to react, her head suddenly jerked and her teeth closed over his finger. He heard the crack before he felt the pain, snatching his hand back as she grinned at him, his blood painting her teeth.

"You crazy fucking whore!" he yelled, scrambling away from her.

"You think that hurt?" she said. "All I did was crack the cartilage between the joints. That's easy to fix. That'll heal in no time. You know what doesn't heal, Ray?"

She was rocking back and forth, her face still struck in a lunatic smile. The robe fell open as she moved and he saw the firm slide of her breast; for a second, he remembered what it felt like to run his hands along those warm, soft places, following the contours of her curves.

For a second, the memory damn near repulsed him.

"What doesn't heal is having your nipples sliced off, then the whole of your breasts, then the skin that covers your ribcage. You know what that does, Ray? It opens two patches where you can see your own ribs and the muscles between them. To die all you'd need would be a blade, stabbing between those ribs to puncture the heart, or the lungs. That's all it would take and it would be such a relief, if only that were what was going to happen. But doing that would kill you, Ray, and they don't want you dead just yet. No, they still haven't got to your legs, or your arms. They haven't cut off your fingers yet, or peeled the skin off your cheeks, and they want to do it all while you're still breathing, Ray. They want to do it all so that they can capture the look in your eyes as it happens and call it a fucking art film. Make themselves money…"

Stacey's narrative had brought back the images, that hell show behind his eyes. Listening to her and knowing that she'd seen more than just the snapshots put things in a new perspective. He couldn't—wouldn't—imagine what she'd seen.

"And do you know what it feels like, Ray?" Stacey closed her eyes. "There's a level you reach where it doesn't even hurt anymore. There's a place you get to inside yourself where all you see is light, all around you, and when the knives come, it feels like heat. Like running cold hands under warm water. Do you know, Ray, that at the end there, before he went for the eyes, it actually felt…beautiful?"

The flat of Ray's left hand caught her hard across the cheek, and she collapsed under the blow as if he'd punched her. She lay still, her breathing suddenly smooth and even, her eyes closed. Her cheek bloomed into the pattern of five blushing fingers.

He looked at his finger, the cuts made by her teeth.

Fucking whore.

He stood, resisted the urge to kick her where she lay. Instead he stooped to pick her up and carry her to her bed. He'd stay here the night so he could keep an eye on her.

God knows what she'd do if he left.

* * *

Justine walks through the redbrick house, her smile soft, her eyes shining.

"This…" she says, running her hands over the satin cushions that smother the couch, "is art."

She takes Ray by the hand, leads him into the living room. She stops before an expensively framed copy of a Matisse, the bright colours and simple line figures clashing against the Baroque pattern of the wallpaper. "This…" she says, "is art."

She leads him to the bedroom, her steps silent on the thick shag of the freshly laid rugs. "This…" she says, walking up to the antique dresser, running her hands over burnished ebony, "is art."

Ray takes her by the hips, turns her around to face him. He pulls up her shirt, squeezes her breasts, watches her nipples tighten under the bruise of his thumbs.

"This…" he says to her, "is art."

* * *

The pain in Ray's finger woke him. He'd wrapped it tight around its neighbour with some bandages, but had loosened it before going to sleep, worried that he'd cut off the circulation. Now, without support, the crack between the joints that Stacey had opened with her teeth was pulsing hot flames, a burning swell that made his hand feel like a heavy, hot rock fixed to the end of his arm.

Getting up to find some aspirin, he looked in on Stacey. She was sleeping soundly, naked beneath her thick down duvet. She was dreaming the empty sleep graced by narcotics. A place free of torments, an unconsciousness almost as total as death.

Maybe she'd feel better in the morning.

* * *

Ray could barely drive with his injured hand and had woken up too late to go home and change his clothes. He brushed his teeth with his finger and went to the office unshaved. When he left, Stacey was still asleep, and he figured she would probably stay that way for most of the morning.

That little slut Rosie Spicer would no doubt be thrilled to fill in on Stacey's spots—Stacey had told him about their schoolyard rivalries before—but Ray figured it wouldn't make much difference in the long run. There was only one Stacey Bishop, and after a few days rest she'd be right back where she belonged, in front of the cameras and then in his bed.

He knew something was off the second he got out of the elevator and walked into the reception. He saw Melinda's eyes widen at the sight of him, then melt down into a gaze of sickening sympathy.

"We didn't think you'd come in today," she said, rising to greet him, her eyes flicking up and down to take in his creased shirt, his stubbled face, his badly wrapped hand.

"Why the hell not?" he asked.

"With the news…"

"News?"

Ray stopped himself. The news, of course. The bastards had aired the piece. Now it was common fucking knowledge that Ray White's sweet, little, failed-actress wife had been killed making the most popular film of her career. That the ceremonial carving of her body was the price she paid for fame.

The price that *he* paid.

"You should go home, Mr. White. I already cancelled your appointments for you. No one thought—"

"Why the fuck would you do that without consulting me?" He

struggled to control his voice.

Melinda stared at him, shocked, her eyes suddenly stinging red with the threat of tears. This he couldn't handle. Not another weeping woman. Not another fucking fragile female moment.

He left her gaping after him while he headed into his office, throwing his stuff on the desk and then lying down on his leather couch.

That was when the phone rang. Not recognising the number, Ray almost didn't answer it.

"Hello, Ray."

"Who is this?"

"I'm shocked that you'd forget me so soon, given that we're business partners."

"Business partners?" he said, and then he knew where he'd heard that voice before. It was thick with mockery, just like that night in the alley. He didn't even wonder how the man had got the number for his cell phone. "Listen here, you sick son of a bitch—"

"Why are you angry, Ray? Especially since I *executed* your requirements so successfully."

"Requirements? I never asked you to—"

"I fulfilled the task. You were clear that I had open range, no? I thought it was a good opportunity for me to incorporate it into my personal project."

Ray's heart boomed in his chest while his mind digested the perverse truth of the man's words. "So, what now?"

"Now? Nothing, actually. I'm just ringing to thank you for the opportunity, and to tell you how pleased I am with how our respective projects have turned out. I never imagined how pleasurable it would be, or how fulfilling. I found the entire experience transformative, not to mention, quite profitable. Whoever thought high art would be so popular these days?"

"You want to blackmail me? Then get about it, asshole. I'll report this call. First you kill the man's wife and attempt to blackmail him afterwards? You think I haven't thought this through? You think I don't have that angle covered?"

The man sighed. "I'm not after anything as mundane as that. I am, after all, a pro-fes-sion-al." The tone in his voice as he spelled out the word had an oddly feminine quality to it.

Pro-fes-sion-al.

Ray's mind raced. Stacey. That's how she'd spoken that word in the bar the other night. Ray's gut wrenched. Had this guy been there, too? Was the freak stalking him?

"Don't ever call me again, you sick fuck. You…" The words died in Ray's mouth. He swallowed hard. His throat was tight, his mouth tasted like ashes. He was starting to unravel, and for all his vast experience orating in courts of law, he couldn't think of a single thing to say. What was there to say to such a person?

"Oh, I won't do that. There's no need. I really just wanted to thank you and to ask if it was everything you wanted? I have the sneaking suspicion that you're getting a whole lot more than you'd bargained for."

Ray hurled the phone and it shattered against the office wall in a shower of plastic.

The office door opened and Melinda peeked in. She took one look at Ray's face and hurriedly closed the door.

Raymond White snapped his briefcase shut and reached for the keys to the Camaro.

* * *

"Stacey?" he called out as he stepped into her apartment. The living room was dark, lit only by a couple of lamps in the corners. He'd never noticed them before. He glanced around the room.

What a fucking time to redecorate. Things must be worse than he'd thought.

Gone was the chic, minimalist furniture, all white leather and glass. Where the Italian leather couches had sat previously was an antique settee and a pair of chairs.

He checked the spare rooms, which were still empty. Whatever fashion virus she'd caught hadn't yet infected her bedroom, which was great, but she wasn't in there, either.

He walked back into the living room and sat down on one of the chairs. The upholstery was soft but it was poorly cushioned. He ignored his discomfort. He should call her, maybe she was out at the bar or shopping. God, not more shopping.

He felt the soft brush of breath at his ear, but before he could react, a thick rope slid over his shoulders, pinning him to the chair.

"Take a seat, honey, I want to show you what I've been working on," Stacey said, in a sweet, husky tone.

Ray laughed, wondering what outfit or costume she'd be wearing, enjoying the tingle of fresh anticipation. Maybe she wasn't mad after all. If she suddenly wanted to go all BDSM on him he could handle that. Hell, maybe he even needed it.

Her hands were cold as they brushed against him, as she worked behind him, looping the ropes around and then pulling them tight at his back. She stooped to lick his neck, and as her hair fell he caught the scent of her perfume, delicate and oversweet. It made him, for a moment, think of dusk in autumn. The drift of dying leaves, the glow of the sinking sun. A girl trembling slightly as he puts his arms around her, the muscles beneath her blouse, beneath her skin, quivering.

Her tongue was colder than her touch, her saliva strangely thick. He could feel it congealing on his skin in a greasy layer. For a moment, he thought it burned.

And then she stepped around to face him.

She was dressed in a white robe, Roman style. Her feet were bare, her smile soft. Her eyes hard and blank and utterly void. The eyes of a fish, the eyes of the dead.

He jolted in his chair, felt the ropes force him back.

"Hi honey," she said, in a voice that was smooth and soft and slightly hesitant, with none of the husky bravado of Stacey's.

"Justine."

He didn't know how he knew. The certainty struck him in a live, electric pulse, crackling through his fingers, stinging all his nerves as he watched her move, watched her step, watched her fingers clench around the fabric of her robe in tense balls, coiling it up, lifting it over her head. She stood naked before him, with Stacey's rounder breasts and wider hips, stood staring out at him through Stacey's vacant eyes.

"Don't tell me I'm more beautiful in this woman's body," she said. "You told me once that people are sincere when they're faced with beauty. But I think the opposite is true. How can I make sure you'll be sincere, Ray? By destroying beauty, maybe?"

"Jesus." The prayer bolted from his lips as she smiled her soft smile, her eyes unblinking.

"The blood will be real this time," she said. "I promise you won't laugh once during this performance." She moved to an antique dresser by the wall, running her hands lightly along its surface of burnished ebony, then opening one of the drawers.

She pulled out the knife, long and flat, sharpened to a taper. For a moment Ray thought she was going to attack him with it, that she was going to kill him here, roped to this ridiculous fucking chair, but instead she lifted her breast and held the knife to it.

"This..." she said, "is art."

He saw her take her nipple between her fingers, saw her pull it until it stretched taut, saw the edge of the blade bite into it.

Somewhere in the depths of his consciousness he wondered how the seat of his pants had got soaked.

He heard the tight, wet sounds of severing, the quick back and forth of a blade moving through raw flesh, once, twice. When he opened his eyes again, Stacey's breasts, her beautiful breasts—the breasts he'd squeezed and kissed and pressed into his mouth—were eyeless sacks, bleeding rivulets of scarlet that raced down her body toward the floor.

Stacey was staring back at him, tears filling her eyes, those eyes suddenly soft and living. She only had the time to say, "It hurts," before Justine was back, closing out the light.

"Don't say a fucking word," she said, her soft voice suddenly hard and firm. And she placed the blade in the soft crease beneath her left breast.

"He did it like this."

Before Ray could close his eyes or turn his face, she moved the blade up with sudden speed and force. She didn't even need to hack. The blade popped through, and the weight of that bleeding sack—that eyeless mound of flesh and fat—dropped to the floor like a ruptured melon.

"You always told me that I look beautiful in red," she said, as blood poured down her body from the gaping wound.

Ray's stomach twisted suddenly, violently, and he vomited down his chest in an acidic choke that burned his breath and filled his nose with the stench of bile. Through the slime that coated his throat, he said, "Please. Don't."

He could see her ribcage. Fine white bones washed pink with her viscera. He could see them moving slightly, see the spaces between them expand and contract as she breathed. The red of her meat, engorged with blood, was so dark it was almost black.

The blade suddenly dropped from her fingers and she doubled over, clutching her belly, racked with hysterical sobs.

"Stacey!" he screamed, helplessly fighting the ropes, the chair.

She raised her head and looked at him with eyes like that of a child when she first sees the true face of life, bestial and leering. When she first learns that her mother and father can break her bones, that a stranger can pin her down and pull her legs apart, opening bloody holes she didn't know existed. When she first realises that there is flesh beneath her skin, and that there are people in this world who would delight to peel her apart so that they can see it.

And for the first time in his life, Ray understood what people meant when they talked about violations of nature, abominations—things that should not be.

"Don't be sorry," Justine said, pulling Stacey's body straight, seeing the words shuddering on his lips. "Didn't I tell you that, at the end, it was almost beautiful? Stacey will be there soon. She'll join me in that place where pain is like warm water poured on cold skin. She'll want to stay there with me, too."

Bending slightly, Justine retrieved the knife from the floor and pinched at the tense meat of Stacey's thigh.

"He did it like this."

This time, even as his eyes streamed hot tears, Ray couldn't make himself look away.

* * *

It was a long night vividly lit by a moving performance of tears and screams and scarlet disrobing. Piles of Stacey's body lay on the floor. Ragged scraps of skin and gobbets of flesh and fat leaked clear fluid through the puddles of blood that spread across the tiled floor. Sticky red puddles that had begun to soak the edges of the new Persian rugs.

At the end of the show the creature faced Ray with bloody black holes where its eyes had been. Its arms and legs were trimmed down to hard white bone that flew the flags of torn muscle, held together by tendons, ligaments and whatever indecent intelligence had hemmed Justine into them.

An entire night of screaming and begging had exhausted him. He was nearing catatonia, his fingers flexing weakly, his jaw opening and closing over unformed words.

As dawn was breaking and the show was just wrapping up, clean, new sunlight brushing against the windows, the thing that had once been a woman raised its blade once more.

"This time," it said, the bare muscles of its throat writhing as it spoke, "we'll do it the traditional way. This time, we'll start with the eyes."

ABOUT THE AUTHOR
JAY O'SHEA

Jay O'Shea is an award-winning author, vegan warrior, and part-time canine swim instructor who lives and works in Los Angeles. An Associate Professor at UCLA, she is currently studying the cognitive benefits of hard-style martial arts training.

O'Shea has written and edited several books on dance. Her essays have been published in three languages and six countries. Her short fiction has appeared in *Bartleby Snopes*, *Toasted Cheese* and in the anthology *Bloody Knuckles*. She has written a novel, *The Alchemy of Loss*.

A PIRATE'S RANSOM

JAY O'SHEA

There is an expression in your language: life is not fair. Well, death is not fair either.

The others were professionals. I accompanied them because I have some English. Despite their being sailors, and I a mere interpreter, it was I who noticed all that went wrong on this raid. I kept silent because I feared their ridicule. Had I worried about the large matters instead of the small, I might live still.

You have another phrase: done is done. Done, in this case, is most resolutely done. Yet, I retrace my steps. It is a false hope that this will help. I cling to it nonetheless, as a man thrown overboard holds to a raft although it only prolongs his suffering.

We call ourselves *badaadinta badah*, coast guard. What we are, in truth, is much simpler. Yesterday, we discussed the raid over a khat picnic. Abraham Abdullah is the leader, the one they call Old Boy, so it sounds like a term of respect, which it is. He talked as we sat and chewed, drinking 7-UP to kill the bitter taste of the leaves and smoking to occupy our hands.

Old Boy has a computer. Naturally. All the good pirate leaders have one. With the money that gets thrown around on khat and cars and pleasure marriages, I am surprised that funds remain. The curse of pirate cash, the land-bound call this. Old Boy is better about these matters. That, I suppose, is why he is the admiral and the rest mere sailors. In any case, the shipping charts are easy to find.

"It is simply a question of using this Google," Old Boy said. He told us a freighter was on its way. Everyone knows freighters are low and open and slow. Everyone laughed and boasted about who would be the first to board.

By morning, my hands twitched and my stomach twisted like the ropes on the side of the fishing boat we use as a mother ship. We left Eyl before daybreak, crammed onto the boat with the skiffs trailing behind. Fareed paced until Old Boy told him to stop. It felt too close on the deck, all of us clustered together, fishing lines tangled like so many snakes. The water did not feel close. The sun turned its surface into a massive, metallic sheet. Pirate season is the hot season. We can't work in the monsoons, and on the Horn of Africa we have only monsoons and heat.

We made way toward the Arabian Sea, a longer journey than before. I have worked for other pirate gangs; it is a job, this working as an interpreter. In fact, it is the only job that pays any kind of good money. But times change. Despite their bragging, they all knew the days of ships drifting past in the Gulf of Aden were gone. The warships patrolled now, sending us further out.

We traveled with five hundred liters of petrol. Five hundred is a large number. It is not, however, enough fuel. Not for a return to land. All pirate gangs travel this way—minimal food, minimal petrol, minimal water. What difference? If one ship doesn't arrive, another will.

We chewed from the old batch of khat to bring back yesterday's high. The acidity burned my throat, and the 7-UP was warm and cloying and did nothing to chase away the bitter taste that sat in my mouth like dread. My thoughts ran to ugly places. What if no ship arrives? If we send a distress call, who would come? Would the warships save us, we who terrorize the gulf and force them to carry out their endless patrol? Would the Yemeni fishermen, whose boats we steal? We could radio to land, but there we live on credit. We cultivate debt and resentment and little else. No one sails for pirates with no ransom.

Finally, the ship appeared at the horizon, heavy and long, like any other freighter. It was gray, resembling a warship in color, if not shape, its deck busy with smoke stacks and masts. Relief washed over me; no false information had appeared on Old Boy's Google. My worries were the product of a mind troubled by sleeplessness and khat withdrawal and the tricks the sea plays on unwary eyes.

The radio crackled. A series of blips followed, syncopated like the French hip-hop we play at the parties that follow a raid. Fareed ran his hand over his jaw. Old Boy strapped his gun across his chest despite our distance from the cargo ship. I chewed a stalk of khat, although it was stale and would do nothing. Old Boy gestured to me.

"It's Morse code," I said.

"Ridiculous. No one uses that anymore," Old Boy scoffed. The others joined in. Bolstered by day-old jitters and bravado, there is little they wouldn't have poked fun at.

A voice cut through the static. It was disjointed, hard to comprehend. Then it came clear.

"I die."

I looked at Old Boy. That much English he understood. He waited to see what I would say. We stared at each other for a long time. I glanced at Mohammed and Jamal to see if they heard it, but nothing registered. It was too hot, they had been awake too many hours, the ship was too close. Old Boy laughed again, tight, not big and full like it should be coming from a man like him.

"It's a distress call," he said.

The men slapped each other's palms, a gesture they learned from the American marines.

Did the voice really say *I die*? Maybe he said the engine died. That
would make sense. But an eerie calm ran through the man's voice. He
sounded as though he had already faced the worst and death came
as a relief.

* * *

Fareed threw down the anchor. We gathered our weapons and the
rope ladders. The men drew in the skiffs and jumped on. I stood on
deck, feet rooted like plants. Jamal slapped my back.

"What are you waiting for, Clever Boy?" They use this nickname
like it's an insult, which it is.

I jumped in the skiff. It rocked under my weight then shot off,
throwing me back. We approached the freighter, aiming toward its
middle, where it sat lowest. The motors rattled and, briefly, it felt like
we were heading toward a moment when everything would change.

The ship was empty.

A freighter carries freight. Cargo boxes stacked one on top of another, from the depths of the hold up to its masts. And a cargo ship,
like any other, has a crew. When we hijack a ship, the sailors move to
the deck, ready to fight or surrender. Usually it is the latter because
who would fight for a ship that is not one's own? Besides, everyone
knows we want our hostages alive.

Perhaps, despite the low morning light and our swift approach,
the mariners saw us and fled to their quarters. Or this could be one
of the ships we've heard about, on which the company stations armed
guards. The mercenaries instruct the sailors to barricade themselves
and they lie in wait. But guards on this broken, ancient freighter?
Never.

There was no crew, there was no cargo. It was that simple.

The vessel was quiet. Other than the complaint of the metal, it made no sound. No whir of the engine, no rumble of ventilators, no splash of water from the dischargers. Its paint was blistered from the assault of the sun, and the white lettering on its side was overlaid in dirt, words sullied by ocean air and debris. I saw it as clear as anything. This ship was damaged in some vital way. Drifting in the current, it did not move of its own accord.

I said nothing. The others knew ships better than me. They were fishermen before they were pirates, and they had worked in a real coast guard when we had one. They will probably do both of those things again if anyone creates a new coast guard, which they will, or launches another incentive to reform the pirates, which they will. And, of course, both those schemes will fall apart. Everyone will return to piracy and it will just keep going. On and on. Forever.

Jamal touched his gun barrel. Fareed and Mohammed scanned the navigation bridge. Old Boy turned toward us but didn't speak. They understood but no one said it aloud: let this one pass. There will be another.

"Throw the ladder." Old Boy never has to say this. The men fight to get the ladder thrown. After all, the first to board gets double pay.

Before I couldn't move when I wanted to. Now, I couldn't stop myself. I grabbed the rope ladder. I swung. It cleared the edge.

"Ah, Clever Boy," Mohammed hissed. I felt a moment's pride until I remembered I had to step on those twists of rope and up over the gunwale onto the deck we couldn't see.

I stepped into the space between boat and skiff, yawning like a ravine.

"Hurry up, Clever Boy." That was mere bluster. They said it because it was expected of them. They were in no rush to mount this steed.

I moved too fast. I put too much effort into clearing the gunwale and tumbled over its edge. The deck seared my bare arms. For a moment, I thought the sun had heated the metal to the burning point. But this was a brittle, shocking sensation, a cold so intense I was slow to recognize it.

My legs fought my attempt to stand. The flesh on my calf stuck to the frigid steel. It tore, bringing blood to the surface. If I moved again, the skin of my hands and forearms would rip open too. If I remained, the cold would overtake me, freezing me as I lay beneath the African sun. I braced myself and pushed the deck away.

When the others saw my head and torso, they shouted, voices weak in the open space. They made their way up the ladder because they knew they had to. I wanted to call out to them. I wanted to tell them to head for shore, although I knew they wouldn't make it. Or back to the gulf. Anywhere but here. But the words tangled up in my mouth. Fareed held my gaze as he stood. I longed to tell him of the dread I felt. But I would not admit fear among these men and, anyway, there was nothing I could name, other than the cold that wounded my skin and seeped through my sandals.

Old Boy was the last up. He didn't speak as Mohammed tied off the skiffs. There was nothing to say on this silent boat with the burning sun and the freezing deck.

I moved toward the bridge. I would find no mariners there. I knew this. But something called me, as clearly as if it spoke aloud. I opened the door to the navigation room. Cold air rushed past. If I had stopped to ponder it, I would have assumed one adjusted to cold as one did to heat. But cold is a different sort of force. It threatens in a way that heat does not.

I walked in before the others. I saw it first.

I come from a country that destroyed itself as the world stood by. I was born into a land torn apart by war and starvation. I witnessed its horrors. My cousins' eyes dull from hunger. Neighbors cast from their homes, walking until thirst claimed them, dead before they hit the ground. I have seen bodies torn apart by bullets and left to rot in the sun because no one dares retrieve them. I have seen barbarity that, I suspect, you can only imagine.

I should have been able to endure what appeared before me.

Corpses lay upon the navigation room floor. There were five of them, Westerners, white men. They were not crumpled in heaps like those struck down in battle. They had not dropped limply like victims of hunger. These bodies were stiff, but this is not what was strange. It was their position. They each lay in a similar pose, hands extended as though to repel something loathsome. Faces frozen in terror. I know well the grimace of fear. I know the expression a face takes on as a person falls in violent death, but I have never seen that look remain once life passes from the body. Yet, here they were, sneering so hard it was a cruel, twisted smile. And most bizarre, next to them, a dead dog, its lip curled, teeth bared. It leaned forward, haunches flexed, front leg raised, ready to attack, hesitating, trapped in that moment of horrified indecision—its terror all the more vivid for its animal realization.

I turned from the bodies and scanned the communication deck. The deck was cluttered with objects I didn't recognize. The equipment had knobs and dials, not screens and keyboards. There was no satellite phone, no VHF radio, only an old-style radiotelephone. One of the crew lay slumped before it, reaching for the handset the way a drowning man yearns for the flotsam of a wreck.

Without thinking, I touched his flesh. He was cold, his skin hard. The radio operator, like the others, wore clothes from another era. Wool coats and blazers, ties, the kinds of things Westerners wear, but wrong, dated in a way I couldn't name.

How long had these bodies lain on this ship?

When I was in school in India, I read of corpses on Mount Everest. Remains that would never decompose because of the cold. So that might be why these bodies endured for decades. Assuming a frozen ship adrift at the equator is an explanation of any kind.

Besides, we received a distress call. It came from this ship. If someone lived yet upon this boat, and he had made the call, he would have knocked this stiff body from its position. If death had truly been close at hand, he would lie here among the others, a new corpse, dressed in modern clothes.

I felt with a sickening certainty that it had to have been this man— this corpse from another era—who I had heard speak. And he had said clearly, "I die."

* * *

We made our way to the crew's quarters, Old Boy still nurturing the fantasy that we would find living mariners barricaded in their rooms. *You daft man*, I thought, *would the ship's hands leave dead people here? Would they tend to minor jobs as the freighter limped in the current?*

We circled around from the bridge. The sun was still hot, the deck cold. We entered a hall, dark, as we knew it would be. I hesitated, blinded by the sudden gloom. A screech filled the corridor. The others flinched behind me. There was no more swagger. Fear was our common state. Fear held us together.

My eyes burned and my gut ached. I searched my pockets for a khat stem. I had nothing. We had made our way through most of the stash yesterday. We chewed the remainder on the boat. My palms leaked sweat and my heart pounded. We would face the worst of our comedown—alongside the hallucinations of insomnia—caught on this cold, desolate vessel.

Metal shrieked again, shrill like the brakes of an out of control truck. I turned on my torch, shining its light onto one wall, then another. The hall was bare. I made my way down its length. At its end, a door stood open. Gently, following the list of the ship, it creaked on its hinges.

"It's the door," I said. No one answered.

I entered the room, steeling myself for more bodies, more expressions frozen in horror. The room was empty, no trace of anyone having spent months floating through waters rough and calm, circling the planet, this small space their world.

It was the same in the next room we checked and the ones after that. Vacant. Quiet.

"The crew is dead," Fareed said.

"The ship is ours." Old Boy tried to make it sound like a triumph. It rang as hollow as our footsteps on the deserted ship.

What good to us was a freighter? What use a ship like this, even if it wasn't disabled, its engine stalled or dead? What would we do with it? Sail it back to Eyl and sell it for scrap, as we waited for the SPF or the National Army to descend upon us?

This ship was old and, no doubt, assumed missing. The shipping company, should it still exist, would pay nothing for a boat it lost long ago.

A ghost ship yields no ransom.

Jamal suggested we go to the hold and search the storerooms for supplies. I wanted to object. Why would there be food, water or fuel below an empty deck? What good were provisions on a dead ship? I peered into the gaping wound of a hold. There were shipping containers after all. They lay cluttered, off-kilter as though dropped from a great height, the discarded toys of a giant. Enough to cast shadows, enough to turn the hold into a maze, but not enough to suggest any kind of order. That sprawling space filled me with a terror that had nothing to do with my certainty that it held no supplies.

"Find the engine," Old Boy said.

He was right. Our only hope was getting the engine started. And I knew, we all knew, we had to go into the hold to reach the engine room.

The stairwell was dark, its shadow deep. I struggled to see even as we turned on our torches. A shiver ran through me, and I wished

desperately for something to cover my singlet and sarong. If anything, it felt colder here. I wondered if I would die, wrapped in frigid
air. The thought was nearly a relief.

A whispering filled the stairway, rushing past like wind. I heard
voices but couldn't decipher their words. Were they speaking Yemeni, English, Arabic? I drove the question away. This isn't real, this
is withdrawal, sleeplessness. It doesn't matter what language they
speak because they do not exist.

The others' footsteps sounded a heavy bass, even though they
are slender men, even though they wore sandals. Light from their
torches bounced around in the shadows, their voices carried. Jamal
and Mohammed loud—as if their shouts were a protection—Fareed
and Old Boy quieter. *Follow them*, I told myself. But I lagged behind,
reluctant to descend into that pit.

I stepped into a pocket of warmth. Hot and cold ran alongside
each other down here, like currents in the sea. I wanted a chew so
badly. *Inshallah*, when I got off this ship, the first thing I would do
was get a batch of khat. Once I made my way through this, I would
sleep long and undisturbed. Then I would stop for good. I would remember this awful feeling and I would make certain never to endure
it again.

I called out for Fareed. My voice bounced back to me. In the darkness, I sensed how vast the hold was. My torch showed me hollow
compartments, catwalks and rows of alcoves, none of them familiar.

I was lost. The realization settled, hard and brutal. The hold was
dark and sprawling, cold surrounded me, and I had no idea how to
get out.

I ran. Without knowing, without caring where I headed, I darted
down one corridor after the next. The cold air burned my throat and
bile rose from my gut. I swallowed, pushing down the sick along
with my fear. I picked a direction, fore or aft, I couldn't determine. I

ran and hoped I'd find my way to the others. I swung my gun back and forth. My gun. They should call me Foolish Boy. What good is a gun in hunting things I have imagined?

I moved into a narrow hallway. It was warm. Relief rushed through me. Perhaps whatever horror filled the rest of the ship was absent here. Then I saw what surrounded me.

Heavy, dark piping cluttered the passageway. Its mass seethed. The pipes breathed as one and slithered around each another—a nest of mambas. An insistent hiss filled the hall. The warmth turned suffocating, sweat poured from my face and hands. My heart pushed against my throat.

I reprimanded myself. This was a hallucination, nothing more. I turned away and walked forward. When I finally glanced out of the corner of my eye, the serpents had become pipes once again.

The hallway opened out into the engine room and another rush of cold. I was almost used to the biting sensation now, although my skin burned where it had torn and my fingers were stiff. I cast my torch over the massive engine, as high as a small building. Ringed with catwalks and punctuated by ladders, the structure, with its dark boilers and heavy gauges, was decades old. It was also covered in ice.

I turned back. My thoughts slowed even as my breath came in jagged gasps. I stopped in the darkness, my every exhale creating a cloud of mist. My legs buckled and I slumped against the wall of a shipping container. Its ridged, cold metal pressed into my back. Exhaustion washed over me, weakening my limbs. I fought an urgent cry in my head to do *something*. What was it? Find the others? Yes. But what would I do when I found them?

Something approached. I sensed it before I heard it. And I heard it long before I saw its form. It wasn't one of the others. They would call out, they would shine a light toward me. Someone else, some *thing* else, was here. I heard its footfall, heavy, nothing like the patters

of whatever ran through the hold. Also nothing like the steps of Fareed, Old Boy and the others. The sound was solid, belonging to a
body well fed and muscular in the way of the West.

I flashed my torch in his face. The man—if I can call him that—
was bigger than me, as I imagined, body broad with flesh privation
never shrunk. Heavy clothes covered a body that no longer needed
warmth. White skin ghastly in death, thin lips blue, mouth caught
in its terrified grin, even as he was predator and not prey. His eyes
glinted with a dead sheen.

Hands touched my neck. Their cold was devastating, turning me
inside out, exposing my organs to a piercing frigid wind. Worse,
it showed me what I would become if I did not resist—dead and
caught on this accursed ship.

In a moment of hope, anger, or sheer animal resistance, I slapped
the hands away. I pivoted and ran, weaving through the pathways
created by the metal boxes, massive and looming in the darkness,
my torch offering only the dimmest light. Panic rose and fell in me
like breath. I wound my way deeper into the labyrinth of shipping
containers, hoping speed could save me.

Something caught my feet, taking my legs out from under me.
I slammed onto the cold floor. A fierce burning shot up from my
ankle. The footsteps behind me accelerated. My torch spun, creating
a mad dance on the walls and blinding me to the darkness. For a
moment, my thoughts, too, were obscured. Then I understood. I had
stumbled over a body.

I crawled toward it, reaching warm skin that cooled under my
hands. I ran my fingers over its face. I felt exposed teeth and taut
cheeks, caught in a grimace. Above that, a narrow face, a long nose.
Fareed. Oh merciful God, am I truly alone? Fareed dead, Old Boy
nowhere to be seen, what hope was there?

I pulled myself upright and fought the pain that raced through me. I limped down the corridor, still pointlessly clutching my gun. I hobbled through narrow corridors and tried to keep my footfall soft. I ignored the sweat coating my palms, the slamming of my heart against my ribs. I fled in terror but also because that's all there was. It was either run or die. I ran.

* * *

I came up into the sunlight, gasping as air, hot and cold, fought within me. Dark spots filled my vision. Once my eyes adjusted, I searched beyond the gunwale. The seawater stretched out uninterrupted. There was nothing but angry, bright sunlight and water. Our skiffs were gone.

A cruel turn of events, marooned upon this ship.

Something moved on the bridge. A man's shadowy form stood out against the glare. I pulled back. It was another sailor, a dead thing, hunting above deck rather than below. But no, the man's dark skin stood before me, its blackness a testament to life. Perhaps it was Old Boy. What a blessing if he yet lived. I ran forward, fear lifting with each step, ignoring the burning that shot up my leg.

The figure turned at the slap of my sandals. For a moment, Jamal's features were cast in shadow, and then they revealed themselves. No frozen grimace, but twisted nonetheless, eyes vacant and mouth wide with terror.

He raised his gun.

I held up my hands. As if a surrender could restore his wits, Foolish Boy.

He fired. I dropped against the edge of the bridge. Gunshot spewed out in all directions, pinging off the gunwale, striking the deck. This was my death, then. A life that could have been stolen by hunger, drone strike or disease would end here, on this icy ship. No gravestone to mark that I once lived, not even the small comfort of my father and sisters reciting prayers, my head facing Qiblah in the hope of redemption.

"Jamal," I called. "Stop. It's just me."

He turned toward me, but his eyes refused to focus.

"You can't kill them," I said. "They're dead."

The decision came suddenly, as if it was not I who made it. I grasped my gun and stood from my protected corner, turning in one motion. My gunfire and Jamal's scattered across the deck, indistinguishable. For a moment, it seemed like the outcome was pure luck. Maybe it was.

After a long volley of shots, Jamal's gun went silent. I kept firing. This, of course, is why we carry the Kalashnikovs. They discharge endlessly.

When I stopped, Jamal lay slumped against the bridge, singlet and sarong darkening, weapon dangling. The air was still. Blood dripped from his body and fell from the bridge. It struck the deck in a steady pattern. I backed away, the sound—the reminder that life oozes from a person—worse than the sight of his limp form.

Shot rang in my ears. I made my way to the bridge. The old corpses were gone. The navigation room lay empty, its cold a relief. For a moment, I was alone.

I sensed movement behind me. Through the window I saw Old Boy. He stumbled and reached forward, condensation gathering on the glass under his palm. The other hand went up in fear. Fear. I had never seen the man afraid.

He wove his way to the door. For a brief moment, I held onto the thought that he could save me. Then I watched as some foul thing extinguished the light in his eyes. I reached for the door, fumbling for its lock. It turned in my hands.

Old Boy stepped in, hands in front of him. His mouth tightened, his lips curled. He was turning into one of those things. Here, before me. I retreated until my back pressed against the navigation desk.

Old Boy collapsed to the floor. He lay still.

Something followed him in. No human form, neither alive nor dead. Instead, a poisonous vapor seared my mouth and nose. With it came a wash of images. Barbed wire fences, white men skinny in a way I thought impossible, in tattered khaki, trapped in cells like cages. Men with black hair and light skin burned buildings, homes and shops. They chased down people who looked much like them, except they were kids, market girls and old men. Soldiers descended upon prone bodies. Blood. Fire. More barbed wire. Men and women stood in their thousands, faded clothing hanging from starving forms. Bombs dropped from airplanes, a city in flames. A much larger explosion, poison shooting out in all directions. People falling in the street, children writhing.

My memories interwove with these pictures of a war I'd never seen. Pirates like me, traveling out in search of ships and dying of thirst. Capturing ship's hands and torturing them. Corpses and sandbags side-by-side on the broken sidewalks of Mogadishu. Children laid flat by bullets as they walked home. Farmers torn apart by landmines. Troops shooting from rooftops. American planes firing from overhead. My mother and my sister's children fading into death as they waited for food that never arrived. My father and I refugees, sailing empty-handed for a foreign land. Homes destroyed, wells drying up, a devastating hunger. Kids sickened by the waste that floated in our seas.

I am certain I screamed. My mouth went wide, even as the sound caught in my throat. I tried to push back against the wretched images that played before my eyes. Pain tore through my skin as it fixed into place, my mouth too large for my face. My sight dimmed and the navigation room turned murky. My vision filled with an ugly gray, full of the recollection of images too horrible to face and too terrifying to deny.

* * *

The ship lists. The waves slap its sides. The radio crackles. I speak, although I know you can't hear me. When you finally do hear my voice, you will be close.

I don't want to hurt you. But I continue to speak. I will bring you here. Like me, you will be filled with dread. Yet you won't be able to halt your approach. You will see what I have seen. And you will join me.

ABOUT THE AUTHOR
PAUL MICHAEL ANDERSON

Paul Michael Anderson is both an author and an editor. His stories, articles, reviews and interviews have appeared in numerous venues.

Anderson's "Survivor's Debt" was published as part of the monthly *One-Night Stands* series. His short story, "In the Nothing-Space, I Am What You Made Me," appear in the anthology *Qualia Nous*.

He is Editor-in-chief of *Jamais Vu – The Journal of the Strange Among the Familiar*, a magazine that features dark fiction, poetry, factual morsels, criticism and more.

Anderson teaches writing, frequently giving workshops on the mechanics and business of writing.

He has recently bought a very charming house, and Harlan Ellison regularly calls him "kiddo."

TO TOUCH THE DEAD

PAUL MICHAEL ANDERSON

People died, and then they received a serial number.

With bodies cremated, a handful of personal belongings became someone's earthly remains, new artifacts in the People's History Project, sealed and placed in metal alloy containers which were themselves stored in great underground Halls.

And if ghosts existed, if these people had souls, they resided in the traces of psychic memory resting like a patina of dust on their belongings, slowly eroding away.

* * *

NOW—

Gregor had stopped wearing the traditional Memory Coordinator robes months ago, so he froze when the seated duty guard outside the Dead Hall said, "You need the proper ID to enter this area, sir." The name on his badge—as shiny and new as the guard, Gregor thought—was Herbowitz.

"I have it," he said, nonplussed, fishing in his pockets for his card.

The guard eyeballed him. "It's against regs to be out of uniform."

Gregor pulled his card out. He looked down the empty metal hallway as he handed it over. "I don't see it offending anyone."

Herbowitz snatched Gregor's identification, face reddening.

At least he's someone who hasn't already heard about me, Gregor thought, and, before he could stop himself, the image of Amelia came to him—pretty Amelia, seven years old, her porcelain skin dotted with blood.

Amelia, who he'd met only in flashes of psychic memory.

Herbowitz was staring at him, his eyes suddenly wary.

Maybe Herbowitz wasn't so shiny new.

"You finished?" Gregor asked.

Herbowitz held the card by the corner, as if it might be diseased, and Gregor knew he'd heard what happened, how wild Gregor had been, trying to save a five-years-dead girl; Gregor sent a guard crashing through a glass door and broke the ribs of a supervisor.

Herbowitz touched a button on his desk. Gregor heard the hiss of air-locks in the Dead Hall's vault door. "I had to check." He wouldn't meet Gregor's eyes.

Gregor sighed inwardly and stepped into the cavernous Hall— more metal plating, more recessed lighting, regimented shelves filled with containers. He pulled the door closed behind him.

Why not just quit? an internal voice asked.

Gregor snorted—and do what? Memory Coordinators were bred for the People's History Project. It might not have always been that way—back when MCs existed on the fringes of a society that called them frauds, or insane—but it sure as hell was now. Some MCs could barely read.

Despair, his friend for the past three months, settled over him like a well-worn coat.

He stopped at the third aisle and pulled a long metal container. The placard on the front displayed only one serial number. He started to think how odd that was, then Amelia's face reappeared to him, and he shuffled to a desk in the corner.

* * *

THEN—

"Looks like a path to Hell," Jerzyck said, looking down at the crater.

Davis nodded. Massive concrete pillars poked into the gray morning air like the crooked teeth of a semi-buried monster. Metal girders twisted together like spliced wires. From where Davis and Jerzyck stood, two lengths of nylon rope had been staked, outlining a path into the dark center.

Jerzyck sighed, a roly-poly man whose hardhat looked too big for his head. "It's safe enough, though. Structural engineers checked it."

"There's nothing left but rubble," Davis said. "Why aren't we just clearing the rest of this out?"

Jerzyck shook his head. "Dunno. Don't think I wanna know."

"Why?"

Jerzyck studied him, as if trying to determine if he was trustworthy. "Gov'ment was out here Sunday. That's why we're here and why the bonus is so fat."

"What'd they do?"

"Marked the path, for one thing. It was four of 'em—two government types and a business guy."

"What about the fourth one?"

"Wore a fuckin' purple robe, like a monk from Vegas."

"The hell?"

"Swear to God. I got here as they was coming out and the monk was, like, 'I think these will last.' And everyone was nodding, like it made a lick of sense."

Davis lit a cigarette with his Zippo. The snap of the lid was particularly loud. "Shit." He looked at the rest of the site. Beyond the crater, the bulldozed and cleared remnants of the Martha K. Dixon FBI Building resembled any other jobsite, its border marked by tall, chain-link fencing, where he heard the morning rush hour heading into downtown Hathaway.

But everything was still and silent in here.

"Where the hell's everybody else?" he asked. "Two people can't do this."

"Thompson and Wilson are on their way," Jerzyck said. "Smith and Glasten, too." He glanced at Davis. "But I'm not waiting around. I don't want to mess with this more than I have to. Too many people died here. If any place is haunted, it's this place. Fuckin' mass grave."

Davis grunted noncommittally. He cared little about death, hadn't even attended his parents' funerals. He thought, but didn't say, *You live, you die, everyone else moves on. Even here.*

Jerzyck turned towards the loaded wheelbarrow. He handed Davis a paper air mask, a walkie-talkie and a clutch of canvas sacks. "Just get what you can. Ready?"

Davis pitched his cigarette.

Jerzyck started down the path, Davis following. It was steeper than it looked and the lip of the crater rose quickly.

They passed blocks of concrete triple their height, their cracks wedged with wires, broken bricks, busted tiles. They flicked on their headlamps. It didn't help much. The sky above was a jagged gray line.

The path split at the end of the staked rope. Jerzyck took the right, which seemed to rise a little, leaving Davis with the lower path.

Davis started down, treading carefully over debris. Up ahead, he spied something small and dusty-red. He picked it up—a novelty pair of Minnie Mouse sunglasses. An arm and lens were missing. He glanced behind him. The end of the trail rope was barely ten yards away.

Maybe this'll be easy after all.

He turned back to the grit-covered glasses. He imagined this in someone's cubicle, a memento from some family trip. A personal touch in an impersonal environment. Maybe the owner had—

Davis shook his head. The owner was dead and gone.

He dropped the sunglasses into his sack.

* * *

NOW—

Gregor set the sunglasses in the container and pulled the recorder studs away from his temples.

Just what he'd expected—a flat flash of memory, almost two-dimensional in its unreality: faint screams, black smoke, a faint vibration as the floor lost support. The bright doorway Gregor imagined whenever his mind picked up psychic energy had barely opened. The artifact was too damn old.

He'd been working for three hours. He should've taken a break by now—it was protocol—but to do what? Sit in the corner of the breakroom while the other MCs ignored him?

He checked the screen of the memory recorder, a tiny plastic rectangle with rounded edges, and saw that everything had saved to the People's History's central data cores.

Did anyone bother to check these things? Pondering the question too much was apt to depress him.

He looked at the single serial number on the container and, curious, pulled the touchscreen from the wall. He tapped the number in and the screen flashed. A file appeared, bearing the title HATHAWAY BOMBING - AUGUST 6, 2018.

Gregor whistled. That was over two hundred years ago.

He scrolled through the file, an ancient PDF document: On August 6, 2018 a terrorist bombed a Federal Bureau of Investigation office—*central government law enforcement agency*, the touchscreen automatically translated—in Hathaway, Pennsylvania—*later absorbed into the Sprawl mega-metropolis in 2156.* There were 356 people killed. Early members of the People's History Project scavenged remaining personal items.

Gregor set the touchscreen back. That many people dying, under such traumatic circumstances—how strong their energies must've been. The artifacts would've been practically screaming back then.

Wait. If that many people died, shouldn't there be more than one container? Something that big should have an entire aisle.

He stopped himself. They probably had gotten through most of the artifacts, but, as the People's History Project grew and the rituals of death became less about cemeteries and funerals and more about creating links in the great chain PHP was forging, the remaining artifacts had gotten lost in the shuffle, winding up down here. The average lapse time between gaining possession of an artifact and when a Memory Coordinator accessed it was five years. Two hundred years ago—

When was the last time anyone had touched these things?

He thought of Amelia. How real that girl's final moments had been; he'd smelled the moist concrete, felt the wet air.

He couldn't have been the only MC who felt something when accessing psychic energy—maybe not as extremely as him because it'd been a murder in a time when murders were incredibly rare, but something.

Gregor shook his head. He knew MCs didn't feel what he now felt. It was a job—push a button, pull a lever, record the last moment of someone you've never met.

Why me? he thought, putting the temple-studs back on his head. *Why do I have to be different?*

Not for the first time he wished he hadn't handled Amelia's artifact, which had been a handful of colorful barrettes. If he hadn't handled them, he wouldn't be here, forgotten in a room full of forgotten things.

But then he wouldn't have known Amelia, and that was its own bitter fruit.

He pulled the next artifact—half of a wooden nameplate and closed his eyes.

* * *

THEN—

The nameplate broke in half when Davis tried pulling it out of a wedge of rock. It toppled to the ground amidst a shower of grit.

Fuck it, he thought, bending over to pick up the busted nameplate and felt someone rush by behind him.

Davis jumped and spun.

His headlamp picked out sharp and irregular walls and the meandering, rubble-strewn path.

But he'd felt the passage of air, heard the harsh pant of breath.

He shook himself. He was alone down here. Jerzyck was in some other portion of the crater—he imagined the supervisor's path was wide as a freeway and better lit—and no one was stupid enough to think they had the experience to go traipsing around.

Then why was the hair on the back of his neck standing up?

A burst of chatter erupted around the corner, like a group of people talking at the same time. It quickly faded away.

"Goddammit," he muttered and climbed around the rubble until he reached the corner.

The path was empty, of course. The mound of rubble he was on petered out, became the tilted, busted tile of a sub-basement floor.

"Too many people died here," Jerzyck had said. "If any place is haunted, it's this place."

Well, you're a dumb fuckin' Polack, Davis thought, wiping the sweat from his brow. *So I don't expect much.*

"What I care about is my bonus," Davis had said. "No ghoulies or ghosties or long-leggedy beasties. Just sacks of junk and a nice nut in my account."

He waited for more phantom footsteps, more chatter, but nothing came. Because nothing would.

He continued climbing, ignoring the way his heart pounded.

* * *

NOW—

"Goddammit!" Gregor yelled, and threw the old, cracked wedding photo. It hit the cubby's back wall and the glass shattered.

He stared at it, a dull headache throbbing in the center of his skull. His eyes dropped to the MR and he read the screen: NO RECORDING MADE.

Of course not. Any residual psychic memory had long since faded away. The people behind the photo were long gone, with no one left to notice.

What was the point if no one remembered or cared? No one looked at the memory cores. Why not just incinerate the belongings like their owners? It was all awful and, what was somehow worse, he hadn't even been aware of it until recently.

And look at the reward for my enlightenment.

On impulse, he reached into the container and pulled out the red sunglasses. He cupped them and closed his eyes, striving to open the mental doorway.

He remembered the last memory, but got nothing. He had the memory of the memory.

The flash was gone. He'd caught the bare residuals just before—pardon the pun—it had given up the ghost. There was no set length of time for how long an artifact's psychic energy would remain; it mostly depended on how traumatic the death was.

Two centuries was a long time.

Like vultures, his thoughts circled Amelia.

Gregor had no idea who Amelia was when he'd picked up her barrettes; he'd been thinking of upgrading his vidcom plan.

But all thoughts were wiped away when he'd closed his hands over her barrettes. He hadn't even had to open his mind. The psychic energy was right there, and—

—he feels the slick condensation on the concrete floor. The air is moist, and each hot exhale beads before him. It smells like a monkey house in here. He looks into the corner and there's Amelia, cowering and shaking. She's been crying ever since the BADMAN—as she thinks of him, and Gregor knows automatically—took her and she can't seem to stop. The heavy steel door opens and he and Amelia flinch as one as an oblong rectangle of dirty yellow light falls on the floor. The BADMAN comes in, his work boots clumping, his huge fists swinging at his sides and Gregor, he, he tries—

Gregor closed his eyes as they grew wet.

And was she still there, in those barrettes? He thought so; her death was too brutal, too fresh. Locked in a container in a busier Hall, Amelia's last moments continued on, ever so slowly eroding away.

And no one would notice. Since Gregor had pulled the psychic energy, there was no reason for any other MC to touch it.

He covered his face while the rows of artifacts looked on.

* * *

THEN—

The voices began as a groundswell, rising up along the twists and turns behind him and, before he could stop himself, he was turning, ready to yell—at the phantom voices, at himself. As he did, his right foot plunged into a hole in the rubble.

Time seemed to hang for just an instant, and a single thought shot across his mind—*I can't believe I just did that*—before his ankle snapped. A hot, galvanizing pain seized his leg. He screamed and fell.

He landed hard, bounced, landed again, and it felt like his ribs exploded. His air mask was torn away and the wind promptly knocked out of him. He heard his ribs break like kindling. His temple hit a rock, and black stars exploded across his vision.

He came back slowly, feeling the rough surface of concrete, the cool touch of steel. He raised his head and a sledgehammer of vertigo smashed his skull. His mouth was full of blood.

He began the slow process of turning himself onto his back, a part of him knowing that was a bad idea and the rest not caring. His helmet was still on, thanks to the chin-strap, but the light was cracked and flickering. He was coated in grit and blood, and his right leg looked like it'd grown two extra joints. Shock was already settling in, taking away the brunt of the pain, leaving instead a jabbing, burning sensation. He would've preferred the pain; it would've sharpened his mind, which wanted to fog over.

He groped for his walkie-talkie, but found only the clip on his belt. It'd been smashed.

"Fuck," he said through gritted teeth. He coughed out blood.

He rested his head back and tried to calm himself. It wouldn't help to panic. Not at all.

And that was when he heard approaching footsteps.

* * *

NOW—

"C'mon," Gregor whispered, "c'mon."

He hunched forward, holding a set of keys. Sweat coated his face. Veins throbbed at his temples. Other objects—wallets, money clips and hunks of plastic with words like "Verizon" or "iPhone 5" imprinted on them—lay scattered around him, their energy gone.

He opened his mind and focused all his mental faculties at the artifact. There had to be *something*.

The bright doorway in the darkness opened slowly, and Gregor launched his mental assault at it, pulling and wrenching and clawing and—

—he's watching a man—Roger Herring, forty-three, a little portly—running down an office hallway filled with black smoke. His shirt was charred, his face burned red, his eyes as empty and terrified as a hunted animal. Gregor can smell his sweat and fear, hear his panting, the slap of his shoes on the tile—

—the doorway in Gregor's mind slammed closed. Vertigo spun through him, rocketing him back into his chair.

He slumped, panting. His migraine felt like a caged bull slamming its meaty shoulders against the sides of his skull.

I had it, he thought.

And look what it did to you, the interior voice said.

Gregor raised a hand to his upper lip and his fingers came away bloody. His nose was bleeding. Not a lot, but enough that if things were normal he'd go to the clinic. If he had a mirror right now, he thought his eyes would appear bloodshot.

Hemorrhage. The word floated up from his years of training in the Academy.

"Does it matter?" he said. His words were slightly slurred.

He set the keys down. Roger Herring. Killed during the Hathaway Bombing, August 6th, 2018.

I remember you. How long had it been since anyone had done that for Roger Herring?

He pulled the final object from the container—a palm-sized metal rectangle with ZIPPO faintly etched on the side. There was nothing immediately there, no easy flash. This was either almost dead or damn near it.

I don't care, Gregor thought, mentally pressing down on the object. Lightheadedness smacked him. Someone needs to see these people.

Even if it kills you? the interior voice asked.

He ignored the voice and pushed at the artifact, willing it to give up its residual energy. Fresh blood flowed from his nose, leaving its hot, salty taste on his lips.

* * *

THEN—

Davis tried sitting up and his chest burst into fiery agony as his broken ribs moved. He spasmed and retched, spewing blood. His head was full of angry wasps.

He collapsed, breathing shallowly.

He couldn't hear footsteps any longer.

There weren't any.

He tried looking up the path. It was like looking through a window smeared with Vaseline, bordered with black.

Wonder if Jerzyck will find me, he thought. *Where the hell is that superstitious son of a bitch? It's all his fault, saying this place is haunted.*

He shook his head, or thought he did. Jerzyck didn't matter. He was alone and dying.

The longer he laid still, the more the agony faded. A great lethargy stole over him. His eyelids begged to close, just for a moment.

I'm dying where a few hundred people did. But those people had done it together. He was alone. He—

Some remnant of his consciousness rose suddenly and he forced himself to scream. All he managed was a wet gargle, but it awoke the pain in his chest, which made it easier to think.

Is this how it is? Just confused and stupid and fading away?

Yes, it is, the interior voice said, somewhat sadly. It was what he'd always thought, he realized, without ever really thinking it. It was how his parents had died, his mother from cancer and, not long after, his father from Alzheimer's. His sister had said neither knew who she was at the end. They hadn't known each other.

He saw movement and he strained to see it. They appeared to be people walking, but he couldn't tell gender or age, just shapes.

"Ya..." he said with his numb mouth. "Ya...rescue?"

The walkers paid him no mind.

'Cause they're not there. Just Jerzyck's... He tried thinking of the word, and, still thinking—

* * *

Gregor poured every ounce of himself into the object, forcing whatever residual spark remained into a brighter psychic flame. Dizziness grew more dominant even as it faded, as everything faded. The feel of the lighter became faint, fainter, gone. Gregor bore down—

—and blinked to find himself standing on a hillside composed of rubble and metal, with walls of the same towering over him.

A man, broken and covered in blood, sprawled on the debris. He gargled out blood, then winced. When he relaxed, he looked at Gregor, his eyes narrowed.

Gregor staggered back into a wall. *He's looking at me.* But that wasn't possible. This was 200 years ago.

His fingers splayed against the rock behind him and he felt its rough solidness. What was this? It made what he'd experienced with Amelia seem like a vague daydream.

"Ya…" the man said and, like a switch had been thrown in Gregor's head, he knew who the man was: Jerry Davis. Was he speaking to Gregor? "Ya…rescue?"

Davis's eyes were slowly opening, slowly losing focus. His face relaxed and, in the center of Gregor's head, he heard Davis's final thought: *'Cause they're not there. Just Jerzyck's…*

Jerry Davis died trying to think of the word ghosts.

And nothing changed.

He touched the wall, himself. Still solid, still present.

What *was* this?

"I'm still here," Gregor said aloud.

Typically, at the end of the final moment, the world as the MC saw it went dark, the doorway closed and the MC pulled the studs from his temples. Something like this did *not* happen.

"But it did," Davis said. Gregor jerked. Davis pushed himself into a sitting position against the wall. His eyes were sharper than they'd been an instant before. "Is this what you wanted?"

"What happened? Am I really," Gregor gestured vaguely, "here?"

"Your consciousness merged with the remaining psychic energy on the Zippo lighter, amplifying it. You threw everything you had at it and this is the result. You are the first Memory Coordinator to go all in, as the saying goes."

"How do you know all that? You died two hundred years ago!"

Davis's face never changed, but, for all of that, he looked at Gregor as if Gregor were simple. "Jerry Davis died two hundred years ago, but the energy remained and whatever energy it has merged with you just as you merged with it."

"You're not Jerry Davis?"

"I am and I'm not," Davis said. "I'm the residual. The ghost."

"And you've been around all along?"

"Not for much longer," he replied, and the sky darkened, throwing the narrow passage into deep gloom.

Gregor recoiled from the wall as the feel of the stone changed, become somehow artificial, almost plastic. "What's happening?"

Davis's face was lost beneath the flickering glow of his headlamp. "The last of the energy's giving out. You gave it a shot in the arm, but you aren't in tip-top shape." He heard the shuffle-rumble of Davis moving. It sounded like a recording of a recording of a recording. "Come here. You deserve a rest."

Gregor did, his legs slightly numb. He felt for Davis's shoulder, and when he touched fabric—*like paper*—he sat down. "What happens now?" he asked. The details of the rocks visible in the glow of Davis's lamp were softening, disappearing at the edges. The feel of solidity beneath him was fading.

"We're going," Davis said, then sighed. "It's the end."

"For me, too?"

Davis didn't answer, which was answer enough.

"I just wanted to see the people," Gregor said. "Feel them for what they were instead of what I and the others made them."

"I know," Davis said, and his voice grew distant, as if he were walking away. The darkness sucked the life from his headlamp. "And I thank you for it, as I'm sure Amelia and Roger and the others would."

Gregor couldn't feel the ground beneath him. The light softened further, becoming gray, then winked out.

Just before the darkness took him, Gregor felt Davis's hand on his. And then that was gone, too.

* * *

Security found Gregor's body the next morning, Jerry Davis's Zippo in his hand.

According to clinic doctors, he died of massive cerebral hemorrhaging.

All the artifacts Gregor used were resealed and put back on the shelf.

Gregor's body was cremated, of course.

Like other Memory Coordinators, he lacked many personal belongings. Because of this, his Memory Coordinator identification card was sealed.

When it was finally unsealed, seven years later, the Memory Coordinator handling it reported a weird doubling in the psychic energy. He told his supervisor that, instead of one mental doorway—the way he imagined his way into the core of an artifact's energy—he saw two, superimposed over each other, with one brighter than the other. However, he caught nothing but darkness beyond the doorways and a queer sense of emptiness.

The supervisor, concerned, gave the MC the rest of the week off. Too much strain, apparently. The poor son of a bitch was crying when he came out of the flash.

Gregor's identification card was resealed and never opened again.

ABOUT THE AUTHOR
STEPHEN GRAHAM JONES

Stephen Graham Jones is the Bram Stoker Award®-nominated author of twenty novels, five collections and more than two hundred short stories. Jones has been named a Shirley Jackson Award finalist. He has won the Texas Institute of Letters Jesse Jones Award for Fiction, the Independent Publishers Awards for Multicultural Fiction and an NEA Fellowship in Fiction.

Jones recently published the single-author collection *After the People Lights Have Gone Off*. The novel, *Floating Boy and the Girl Who Couldn't Fly*, was written under the pseudoynam P.T. Jones and is a collaboration with Paul Tremblay.

Jones likes hackysack and slashers and hair metal and old trucks.

YOU ONLY DIE ONCE

STEPHEN GRAHAM JONES

So, my boyfriend's what I think they call a "scabhead."

He wants to keep on, like, kissing and stuff, but I don't know.

If he just had cigarette breath or something, that'd be one thing. But flames don't even work here. I mean, you'll see a candle on the table by the open door of a cafe sometimes, but its flame, it'll be this flickering blackness.

Anyway, I think Josh has maggots too.

It's not his fault—we *are* dead, I'm pretty sure—but, where maggots are involved, it's not about whether you meant to have them or not. It's about if I can see them at the corners of your mouth sometimes.

You're not fooling me, Joshua.

I can't just leave him at some corner watching the streetlight click either, though. Not because I love him or anything—*please*—but because that thin bone right behind your ear, that if it gets infected then you might as well stick a blender in your brain and turn it on. That bone on Josh, it's got kind of a white glow to it now. On both sides.

I don't know what it means. I can't even imagine what it could mean. I wouldn't have ever even seen it except, when we first landed here and those things were in the sky, I did what you do: dove for the basement, dragging Josh by the collar.

Down in that moist darkness, Josh cranked his head up to watch the sound of footsteps crossing the wood floor overhead, and I saw the glow from the back of his head.

I cupped my hands over it, held my breath. After a while, the footsteps crossed back, left by the front door.

I was crying by then. I hit Josh with the side of my fists, but it was really more of a hug.

Josh just looked at me like he would a utility pole, or graffiti in another language.

I guess some of us, we come through as ourselves. Others, they bring in the corruption from the other world.

Josh swallows the maggots down when he thinks I'm not looking.

The skin behind his ears, it's warm.

* * *

The reason I know Josh is a scabhead is that that's what one of the women at the edge of town called him.

What I call her is an inkfoot.

I think it's a form of suicide, what they're doing out there.

Those things in the sky? There's something about their shadows. The people at the edge of town, their new religion tells them that if they can run for twenty steps in a single thing's inky shadow— they're so black they're blue again, like in a comic book—then that shadow will become a trapdoor they can fall through.

I like to watch them run.

Josh, he watches the things in the sky instead. I don't know what they look like to him.

"You killed us, you know," I said to him once, out there.

He just kept watching the sky.

The people who run out there, I've never seen any of them get more than sixteen steps in a single shadow.

The time that happened, I was holding my breath.

I was waiting.

* * *

The way you get here is you're suddenly standing in a closet, and it smells exactly like the closet you used to hide in at your grandmother's house, or your uncle's—wherever it was you played hide-and-seek best.

You can't hear it, but outside there's the distinct sense that someone's counting you down.

When you open that door, it's not onto the hallway that should be there, but into another closet.

The smell is all different. Then you get it: that time you took too many at that one party and went and hid in the closet to call your dad and say you're sorry, but fell asleep instead, woke the next morning, stumbled out into a kitchen of people who didn't know your name but were happy to see you anyway?

This is that closet.

Stumble out of it again. Not into a strange kitchen but into a closet that's dusty, like a vacuum cleaner died in here. Outside, in what you are suddenly sure is a bedroom with a hardwood floor and white curtains gone yellow with nicotine, somebody's sleeping.

This is when I tried to go back, when I felt the wall behind me for a doorknob, because I didn't belong here.

My grandfather, when they found him, he'd been dead for eight weeks. In his bed.

He never went into his closets anymore, by then. Just one pair of clothes, and the closets had too many photo albums in them anyway. And shoes of children long gone.

Instead of finding a doorknob when I reached back, I found a hand.

Josh. He was just standing there.

"What happened?" I said into his chest.

It was dark, so there was probably a fly crawling across his eyeball or something, for all I know.

And then my grandfather's slippered feet were scraping across the floor.

He'd heard us.

I closed my eyes, screamed, spilled us out the door to rush for the hall and the front door and the porch and the yard and the driveway and the world we used to know, that we could still live in if we could just find it. But where we fell out into, it was the loft over a bar nobody was in.

I nearly fell over the railing but had Josh to hold onto. My dead-weight boyfriend.

The reason he's a scabhead, it's because the headliner of his Monte Carlo, it scraped all the hair and skin off up there after he'd locked his elbows against the steering wheel.

That's the way inertia works: he couldn't go forward, so his arms pendulumed him up into the maroon roof.

The other way inertia works, the way it works best, really, is if you're a passenger, one not wearing a seatbelt. One about to say something funny that you now can't remember. But it's right there on your tongue, wriggling and unborn.

* * *

What I kept doing at first—what anybody would do—was go back to that first bar.

Right?

I would hold Josh's hand, pull him up the rickety ladder and we'd try every door up in the loft—all *two* of them. Because this had to be a mistake.

The first door opened onto a closet that was just a closet.

The other was just a spare door someone had stashed up here. It was leaned against the wall.

Still, I tried.

My handprints were in the dust on the rail, from our first day.

Since nobody was ever down in the bar smoking and drinking, then this dust, it wouldn't be powdered skin, would it?

Then where did it come from?

But barns the world's forgotten about, they're always dusty.

Moths, I told myself.

Every time a moth launches off toward what it probably thinks is a sun, there's a small breath of dust puffing up from its wings. Dust that has to go somewhere.

When I was kid, we thought that dust was poison, like the dust in a rattlesnake's tail, or the white powder inside certain beetles, if you cracked them open right.

Standing up there, I licked my lips. But not the rail. Not even where it was clean from my hand, however long ago that had been.

Behind me, Josh made his groaning sound and secretly swallowed a maggot.

Soon he was going to open his mouth, and flies were going to crawl out.

Maybe this is what love is, here.

* * *

If Josh is a scabhead, he's the only one I've seen.

Aside from him and his decaying breath, there's the inkfeet—I should have called them shadowrunners, but it's too late now—and there's the standers.

I think I might be a stander.

I didn't even see them for the first few days.

All they do is stand flat-backed up against a wall, and stare. Soon enough they get coated in the same grime as the walls, as the bar, as the loft. They're easy to miss.

In the mornings, though, their footprints give them away.

After dark, they drift through the streets, feeling around for a better vantage point. For some span of days early on, two of them were standing back-to-back against each other right by a doorway, like they'd been caught out by this version of the sun, and were just standing very, very still, waiting the day out. I don't think they even knew it was another stander behind them, not a wall.

The reason I think I might be one is that I always wonder what they're looking at.

One of them is a scraggly-haired girl, always hiding her face in the corner.

Josh is drawn to her. I have to guide him away each time we get close enough for him to sense her, however he does that.

One time I found him with a mouthful of blonde hair. He wasn't chewing it, it was just packed in, some of the strands even down his throat.

I pulled it out carefully, smelled it.

It was like a battery.

I looked at Josh. He knew things I didn't. I could tell. He'd traded in his higher functions for a set of low ones. For instincts. He could navigate here in a way I couldn't. Because he'd forgot about the Monte Carlo, about the party, about my sister. About me. None of that was clouding his head, now.

It's not his fault, though.

It had to be one of us.

* * *

Two mornings before I'd decided this was it, that something had to be done, something was burning on the horizon. With those oily black flames.

We walked out together, me leading Josh by the hand.

He tried to pull away but I insisted.

It was a corrupt mattress. One a body had decomposed into.

I threw dirt at it and finally fell down onto my knees and cried.

Josh was watching the sky again by the time I looked up to him.

The woman who'd called him a scabhead, she was watching *him*. The flames from the mattress were throwing his wavery shadow behind him. It was doubling and reforming, but in the middle where it crossed itself, there was a deep blackness.

The woman looked from that blackness up to me.

And then she was running for us.

I met her ten steps out, and we clawed into each other, but I wasn't spent from running my days away. I drove her back, screamed after her like an animal, so she would know to stay away.

In reply, she pointed behind me.

Josh was standing on the mattress. In the flames.

Above us, the things in the sky screamed.

* * *

The bar nobody comes to is ours now. I've decided.

I keep Josh laid out on the part of the bar that lifts up like a door.

The fire burned most of his features off, but you can't really die here. It's like a rule. You only get to die once.

The bone behind his ear is still infected with light.

Not everybody comes here through closets, either. The day after I pulled Josh from the flames, a man fell from the sky. For a long time he lay facedown in the street.

He's in the basement now, and is staying longer than we did.

Maybe that's a fourth option. The basement people. There were probably already generations of them down there watching us when we'd tried to hide.

To try to keep Josh alive, I pried his mouth open to spit into it—there's no water, nothing in the bottles on the shelves—but what came up from his mouth, it was that same light from behind his ears.

It was grainy light, too. I could put my fingers in the glow and feel the grit between the pads of my finger and thumb.

If the door wasn't barricaded, the inkfeet would all be in here already, looking over my shoulder.

Instead, they have to mill around on the street. Because they've been in motion so long they can't stand still anymore, have to walk back and forth, doing neat flip turns at the end of their round. It's like the street's a big waiting room.

I've tried stacking bottles and clothes and broken off chair legs under Josh's chin to keep his mouth from spilling light—it settles in odd, now-phosphorescent places—but every time I nod off, I come back to my boyfriend, the flashlight mouth.

Finally what I do is find a right-sized bottle, one with the narrowest base of them all, and work it into his mouth, careful of his teeth, trying not to pinch his dry tongue.

The bottleneck focused the light into more of a beam. Which I then corked off.

He's not a flashlight anymore. He's a lantern.

From the side, it's like he's got a beak but ate too many fireflies, and now they're swarming, trying to get out.

I don't know how much longer this can go on.

* * *

In the clean spot I elbow-rubbed in the mirror, I see the bones behind my ears aren't glowing. Not even a little.

I've figured out there are standers in here with me, too.

I don't mind them so much. I think they've been there too long, have forgotten what they are, or used to be.

But they've started opening their eyes. For Josh. Josh who, before the wreck, before this place, used to always cut the inside seam of his pants legs up about two inches from where they stopped. He said it was because he'd grown up with uncles who wore bellbottoms, and now his pants, opened into a flare like that, looked the same over his boots.

It was a big part of why I kept walking out to his Monte Carlo when he pulled up. Because I was the same age, and didn't remember any of that. My pants all tapered down to my ankles.

But I wanted to have more of a connection to how it used to be, I think.

Josh gave me that, if I squinted just right.

Maybe that did count for love.

Or close enough.

* * *

Because I let Josh lie in one place too long, with that glowing bottle jammed down his throat, the burned skin and clothes between the inside of his arms and his side has congealed together.

I woke to him jerking his left arm and moaning into the bottle.

I kissed him on the cheek.

The bottle had a single fly in it. It was banging against the glass walls, its eyes splintering the light.

There was no sound, though. Any buzzing would have driven me to scream, I know.

In the street, they're moaning. The inkfeet, whatever standers have been roused, and maybe even the basement people.

One of them is my grandfather, I'm pretty sure.

When the family was trying to establish a last live sighting of him, my mother had come to me and I'd lied that I'd taken those cigarettes to him last month, and he'd been fine, okay?

To everybody else, my grandfather lay dead on his bed for four weeks.

I know it was two months, though.

I was still smoking from that carton then, even.

I don't think he remembers me, though.

He's a stander now, I'm pretty sure. Judging by the accumulation on his shoulders and brow ridges.

His lips are cracked and dry.

We're reborn here, though. Made whole again, in a way.

Except some. The Joshes. The scabheads.

When I'm watching for my grandfather in the crowd, my hand ready to wave to him, to say I'm sorry, a door opens upstairs and a boy steps through.

Not from the cast-off door, but the closet.

He closes it before I can crash the stairs. When he sees me coming, when his face catalogues Josh on the bar, and what's been done to him, he crashes through a window up there, falls out into the street and keeps running.

"Go," I tell him.

His feet are so sure for now. So fast.

That's where I want to go, I know. That's what I should have done in the first place. Except for the dead weight of Joshua, my scabhead boyfriend, who, instead of looking both ways, figured he could just put his foot into it, surge through the red light.

But the Monte Carlo never was a muscle car.

I think the funny thing I was going to tell him, it was related to that.

When I try to pry the bottle from his mouth, it won't come. So I stand him up. At first he's unsteady, has to lift his arms for balance.

The congealed matter stretches up from his side.

It's wings.

I fall back, a new coldness welling up in my throat.

Outside now, the crowd is silent, holding its breath. Waiting.

Then, as one, a humming seeps in from them. From their throats, their lips all closed, their eyes so open.

How long have they been here? How long have they been waiting for a scabhead?

Josh coughs and, even though the bottom of the bottle has to be whole—there's only soft tissue at the back of the throat, nothing to crack the eyeglasses-thick bottom of a bottle—still, his cough dislodges the cork.

It doesn't shoot out like a cartoon, just tumbles down to the hardwood.

From behind it, that single fly buzzes, and then the light from inside Josh's head, the light bottlenecked through that glass funnel, it spotlights that little fly for a moment, casting its blurry shadow huge on the wall, right beside a stander.

Neatly, like he's been timing this for ages, that stander rolls from back to front along the wall, and slips into that shadow, is gone.

I pull back and reach forward at the same time, one confused motion, and by the time I know I should have ran across the bar, dove through that fly shadow, after that stander, Josh has his bottle-mouth directed somewhere else.

At me.

He's remembering. I can tell from his eyes.

They're crinkling up like from a smile, like he's hearing the funny thing I had been going to say—it was something to do with "Monte Carlo," how that's a gambling place, isn't it? Like this car was *born* to take its chances through an intersection—but then he jerks his head towards the batwing doors that open onto the street.

Goodbye, I want to say to him, because I know, because I can tell from the way he's shifting his weight on his feet, but what I say instead is "Wait."

I'm too late.

He's already running, pushing through the doors, through the wall of bodies opening before him.

He's leaned forward like a kid, pretending to fly.

Maybe this is how old he was when he first saw how his uncles wore their pants. Maybe this is where he gets to stay.

I hope so.

Behind him, the wall closes. I crash against the people, the bodies, the standers and the inkfeet and the basement people, and I fight through, over, under, but still only get to the edge of town with the rest of them.

Josh is already aloft. He's already up there, swooping back and forth.

Scabheads, they're eggs.

I want to smile, I want to laugh.

But his shadow seeping across the ground like oil, like ink, it's still so fresh.

What I do is what I have to do: I run after it.

Inside it, bathed in it, it's cool, it's quiet, it's perfect.

If he can just keep his flight straight for two steps more. For four. Steady now. Steady.

I run faster, harder, lighter, my skin so tuned to the coolness under his leathery wings, trying to track it, anticipate it.

I can keep this up. I can do this.

The tears, they're streaming back from my eyes, cutting through the dust on my face, tracing coolness onto my scalp.

And I'm smiling.

Because I can, I can do this.

You only die once. I know this now.

But it lasts forever.

DECLARATIONS OF COPYRIGHT

MORE DARK FICTION FROM
GREY MATTER PRESS

THE **REAL MONSTERS** ARE IN YOUR MIRROR

PEEL BACK THE SKIN

FROM BRAM STOKER AWARD® NOMINATED EDITORS

ANTHONY RIVERA | SHARON LAWSON

PEEL BACK THE SKIN
ANTHOLOGY OF HORROR

They are among us.

They live down the street. In the apartment next door. And even in our own homes.

They're the real monsters. And they stare back at us from our bathroom mirrors.

Peel Back the Skin is a powerhouse new anthology of terror that strips away the mask from the real monsters of our time – mankind.

Featuring all-new fiction from a star-studded cast of award-winning authors from the horror, dark fantasy, speculative, transgressive, extreme horror and thriller genres, *Peel Back the Skin* is the next game-changing release from Bram Stoker Award-nominated editors Anthony Rivera and Sharon Lawson.

FEATURING:

Jonathan Maberry

Ray Garton

Tim Lebbon

Ed Kurtz

William Meikle

Yvonne Navarro

Durand Sheng Welsh

James Lowder

Lucy Taylor

Joe McKinney

Erik Williams

Charles Austin Muir

John McCallum Swain

Nancy A. Collins

Graham Masterton

GREY MATTER
P R E S S

greymatterpress.com

EVEN MONSTERS CAN LOVE

SEEING DOUBLE

KAREN RUNGE

SEEING DOUBLE
BY KAREN RUNGE

A trio of expats living in Asia form a tenuous bond based on mutual attraction, sexual obsession and the insatiable desire to experience the deadliest of thrills.

As their relationship matures, the dangerous love triangle in which they've become entwined quickly escalates into a series of brutal sexual conquests as they struggle to deal with lives spinning out of control and the debilitating psychological effects mental and physical abuse.

Known for her distinctive brand of unsettling fiction, author Karen Runge is at the top of the modern horror game in this, her premiere novel. Seeing Double is a beautifully evocative and stunningly dark coming-of-age exploration of human sexuality and the roles of masculinity and feminism, polyamorous relationships, social and psychological isolation, and the humiliation of ultimate betrayal.

———————

Karen Runge is an artist and horror writer whoe teaches adults English as a second language. Her fiction has appeared in *Pseudopod*, *Something Wicked*, *Pantheon* Magazine and *Structo*.

Her story with editor and author Simon Dewar, "High Art." is featured in the Grey Matter Press anthology *Death's Realm*. Runge's short story "Good Help," which appears in *Shock Totem 9*, prompted horror icon Jack Ketchum to tell her, "Karen, you scare me."

———————

GREY MATTER
P R E S S

greymatterpress.com

A DARK THRILLER

MISTER WHITE

THE NOVEL

DO
NOT
SPEAK
HIS
NAME

JOHN C. FOSTER

MISTER WHITE
BY JOHN C. FOSTER

In the shadowy world of international espionage and governmental black ops, when a group of American spies go bad and inadvertently unleash an ancient malevolent force that feeds on the fears of mankind, a young family finds themselves in the crosshairs of a frantic supernatural mystery of global proportions with only one man to turn to for their salvation.

Combine the intricate, plot-driven stylings of suspense masters Tom Clancy and Robert Ludlum, add a healthy dose of Clive Barker's dark and brooding occult horror themes, and you get a glimpse into the supernatural world of international espionage that the chilling new horror novel *Mister White* is about to reveal.

John C. Foster's *Mister White* is a terrifying genre-busting suspense shocker that, once and for all, answer the question you dare not ask: "Who is Mister White?"

"*Mister White* is a potent and hypnotic brew that blends horror, espionage and mystery. Foster has written the kind of book that keeps the genre fresh and alive and will make fans cheer. Books like this are the reason I love horror fiction." – RAY GARTON, Grand Master of Horror and Bram Stoker Award®-nominated author of *Live Girls* and *Scissors*.

"*Mister White* is like Stephen King's *The Stand* meets Ian Fleming's James Bond with Graham Masterton's *The Manitou* thrown in for good measure. It's frenetically paced, spectacularly gory and eerie as hell. Highly recommended!" – JOHN F.D. TAFF, Bram Stoker Award®-nominated author of *The End in All Beginnings*

GREY MATTER
P R E S S

greymatterpress.com

"Paul Kane is a first-rate storyteller."
— Clive Barker, Bestselling author of
The Hellbound Heart and *The Scarlet Gospels*

BEFORE

PAUL KANE

BEFORE
BY PAUL KANE

In 1970s Germany, a mental patient at the end of his life suddenly speaks for the first time in years. A year later in Vietnam, a mission to rescue a group of American POWs becomes a military disaster.

In present day England, the birthday of college lecturer Alex Webber sends his life spiralling out of control as a series of disturbing hallucinations lead him to the office of Dr. Ellen Hayward. And things will never be the same again for either of them. Hunted by an immortal being known only as The Infinity, their capture could mean the end of humanity itself…

Part horror story, part thrilling road adventure, part historical drama, Before is a novel like no other. Described as "the dark fantasy version of Cloud Atlas," Kane's Before is as wide in scope as it is in imagination as it tackles the greatest questions haunting mankind—Who are we? Why are we here? And where are we going?

The author and editor of more than sixty books, Kane's work includes *Sherlock Holmes and the Servants of Hell*, *Lunar*, *The Rainbow Man*, the Arrowhead trilogy (later released as the *Hooded Man* omnibus), *The Butterfly Man and Other Stories*, *Hellbound Hearts*, *The Mammoth Book of Body Horror*, *The Hellraiser Films and Their Legacy* and more. His work has been optioned and adapted for the big and small screen, including for US network television.

"Paul Kane is a first-rate storyteller, never failing to marry his insights into the world and its anguish with the pleasures of phrases eloquently turned." — Clive Barker, author of *The Hellbound Heart* and *The Scarlet Gospels*

"I'm impressed by the range of Paul Kane's imagination. It seems there is no risk, no high-stakes gamble, he fears to take… Kane's foot never gets even close to the brake pedal." — Peter Straub, author of *Ghost Story*

GREY MATTER
P R E S S

greymatterpress.com

BRAM STOKER AWARD-NOMINATED

JOHN F.D. TAFF

MODERN HORROR'S KING OF PAIN

"Accomplished, complex, heartfelt.
The best novella collection in years!"
— JACK KETCHUM

THE END
IN BEGINNINGS
ALL

INTRODUCTION BY SHANE DOUGLAS KEENE

THE END IN ALL BEGINNINGS
BY JOHN F.D. TAFF

The Bram Stoker Award-nominated *The End in All Beginnings* is a tour de force through the emotional pain and anguish of the human condition. Hailed as one of the best volumes of heartfelt and gut-wrenching horror in recent history, *The End in All Beginnings* is a disturbing trip through the ages exploring the painful tragedies of life, love and loss.

Exploring complex themes that run the gamut from loss of childhood innocence, to the dreadful reality of survival after everything we hold dear is gone, to some of the most profound aspects of human tragedy, author John F.D. Taff takes readers on a skillfully balanced emotional journey through everyday terrors that are uncomfortably real over the course of the human lifetime. Taff's highly nuanced writing style is at times darkly comedic, often deeply poetic and always devastatingly accurate in the most terrifying of ways.

Evoking the literary styles of horror legends Mary Shelley, Edgar Allen Poe and Bram Stoker, *The End in All Beginnings* pays homage to modern masters Stephen King, Ramsey Campbell, Ray Bradbury and Clive Barker.

"Taff brings the pain in five damaged and disturbing tales of love gone horribly wrong. This collection is like a knife in the heart. Highly recommended!"
— Jonathan Maberry, *New York Times* bestselling author of *Code Zero* and *Fall of Night*

GREY MATTER
P R E S S

greymatterpress.com

BRAM STOKER AWARD–NOMINATED

JOHN F.D. TAFF

MODERN HORROR'S KING OF PAIN

"A compelling and frightening read!"
— AIN'T IT COOL NEWS

A LEGENDARY AMERICAN HAUNTING

THE BELL WITCH

FEATURING "A SKEPTIC'S GUIDE TO THE BELL WITCH"
AN INTRODUCTION BY BRACKEN MacLEOD
AUTHOR OF STRANDED AND MOUNTAIN HOME

THE BELL WITCH
BY JOHN F.D. TAFF

It's 1817, and Tennessee is on the western frontier as America expands into the unknown. In idyllic Adams County, home of the Bell family, there exists a collection of tight-knit rural communities with deeply held beliefs. And even more deeply buried secrets.

Jack and Lucy Bell operate a prosperous family farm northwest of Nashville where life with their many children is peaceful. Simple country life. That is until those secrets take on a life of their own and refuse to remain unspoken.

Much has been written about the legend of the Bell Witch of Tennessee, but the details of the Bell family's terrifying experience with the supernatural have never been told in quite the way that Bram Stoker Award-nominated horror author John F.D. Taff has conceived. In his novel, for the first time, the Witch has her own say. And what she reveals about the incident and the dark motivations behind her appearance reaches way beyond a traditional haunting.

Forget what you've read about this wholly American legend. What you believe you know about the mysterious occurrences on the Bell farm are wrong. Uncover the long-hidden reality that's far more horrifying than any ghost story you've ever heard.

Because sometimes the scariest tales are true.

GREY MATTER

P R E S S

greymatterpress.com

www.ingramcontent.com/pod-product-compliance
Lightning Source LLC
Chambersburg PA
CBHW030420180626
46812CB00005B/2095